Operation SECOND STARFISH

A Tale of Submarine Rescue,
Science, and Friendship

Susan R. Kayar

The use of the trademarked names of Indian Motorcycles and Harley-Davidson Motorcycles was generously granted by written permission. An excerpt from *The Journals of Lewis and Clark*, edited by Bernard DeVoto, was included with written permission from Houghton Mifflin Harcourt Publishing Company, with the author's thanks.

First publication: June 2017.

ISBN: 0692868585
ISBN-13: 978-0692868584
Library of Congress Control Number: 2017908221
LCCN Imprint: **Sabella Press, Santa Fe, NM**

Dedication

Down with divers. Up with love.

Acknowledgments

The telling of tales, true, tall, and betwixt, is a tradition among seafarers of all kinds. Ideas for this book started many years ago as a way for friends to pass the long hours of hydrogen chamber tending at the Naval Medical Research Institute. We did good work together and had fun doing it. Among these friends are Richard Ayres, Andreas Fahlman, Tom James, Walter Long, Roland Ramsey, and Anthony Ruopoli. I am grateful and honored that they shared with me.

In more recent days, other people, some longtime friends and some new acquaintances, generously shared their special technical skills or editorial advice. These include Kathleen Antona, Christine Bird, Steven Cassell, Sue and Jack Drafahl, Cynthia Fowler, Mark Helmkamp, Carol Hunter, William Orr, Bobbie Scholley, Jacqui and Rod Stanley, Maida Taylor, and Paul Weathersby. Information on Navajo language and culture was kindly supplied by many people, with special thanks to Jason Harvey and Elizabeth Wallace. I hope you all feel I have done justice to what you entrusted to me and that I have presented these stories with compassion.

My deepest thanks go to my husband, Erich. His love and support in all my efforts have contributed more to my life than I can express.

Any residual errors are solely the fault of the author.

Operation SECOND STARFISH

April 9, 2013
0203 Hrs
Aboard *Whatever*, Naval Air Station Key West
Key West, FL

"He's dead."

Stella's head drooped forward, loose strands of her long black hair veiling her face. The two men standing near her stared at the deck, slowly shaking their heads.

"Doc?" came the voice again over the communications system. Stella did not look up from where she sat on the deck. "Doc Stella? What do you want us to do now...? Doc...? Are you there?"

The two men looked at Stella. She had begun to rock gently to her own rhythm, her arms wrapped around herself, her face still obscured by her tangled hair.

"Stella?" drawled Hank Johnson, a tall, lanky Texan in his fifties. "You have to say something. The Team is waiting. We're all waiting. I want to know how you're planning to talk your way out of this one, Little Miss Know-It-All."

"Shut up, Hank, you jerk!" hissed Art Moore. He moved toward Stella with more grace than one would expect for a largish man over sixty. "Stella, come on, let's get you to your cabin. You haven't slept more than a couple hours at a stretch in your bunk in far too long, and you can't do anything here now. We'll take over while you get some rest. Your head will be clearer after some sleep."

Stella rocked, unresponsive.

1

Hank made an impatient gesture. "Oh, great. She picks now to go Navajo on us!" He reached for the comms switch. "Uh—the Doc's gone to her cabin to do—uh—some calculations—er, something. I guess we're going to have to start thinking about what we're going to do next. Sit tight for now, and we'll get back to you." He switched the comms off.

Art stepped irritably back toward Hank and muscled him aside to switch the comms on again. "Doc Stella is going to her cabin for some much-needed rest. She'll get back to you soon. Hank and I will help you. Doc Balinski and Lieutenant Commander Costello too. You should all try to get some rest yourselves." He returned to Stella's side and touched her arm. "Come on with me now, Stella honey, we're going to your cabin." He pressed more firmly. Stella slowly lifted her head, her neck as rubbery as a sleepwalker's. As her hair fell back, Art was startled to see her strong, young face look gray and ancient, her dark eyes vacant. She did not respond.

"Jesus, Art, get her out of here now before Costello sees her like this, or we can kiss the Hydrogen Project good-bye!" Hank whispered hoarsely.

Art clenched a fist at Hank. "*You* are worried about *your job* at a time like this?" he spat angrily. Art then turned his back on him to lean over Stella. "Come on, Stella hon. Don't jump to conclusions. It could be anything. We won't know what happened until somebody has a chance to look at him. And as far as we can tell, the rest of the Team is fine. We shouldn't look for more trouble before it comes to us. Let's get you to your cabin now." Art tugged her carefully to her feet.

The young woman slowly unfolded to stand a hand's breadth

2

above him. He steered her across the deck, through a hatch, and down a gangway to her cabin, as if leading a blind woman. Opening her cabin door, Art gently pushed her inside and pulled the door shut in front of himself. He stood staring at the door a moment, then opened it and looked inside. She was standing where he had left her, silently rocking. Art stepped into the tiny cabin, pressed her slowly toward her bunk, and got her to lie curled on her mattress. He tugged off her sneakers and smoothed a sheet over her. After another moment of deliberation, he pulled back the sheet, fished for her chunky belt buckle, tugged the belt free, and dropped it on the floor. He readjusted the sheet. Then he left the cabin quickly, without looking back at the rocking, mute form.

February 14, 2013
0800 Hrs
Operations Facilities, Navy Experimental Diving Unit
Panama City, FL

Stella strode through the cavernous hangar of the building's operations deck, where the control facility for the test chamber was housed. She approached the nearest porthole on the chamber and was presented with a rather large, tan shorts-clad butt waggling excitedly inside. She stepped back startled, then looked in again to identify the porthole containing the anterior end of this test subject. It was Petty Officer Bill Murphy, a big, sandy-haired Coloradan. He was something of a goofy kid, despite his three decades and change (a much shorter time span when recorded in what friends called "Murph years"), with a faint look in the eyes when you spoke to him as if he were not really listening to you but to some private joke. But Stella and the other team members appreciated him for his big spirit and big heart.

At present Murphy was trying to gain the attention of anyone in the control room. Numerous people were pressing their own noses to control panels, but with communications switched off, Murphy's dance was as yet unwitnessed. Stella stepped within his view, waved a greeting, and offered an index-fingered admonishment to wait until she could perch on a stool by the porthole and switch on communications.

"Hey, Murph!" she greeted him. "Got a problem I can help with?"

"Hey, Doc!" he responded cheerfully, his incongruously squeaky, thin voice resonating strangely in the low-density chamber gases, despite the electronic voice descrambler. "I sure could use some ketchup. We got any?"

4

"Ketchup? Oh! I can ask around for that, but I've got something even better than that right here." She unslung her daypack from a shoulder and dug around inside for a moment. "My Grandma Nellie just sent me her latest CARE package, and I've got…" She dramatically pulled out a small can and waved it slowly within his field of view.

"Hatch green chiles! You spell 'em with an *E*!" His little dance of happiness made Stella smile.

"Yes, indeed! I can see my corrupting influence is creeping into your dining. I'll get someone to lock those in to you, along with that ketchup. Nothing more exciting than that on your mind this morning at one thouuuusand feet?" Stella asked him.

"No, Doc, not yet. They brought us scrambled eggs this morning, but as soon as they were locked in, everybody ran off to do other stuff before we could check it and ask for anything else. Gotta love this new cook, though. He makes the food look like something you'd wanna eat, not like a pile of catfish barf, like the last guy."

"Yeah, I heard you guys were having trouble with your appetites for the first couple of days in there. We can't have you all wasting away. If you don't eat, your bugs can't either. Your bug caps went down OK with breakfast? Good. I'll see what I can do about perking up those eggs of yours," she assured him. She hailed a staff member and passed on the request and the small can; he nodded and scurried off at a brisk trot.

Stella turned back to the chamber and called out greetings to the other three divers inside. "Hey, Soapy! Hey, Cal! Hey,

5

Jake! *Yá'at'ééh*, buddies." Stella reserved her Navajo greeting for close friends and family. "Good morning, Hank," she added, addressing the man running the chamber controls that morning. His chin tossed in her direction was his full reply.

Chief Petty Officer Byron Soaps was a relative rarity in the US Navy, even in modern times: an African-American diver. A native of the Florida Keys, he considered a life on and under the water an obvious choice. He was trim and precisely erect, smart, remarkably calm in danger even by Navy standards, and incredibly patient with dumb guys. Sadly, Stella thought, the lattermost skill was called into service all too frequently. Stella loved his deep, rich voice, which contrasted with his compact stature. A genuine "still waters run deep" man, in her estimation.

Chief Petty Officer and Medical Corpsman Calvin Sorensen was the Navy Diver poster boy of the group: tall, blond, sculpted with swimmer's muscles. As a Medical Corpsman, most divers used the standard honorific of *Doc* for him, and she had to agree he was often more useful than many a doctor of her acquaintance, her dad excepted. He was endearingly cheerful about life and everything in it, always full of hypercaffeinated energy, but mature and intelligent enough to channel that energy to good use. He had a lovely wife and two budding beauty queens for young daughters; his was the longest marriage and happiest home life of not just the Team but of all the divers stationed at NEDU. He wore his Christian faith more gracefully than any man Stella had ever met. It took her some time to learn to understand his usual Texas/Arkansas/Missouri mush mouth. He could speak with razor-sharp clarity and textbook grammar when motivated, she noted with curiosity. But she considered it a worthwhile effort to master an understanding of his preferred

6

modest patois, given the great good sense of its usual content.

And then there was Jake. Senior Chief Petty Officer Jacob Henderson Webster. Even when she was standing in a room filled with hunky young divers, all shirtless and tricked out in those distracting little tan UDT shorts, her eyes would rove until she spotted his light-brown, spiky brush cut and striking blue eyes. (It was Underwater Demolition Team members who made the shorts the universal divers' fashion statement they are today, which were by tradition left unfastened at the waistband; distracting indeed.) Jake was rather short by the standards of his peers. Her five-foot-eight frame in cowboy boots noticeably cleared the top of his spikes by a good inch. But years of agonizing work in the gym had given him an athlete's body to rival any around him. *Smart* did not describe him; he was a genius, which was indeed a continuous burden to him. Born into a prosperous Boston family, he had been expected to take his sky-high IQ to Harvard Business School and groom to be the third generation in Webster Marine Salvage. But salvaging had not always been the most respectable of ventures in previous generations of the family, and genes will express themselves when they will. Jake's streak of pirate made him act impetuously, doing the wrong things for the right reasons and vice versa, at random and inconvenient intervals.

Three years into his Harvard bachelor's program, he wearied of being what he viewed as the skinny little intelligeek puppet of his parents. With no word of warning or explanation to parents or hometown girlfriend, he left Harvard, enlisted in the Navy, bought a motorcycle, and rode it directly to Panama City. He worked doggedly to pass the physical tests to enter dive school, graduating (of course) at the top of his class, and was now advancing smoothly

7

through enlisted ranks. His Boston girlfriend, with pirate blood of her own, countered by "accidentally" getting pregnant during a visit home. Shotgun wedding, awkward on-and-off attempts to have a Northeastern fancy girl living in enlisted housing, messy marriage collapsing around a beloved young son, the whole catastrophe of a "good boy dripping with bad boy icing," as Stella framed the metaphor. "He's married," Stella lectured herself. "He's married. Be a professional. And even if he weren't, you certainly do not need another Harvard boy."

What did this group of four divers—the Hydrogen Diving and Biochemical Decompression Project Team, as line-itemed in the NEDU budget, or just *the Team* in usual parlance—think of her? *The world* would hardly cover it. Stella Nellie Curtis, PhD, was the product of the happy but tragically short union of a Yankee doctor and a Navajo teacher. Consequently, hers were a blend of features that did not quite suit many in either population. Dark, thick hair and large dark eyes in a light-tan face of strong bones did not quite succeed in making her look any more ethnically identifiable than Mediterranean to anyone outside of family. A Turkish man she'd once met at a science convention had unintentionally hit the nail on the head most accurately; he had stared at her briefly and cautiously asked her, "Are you Oriental or Accidental?"

"The latter, definitely," she had responded gravely. Her preference for Western wear did not help clarify her ethnicities as much as she hoped. Her tall, sturdy frame was a bit too androgynous to many a critical eye. Until she smiled. Not her quotidian "thanks a lot." Her really big, full-blast from-the-heart smile. Stella had a smile like morning sunshine on a glittering mesa in her New Mexico homeland. Any sensible man who had basked in the radiance of that

8

smile thought, as her Team did, that she was graced with a rare beauty.

But the Team's admiration of her was more than tooth deep. Not all Navy divers were as happy as they were to spend a tour of duty at NEDU as subjects in test and evaluation efforts, instead of actually diving in the ocean on Navy operations, such as with the Mobile Diving and Salvage Units, usually pronounced by their attractive acronym "Mud Sue." In the years they had each spent as test subject divers at NEDU, they had never seen a scientist like her. Stella was the first scientist to insist on explaining to them, as if they were intelligent people, the underlying concepts of her project: what is hydrogen biochemical decompression, how does it differ from what they already knew about diving and decompression sickness, and why is it potentially so important to the US Navy? She lectured to them repeatedly on the intricacies and novelties of the science and then quizzed them on their understanding of what she was telling them, until she was convinced they actually got the ideas.

Not all scientists knew as much as the Team learned from her. Together they would prove that gases could be safely eliminated from inside divers, not just from rats and pigs, as had been shown a scientific generation ago. This gas removal would reduce their decompression sickness risk, or increase their bottom time, or permit a deeper dive, or whatever combination of those three things their mission required. Together they would make this work with hydrogen, and then they would carry it forward to nitrogen. She made them understand they were a part of something, if it all worked out, that would be completely game changing in the realm of decompression sickness avoidance and safe dive profiles.

In short, the biodec Team loved Stella because she made them feel important.

What also made Stella so special to her Team was her devotion to them, not as guinea pigs for her admittedly bizarre-sounding experiments but as human beings toward whom she felt personal responsibility. They had seen her go to bat for each of them, and the Hydrogen Project as a whole, in some occasionally brutal transactions with Navy Brass. They liked to brag that she might get knocked down in some of these fights, but she would never stay on the floor until every knuckle was broken, which had not happened yet in the past two and a half years.

Of course having to fight for what you believed in was part of the Navy Way. Nobody believed you were sincere about something genuinely important unless you fought for it repeatedly and with your own skin in the game. Seeing you willing to fight saved the people in charge of making policy decisions the effort of figuring out for themselves what was important. When the first batch of what they called *bug caps* arrived, she demanded to be the first and only one to take them. Stella tried several times unsuccessfully to explain that the freeze-dried cultures of *Methanobrevibacter smithii* in their enteric-coated capsules were not populating their intestines with bacteria but with another category of microcritters called *archae*. She wanted to personally perform the safety test showing that trace quantities of hydrogen gas, made normally in human intestines by resident bacteria, could be grabbed up and safely metabolized by the *M. smithii*, also native to the intestinal flora of humans but amplified by the capsules.

They watched her spend hours in what was basically a clear body bag, her air supply provided by a regulator threaded in and stuffed in her mouth. She needed to capture her body's release of methane, an end product of *M. smithii* hydrogen metabolism, from every possible orifice, snout to tail, as she called it. When the very first gas chromatographic analysis was printing out, she was writhing with anticipation in her bag to see the trace. What can probably best be described as a war whoop, sending chills (and not the good kind) down the spine of every rough 'n' tough in the room, emerged from her bared teeth when she saw her beloved methane chromatographic spike for the first time. Yes, this was probably the world's most enthusiastic response to a fart.

For a bunch of hairy-chested Navy divers, it struck Stella as odd to see how she could make them squirm over the part of the research that accompanied her chromatographic analyses of gases going in and coming out of a biodec subject. The farting parts they could handle with no more than the obvious little boys' jokes. The squirmy bit was that she also needed to analyze the *M. smithii* as they inevitably were shed from their new but temporary intestinal home. That translates to exactly what you'd think: she needed to collect her own feces and perform a microbial cultural analysis of it. Clearly their turn to poop into containers and hand it off to her would be coming. The divers had spent years passing out cups of their own urine for one reason or another, but feces?

For Stella all of these scatological labors and tribulations were only the one-atmosphere, air-breathing part of the preliminaries. Then came Stella's solo safety tests of the capsules in the minimum pressure of hydrogen in a chamber: that magic point at ten atmospheres total pressure (equivalent to a depth of almost three hundred feet of sea water) at which the initial press of helium and oxygen could be exchanged for a mix of hydrogen and oxygen. At ten atmospheres, the gas mix could be both enough oxygen for a person to breathe (0.2 atmospheres partial pressure of oxygen) and little enough oxygen in hydrogen (2 percent) to be well within the non-explosive limits for what can be a highly volatile gas mix at oxygen-richer concentrations. This gas blend they verbally as well as physically compressed into *hydrox*.

Stella remained the only one of them with hydrox experience, strictly speaking. Research of past decades in France had shown there is a limit of twenty-four or twenty-five atmospheres of hydrogen pressure that is safe to breathe, beyond which there is a risk of a psychotic hydrogen narcosis. Consequently Stella's safety tests to ten atmospheres were the only dives to utilize a flush-out of perfectly good helium, as anyone working the chamber would say, to replace the chamber gases with hydrox.

For today's dive to one thousand feet, about thirty-one atmospheres, once the chamber was pressed to the ten-atmosphere safety point on helium, all the chamber tenders needed to do was to continue the press with hydrogen. They would thus wind up at one thousand feet with more or less the original one atmosphere of air, plus nine atmospheres of helium, plus almost twenty-one atmospheres of hydrogen. That blend of gases goes by the highly ineuphonious term of *hydreliox*. This led to a distinction that was really not as important to Stella and the Team as they joked it was: she was a hydrox diver, and they were hydreliox divers. After all, there was no surprise in the motivations for the differing gas mixes. Stella was studying hydrox as the scientifically most relevant gas mix for hydrogen biochemical decompression. The Team was being given hydreliox to breathe as the operationally more relevant gas mix while still leaving the option available for hydrogen biochemical decompression.

Everyone was breathing more easily, in the metaphoric sense, when Stella's research on herself was completed and she could start using the Team for their jobs. While they would not have wounded her pride by saying so, the Team was nervous watching Stella pushing herself so hard. In order for Stella to be permitted by Navy rules to be pressed in a dive chamber with hydrox or air or any gas mix to any depth whatsoever, first she had to graduate from Navy dive school. While there is a significant and growing number of fine Navy women who have accomplished this feat, it is never easy for them, or even for most men. The four team members spent countless hours with Stella, training her in the gym, in the pool, and in the surf. She was tough and earned their respect daily. Seeing Stella graduate from dive school was an exciting day for all of them. Hearing Stella declare that her research on herself was over was an even better day for the Team.

As if they needed anything else to bond with this glorious, golden Amazon, Stella had unwittingly found the final key to any diver's heart: she'd designed an amazing Team T-shirt, in the traditional colors of dark blue and gold. She'd had the shirts custom silk-screened for them at one of the supernumerary silly souvenir shirt and beach towel shops on the PC main drag. On the shirt front, an improbably brawny cartoon diver, bristling with chest hairs, was breathing from a closed-circuit rig emblazoned with "H_2-He-O_2" and staring down a quavering little diver wearing conventional air-filled scuba tanks. The message that wound on a banner through the image was "If you aren't diving hydrogen, you're just putting on airs!" The Team considered these shirts prized possessions, the proof of which was the irritation the shirts evoked in all other NEDU divers.

The Team watched over Stella like a group of big brothers. No man outside the Team was permitted to make an off-color remark at her expense without paying a very severe penalty for it. The Team acted as her cultural attachés into the arcane vocabulary and habits of the Navy in general and Panama City in particular. They taught her the proper and frequent use of the broad-spectrum accolade "hoo-yah!" Several months into her Florida residence, when she registered her family heirloom 1947 Indian Motorcycle, which she and her father called *Red Chief*, the Team explained to her why she had to stop telling everyone she had just gotten a Panama City license plate or accepting other divers' requests to take them into the back parking lot to show it to them. In local parlance, her new acquisition would have been obtained not from a Division of Motor Vehicles office but from one of the vast array of local tattoo parlors. Of course there was one advantage to being like her big brothers, but not actual biological brothers (of which she had none): they could end that particular vernacular lesson with the friendly request that if she actually ever did get a PC license plate, would she kindly turn around and lift her shirt tail for their inspection of it? Carefully respectful though they were of her when professionally appropriate, they were, after all, no better than they had to be as Navy divers. Nor would she have wished it otherwise.

Their one failing with her, despite their best efforts, was to get her to use the long list of Navy acronyms and compressed words for almost everything. Oh well. They would not say "Archae," and she would not say "DivSup." Or was that "SupDiv"? In case you were wondering, there is one of each, but the latter is correctly presented as "SUPDIV."

Stella's morning salutations to the men in the test chamber were followed with her now standard question: "How are you all doing in the belly of the beast? Yeah, I know: It's a lot smaller on the inside," she said in slow unison to the quartet of quacking voices. "Any requests? Special issues we should know about?"

"Can anybody do anything about the temperature in here?" asked Webster.

"Too hot or too cold?" Stella inquired. A cacophony followed. "Whoa, boys, when you all squawk at once, I can't make out a thing you're saying. Too hot? Too cold? Sounds like I am getting two votes for hot and two for cold, right?" Affirmative noises confirmed her suspicions. "Sorry, buddies, but that's just the hydrogen talking. It's a recognized feature of your gas mix and pressure. First of all, the thermal conductivities of hydreliox at one thousand feet are crazy high for draining your body heat. And second, the hydrogen is messing a little with your nervous system. Your body can't tell what it wants for thermal comfort. Top bunk guys may say 'too hot,' bottom bunk guys may say 'too cold,' guys with a sheet for covering will say 'too hot,' but the moment they take the sheet off, 'too cold,' skin on the mattress boiling, skin in the gas freezing. Does that sound about right?"

A mix of more or less yeahs and uh-huhs followed. "Sorry, gentlemen. Ask me again when all four of you are simultaneously too hot or too cold, and then I'll try to do something out here. For now just try to do the best you can with clothing and bedding, and then try to take your minds off it. The good news is that as we whiz you through the decompression, it will get better," Stella assured them. "Speaking of diversions, what cool thousand-foot chamber tricks do you have to show me this morning?" she inquired of the four men.

Murphy was the first to squeak up. "Ooh, watch this!" He reached for a can of soda on his breakfast tray. It was not the best of nutrition, to be sure, but an authorized indulgence in hydration and appetite stimulation they needed today. Checking that she could see him clearly through the porthole, he shook the can with exaggerated vigor. When he popped the tab with a dramatic flourish and a quacky "ta-daaah!" no spray came out of the can. Stella applauded and cheered.

"I've got something cool to show you!" Webster offered. He reached for a paper tissue from a little box on his narrow bunk. Holding it aloft and watching her closely, he let go of the tissue. To her amazement, instead of falling directly to the chamber floor, the tissue stayed briefly aloft before floating downward, lazily drifting this way and that.

"The wonders of high-density gas! Very cool!" Stella enthused.

A weird and unidentifiable screech suddenly made Stella jump. The three divers in her field of view were all staring at something in the far end of the chamber that she could not see. Then they cackled.

"What in the world was that?" Stella asked with alarm.

"S'OK," Cal Sorensen assured her. "Soapy sneezed. Just about blows yer head off sneezing at a thousand feet."

"Oh! You scared me! You OK, Soapy?" she enquired.

16

Byron Soaps leaned himself into her view and fingered an OK to her while wiping his nose and a few tears with a tissue.

"On to business, gentlemen," Stella said crisply. "I've checked the gas chromatograph this morning, and the Oracle of the GC says that you are all a rootin' and a tootin' out your methane at the rate I've predicted to be on schedule. We don't of course know how much hydrogen each of you is scrubbing individually—and trust me, you don't want the body bag trick in there—so we'll have to expect that the total amount, divided by four, is a reasonable estimate for each. Carry on, gentlemen. I'll check back with you in an hour or so, before my noon shift."

"Wait!" they chorused out in ragged protest.

"Did you get any interesting mail this morning?" Jake Webster hinted broadly.

Stella smiled. "I do believe our deal was official business first, fun and games and sea stories at bedtime. I'll keep these," she tapped her daypack with an outstretched finger, "safely in here until after dinner this evening. Don't worry. I won't peek," she assured them.

She turned to head back to her office. She was startled to see a man standing steps behind her, quietly waiting to get her attention. It was Lieutenant Commander Bob Costello, a tall and distinguished-looking man in his early forties. His dark flat-top, with touches of silver at the temples, always looked freshly cut. He was Executive Officer of NEDU and an Explosive Ordnance Disposal Officer, titles that in Navy terminology were usually shorthanded down to XO and EOD, respectively. He was formally in charge of all activities involving divers, including her experiments with her Team.

"Good morning, Lieutenant Commander Costello!" Stella greeted him cheerfully.

"Good morning, *Doctor Curtis*," he responded with a formality meant to be a mild reproach, despite his friendly smile.

"Sorry. Good morning, *Bob*," she corrected herself. "I know, I know. You've been kind enough to tell me many times that I'm welcome to call you Bob. But it feels weird being the only person in this whole building who speaks so casually with you, when everyone else salutes and uses your full formal address."

"I get that. But nobody is listening to us now. Anyway, I just wanted to check in with you and with Johnson and the Team, and see how things are going. Everything OK?" he asked.

"Everything is just great!" she enthused. "Methane release rate is tracking along as predicted, and so far so good on any issues with the gases and depths. I'm really encouraged," she summed up happily.

"Good. Glad to hear it," he responded. "Anything else interesting happening today? How's your day shaping up?"

"You mean anything more interesting than an experiment with the rarest gas in diving at pressures that exceed any the Navy has used in years?" she asked, startled at his line of questioning. "Oh, well, yes, now that I think of it. The Team has promised me a Valentine's Day surprise for later this evening, after my shift at chamber tending. I've been given valentines from them already, which I am sworn not to open until then," she told him.

"Uh," Costello replied. Stella could not interpret whether his uncharacteristically inarticulate response indicated sadness, boredom, or indigestion.

"Anything else, Lieu—I mean Bob?" she asked him, already assuming a negative answer and turning away but leaving a smile pointed in his direction.

"Nope. Guess not. Um, happy Valentine's Day," he mumbled as he turned away himself.

"Thanks! You too," she called brightly over her shoulder as she headed down the hall. She did not see him pause and turn back to watch her energetic march.

April 3, 2013
0930 Hrs
1700 Feet Below the Ocean Surface
Straits of Florida

"Thanks for coming to find us. How'd you get here so quickly? Over."

"The FBI will tell you what our missions are when the US Navy tells us yours, Captain. Over."

"Oh yeah. Well, what the hell happened out there? What do you see? Over."

"I guess you already know about the ugly holes in your sides. And I see you're sitting pretty precariously on a pile of rocks. Is your nuclear power system running? I'd be worried about your cooling water supply right now. The intakes might be restricted by your position."

"You think you're worried! When the explosions blew out our ballast tanks and we dropped onto the bottom, we had to shut down the nuke power plant right away because the system was heating up and we didn't want a meltdown. The last men in the power plant control room said there seemed to be just enough water flow to keep the system from going critically hot, or at least it hasn't melted down yet. I called for an evac of the mid- and after-sections when we started taking on water, so we don't know temperatures back there right now."

"How are you on environmental controls, Captain?"

"We're on battery power for them, and that room was secured from flooding by a crew member, so we should have about a week of good air. We've got heat, lights, potable water, food. All we need is a ride outta here and the luck to stay in one piece until it arrives."

"That's a relief. But you're not going to like what else I see out here. There's an ongoing threat to that staying in one piece issue and not a damned thing I can do to neutralize it. Over."

"Ongoing threat? Don't like the sound of that. Go ahead. Over."

"There's a small submersible out here, covered in Russkee lettering, and it's hanging upside down, attached to your sail by big loops of cable, over your forward hatch. Its props are fouled in what must have been that first SEPIRB comms cable you sent up. About the only way I think they could have made this big a mess is if they fouled first one prop, and then they spun and flopped around for a while, powered by the second prop, trying to get loose until they got so tangled that they eventually fouled and froze the second prop. I'm surprised that a fiber optic cable could be strong enough to do all this, but I guess if you've got over a thousand feet of it playing out, and you knot it and twist enough strands together, it gets to be pretty darned strong. The idiots. They look about as ridiculous as a mad cat tangled in a ball of your granny's yarn. Over."

"That would explain all the weird bucking bronco sounds we heard after the explosions. Over."

"Speaking of sounds, didn't you hear them before they hit you, Captain? Over."

"We did hear something, but it was so intermittent and full

21

of echoes, probably from that rocky bottom you're seeing, that we couldn't interpret it, and we thought we could finish what we were doing here before we moved off. If the mad cat is now immobilized, what's the ongoing threat? Over."

"I can see a limpet mine in one of the robotic claws of the mad cat, but the whole claw assembly is so wrapped in cable that they can't manipulate it any more. If I had to guess, I'd say what blew those holes in you were other limpet mines. They must have planted a couple of those on you, backed off, and remotely detonated them to watch the effect. But when they decided to come forward along your boat and tag you with one more, that must have been when they fouled on the SEPIRB and got stuck. Maybe you got lucky about when you deployed it, when they were past the point where they could see it was coming up around them. Or maybe they saw it and got careless in their rush to tag you again before it could reach the surface and send out your distress call. Over."

"We're sure glad they couldn't plant that last one. A hole in us up forward might well have taken us all out. Can you see the operators in it? Over."

"Yes. Guess who? Dark bushy beards, mean look in dark eyes, white pajamas. And trust me, those beards don't look any better for being upside down. Over."

"They're looking at you? Over."

"Yes. Want me to give them a one-finger salute for you? Still alive, but they must be running out of life support in there. That's the ongoing threat I can't neutralize. I'm worried they can still detonate that limpet mine. It would be easier on them to take themselves out with their own mine on their own time than to just wait to suffocate in there. It also gives them one more chance to harm you. Even though the explosion won't be against your skin, it might still do some damage to your boat. And there's one more threat. Over."

"You have my attention. Over."

"They're carrying a mesh bag of what looks like scraps of old US ordnance. I wouldn't want to bet your life on whether all that stuff was completely deactivated before being thrown into one of those trash heaps we've got around here. If the limpet mine is blown so close to that grab bag, I don't know what can happen. Ov—wait. Aw, shit! They're praying! Brace for impact! I'm bugging outta here. God be with you. Out!"

February 14, 2013
2000 Hrs
Operations Facilities, Navy Experimental Diving Unit
Panama City, FL

Jake Webster pressed his face to the porthole separating the Team from Stella, who was perched as usual on her stool. "We've finished our dinner. I see Art is here, so your shift at chamber duty is officially over. Don't you have something you'd like to share with us?"

"Oh, my goodness, how could I have forgotten?" Stella warbled, hand theatrically pressed to cheek. "I do believe I found something under my office door this morning. Let's see what I have here…" She sifted through her daypack and fished out the stack of envelopes she had retrieved early that morning. "Is it really Valentine's Day today? And can these be my valentines? Who could be sending cards to a poor girl stuck working all day on Valentine's Day? My oh my." Her vague attempt at sounding like a simpering Southern belle was lost on her listeners.

She selected and scrutinized the top envelope. "What lovely um…green bananas these are?"

"Let us see," came the jumbled chorus from the chamber. Stella held the crayon-scribbled envelope up to the porthole for the divers to view. "I'm just guessing here, but those might be green chile peppers," suggested Bill Murphy helpfully. The other men squeaked their agreement.

Stella opened the envelope. She scrutinized the messily written note inside briefly, then collapsed with a laugh.

"Read it! Read it!" they chorused.

24

"Must I?" she asked, a touch of red showing on her cheeks.

"Rules are rules," Cal Sorensen reminded her. "Ya got to read 'em, no guessing who wrote 'em."

Stella nodded with resignation. "Roses are red. Violets are blue. Hatch chiles are hot."

There was a moment of silence as it registered on three out of four men that the note truly ended there. Then came the peals of high-pitched laughter. Three pairs of eyes swung toward Bill Murphy, who was taking this moment to inspect the chamber ceiling, lips pursed in a physically impossible whistle.

"Dude. Really?" asked Jake Webster, as sotto voce as he could manage in the strange gases.

Murphy shrugged slightly. "Sorry, Shakespeare. What you got?" he murmured back, cupped hand hiding nothing in that acoustic sound trap.

"Uh, thanks very much, I guess," Stella concluded. She was already inspecting the second note while displaying with one outstretched hand the collection of colorful arrow-pierced hearts on its envelope. She read:

> Doc Stella had four little lambs
> Of fleeces black, brown, red, and hay.
> And everywhere Doc Stella led
> Her lambs would go and stay.
> She kept them safe, she did her part.
> And in return, they gave a fart.

More quacky peals of laughter from the chamber mixed with Stella's own laugh. "Very good! Thank you!" she pronounced, this time with more enthusiasm. Eyes within the chamber fairly quickly came to rest on Sorensen. "Pretty good, Doc," they assured him.

Stella was already hard at work scrutinizing the third note. "We have a genuine work of literary art, here," she announced, clearly impressed. "Oh yes, and a nicely decorated envelope," she added, waving a collection of scratchings that seemed to be muddy piglets brandishing bows and arrows. She read:

> Once within a chamber dreary,
> While I pondered, weak and weary
> Over many a quaint and curious table of forgotten dives,
> While I nodded, bored and napping,
> Suddenly there came a rapping, as of someone gently tapping,
> Tapping at my chamber sides.
> "'Tis some janitor!" I muttered,
> "tapping at my chamber sides.
> Only this, and naught besides."

> Ah! distinctly I remember those long tables
> Full of numbers, numbers marking off the months that I'd be here.
> What am I, a young man doing,
> When I could be out and drinking beer?

> Open then I flung my porthole,
> Where with many a laugh and chortle,
> In there stepped a stately maiden
> from a far Southwestern lore.

"You won't need those!" she said pointing,
Pointing at my lengthy tables.
"You will need those nevermore!"

"But these tables, they are sacred!"
I called out with fear and more.
"Will I not grow old and gray here?"
Quoth the maiden, "Nevermore!"

"Thanks, o thanks!" I cried out to her
As she sank into the floor.
I saw my future freedom shining,
My manhood wasted
Nevermore!

A mix of "holy cows" and "daaaangs" came from the chamber. Byron Soaps softly muttered, "Mama made us learn a lotta poetry is all I'm saying."

But Stella was already lost in amazement, reading the only plain white envelope in the group, with a typed name and message.

A Valentine to Stella

You excite me like
a dive in cold brine
a 'chute made of twine
a run through fields of mine
covert ops in Palestine
rough seas sans Dram-o-mine
a "navigation hazards" sign
a swordfish on the line
a sports car engine whine
batteries of alkaline

27

a torch for Frankenstein
a match in turpentine
a steak and spuds to dine.
No rhymes made with *sparkling wine*,
no shirts pink as calamine.
But I'll be yours if you'll be mine.

So please, please, please be my Valentine!

Three of the four divers were literally rolling on the deck plates, holding aching ribs, by the time Stella had finished the recitation. Webster sat in uncomfortable silence. Stella was wiping away tears of laughter as she rocked precariously on her stool. Cal Sorensen clapped Jake Webster on the back in congratulation. "Not my poem, dude," Webster muttered through clenched teeth.

Bill Murphy looked at Jake in surprise. "Even I can count to four, man. We all saw you writing something and sending it out in the same lock-out as ours."

"But it's typed," Webster reminded him, eyebrows lofted.

"You coulda asked Art or someone else outside to type it up for you, to make it look nicer," Murphy observed, not unreasonably.

"Not my poem, Murph," Jake muttered more forcefully, glancing sideways out the porthole in the hope that Stella was not listening. "I wrote a request for something else that isn't here yet," he said, with a solemn enough face to be believed. "So who...?" The four men looked at each other in bewilderment but could only lamely shrug. An awkward silence ensued.

Jake glanced at his watch and then scanned as far as he could see out into the control room. "Showtime!" he suddenly announced to his buddies.

Stella felt a gentle tap on her shoulder. She looked up from her third reading of the typed note. "JB, good to see you," she greeted him. It was Petty Officer James Brown ("no relation!" the manscaped, golden-blond surfer boy always told people). He was notorious among the divers for his freelance moonlighting career at bachelorette parties and the like, and a very lucrative one it was, under the stage name of Ripp Tyde. He reached into a pocket and pulled out a small device, which he set carefully onto a shelf and switched on. Stella nodded with pleasure when she recognized the velvety rumble it emitted: "A little less conversation, a little more action…"

Despite the musical refrain, Stella would not be the one expected to satisfy Elvis this time. JB swirled a finger at Stella, his eyes boldly engaging hers. She adjusted her position on the stool to face him as requested, with a growing look of surprised consternation in her widening eyes. An oddly warm smile slowly painted his lips as one hand crushed his T-shirt front, just before he gave it his signature rip. A second rip of clothing at below-belt level made Stella nearly topple from her stool.

Bruises on knees and elbows acquired in the ensuing melee of rubbernecking inside the chamber persisted for the remainder of the experimental dive. Let us be clear: Stella was watching JB; the Team was watching Stella.

April 3, 2013
1015 Hrs
1700 Feet Below the Ocean Surface
Straits of Florida

"We're OK. A few new bruises from the shock wave, but at least our dry parts are still dry. And we're still sitting pretty level. Over."

"Whew. I'm glad you're all OK. That was scary to watch, Captain. Looks like their goody bag of ordnance was stable after all. Now for the bad news. Over."

"What more bad news can there be? Over."

"The damned mad cat blew big chunks of itself all over your forward hatch and pressed up against your sail. Major sections of the wreckage are still bound together by that cable wrapping. I've used my vehicle to try pushing some pieces away, but nothing is budging. I'm afraid if I keep trying to do that, I might compress wreckage together harder and wind up doing more harm than good. It's going to take some heavy work to free your hatch enough for a rescue vehicle to dock. I can take photos for your guys in Key West to see for themselves and have them come up with an action plan for pulling you all out of there. I don't envy them that job. Hang tight till the cavalry gets here. I'll check back with you again later. Wish I could do more. Over."

"Photos would be great. We'll have to let Key West take it from here. Can't thank you enough. Keep us in your prayers. Over and out."

"You're already in them, Captain. Out."

February 14, 2013
2030 Hrs
Operations Facilities, Navy Experimental Diving Unit
Panama City, FL

She had needed an extended trip to the ladies' room and another to the junk food room to restore her professional calm. Now Stella was reinstalled on her stool outside the chamber, a can of soda resting on a knee.

"That was ahhhh…thank yuh, thank yuh verra much" was as much as she could think to say regarding her final Valentine's Day gift of a solo dance performance.

"Fair is fair! We gave you ours, now you have to give us yours. And no fair telling us that your worst Valentine's Day ever story was today," Jake Webster admonished her, all potential for sternness lost in the quacked-up delivery.

Stella sighed heavily. "Good thing you guys aren't going anywhere this evening. This will take a while to explain." The four men settled into their narrow bunks in the chamber and prepared to listen to her.

"The short answer is that on my worst Valentine's Day ever, about a dozen years ago, my college boyfriend proposed marriage to me," she said flatly. Squeaky murmurs of protest and disbelief emanated from the chamber. "The problem," she explained, "was that this was more of a trial balloon he was floating rather than a full proposal, and it was accompanied by a list of personal defects I was expected to fix before the offer was final," she enunciated with distaste. More squeaks and quacks from the chamber.

"The long version is that I had known this guy since we were both kids. His family spent summers on Cape Cod, in the cottage next door to my Grandma and Grandpa Curtis's, and we hung out together whenever I stayed with them, which was usually a month or more every summer. We were both pretty conservative kids, and so we never...well, we both knew quite early on that we were going to different colleges, which did not seem likely to keep us together, so we were careful not to let ourselves get...you know...carried away with any fooling around. Then he went to UMass, and I went to UNM, and even though Amherst and Albuquerque were that many miles apart, we kept thinking of each other and wanting to be together. So on the summer break between my sophomore and junior years at UNM, while I was visiting Grandma and Grandpa, Todd and I...uh...took our relationship to the next level."

Stella squirmed on her stool, suddenly very uncomfortable divulging so much personal information. "You guys awake in there? Is this getting too boring?" she enquired nervously. Sounds she took to be urgings to continue made her return to her narrative.

"Everything was great for about a year or so. We didn't get to see each other that often, but we could phone and e-mail, and it seemed what we had was great. Well...except there was this one problem early on. Todd told me what he called 'crusty New England men'—and remember, this guy was twenty-one at the time—never used the *L* word, so I should never expect to hear him saying *that* to me, or any other terms of affection or endearment. I told myself it was OK. I knew how I felt, and I thought I knew how he felt, even if he didn't want to say it."

Murphy sat up in his bunk and was about to speak, but the other three men hastily slashed fingers across their throats.

32

Murphy slowly returned to horizontal, his lips pressed.

"Once I graduated from UNM, I went straight on to grad school the next fall at SUNY Buffalo, in their environmental physiology program, and Todd went straight to Harvard Medical School. We were finally at least on the same coast together. Dad was ecstatic." Stella shook her head ruefully at the memory. "He had always wanted me to follow in his footsteps and go into medicine, but I was busy following other footsteps of his than medicine." She gestured widely to the room around herself. "So he was dreaming of having a doctor at least for a son-in-law. But the problem was Harvard. Todd really changed when he got there. Or maybe he was just showing a side of himself I hadn't recognized before."

Stella took a pensive sip of her soda. "You see, Todd's family was doing pretty well, with a small-town Massachusetts hardware store that was handed down from his grandfather, but they were no wealthy blue bloods or DAR members or anything like that. Good people, really. Todd was acutely aware of being the first member of his family to go to college, and here he was—drum roll, please—at Harvard and in medical school with the uppercrustiest of uppercrusties. So he began thinking he needed to start looking like this role he was going to play as a Harvard God-King Doctor. And that included having a God-Queen for a wife to put on display with him."

Not a sound came from the chamber. She sipped some more on her soda. "He told me he had been to some med school social events, which gave him a chance to see the kind of women his classmates chose. They were all better looking than I was, his words exactly," she stressed, "and they talked only about mainstream American things, so would I please—

and here started his official list." She tugged with growing irritation on her fingers to help count. "Number one, fix myself up to look better; number two, stop using the occasional Navajo words and phrases and making references to life on the Rez in public, or for that matter with him in private; and number three, get rid of my motorcycle, as it created too edgy an image. I asked him, 'So what am I supposed to do here? Dye my hair blond, get a nose job and some breast implants, or just what did you have in mind?' You know what the little stuffed-shirt snot said to me?" she asked with heat in her voice. She did not wait for their answer. "He said, 'Only if *you* want to'."

Now there were audible high-pitched noises that under other circumstances would have been manly groans. "So when do we get to the part where you punch this jackass out?" Webster enquired.

"Oh, the conversation got worse," Stella assured him, her voice now a rough growl. "He proceeded to tell me he was liberal-minded enough to overlook the fact that my mother was, and I quote exactly, not even White." Stella swiped a hand across her face at the painful memory. "True statement: my mother was Navajo, my mother's entire family for countless generations was Navajo. And thus *I am* Navajo. My family is proud to be Navajo, dammit! In equal measure, I am White and proud of that as well. I'm not apologizing to anyone anywhere for either side of my family. Sure, I've encountered bigotry before, and it has been dished out by Whites and Navajos alike, but never in this form or to be expected in this context, by someone I was inviting into my life. It was not the 'not White' but the 'not *even*' part that really pissed me off. Like whiteness was some necessary entry-level qualification for proper motherhood, or at least mother-in-law-hood. I never thought of Navajo-ness as a deficiency of Whiteness and thus a flaw one had to be gracious to overlook in my mother—or in me. Overlook indeed! The little racist prick!" she snarled.

Stella struggled to get her mood back under control. Rarely has an empty soda can been crushed so flat and so quickly by a human hand. "So, you asked for it, boys, you got it. My worst Valentine's Day ever," she concluded. "Care to top that, anyone?"

After some period of thoughtful silence, Byron Soaps was the first team member to make an effort to say something that might defuse some of Stella's heat and restore their evening together to pleasant chatting and clowning. "Sounds like he needed a good kicking to the curb, Doc. You did the right thing. But you said this was like a dozen years ago, so best you try letting some of that anger go, if I may say so," he ventured. "Gotta say, picturing you with a blond flippy hairdo and maybe one of those weird-ass English girl hats that looks like a pie plate nailed to your forehead, driving some fancy suburban mom minivan, trying to pahk yo cah in Haavad Yaad—that's a really funny image there."

Even Stella had to laugh.

Soaps, who had been staring at the chamber ceiling, heard a small tap at the porthole. Stella had placed her face near it so they could see each other clearly. She pressed fingertips over her heart and tossed them slowly toward him. He smiled and nodded back, a little embarrassed. "Chief Soaps, you're a good man," she said gently, embarrassing him further.

"Oh! Nevermore! Nevermore!" quacked out Bill Murphy excitedly from his bunk.

35

"Yes, Billy, very good! Your mother and I may have to start watching what we say in front of you," Jake Webster needled him. He received the not-so-secret hand sign he expected and deserved.

"Sooooo, to be clear here, the fool said, not realizing he was skating onto thin ice," Webster said with a touch of theater, "blond dye job—ridiculous idea. Nose surgery—terrible idea. Breast implants? Where did we come down on those? Negotiable? Non-negotiable?" He waved palms up and down to balance the odds.

"Ohhhhhhh, duuuuude!" was the best Stella could make out of the racket that followed for some seconds. Pillows and socks flew with the greatest of low gas-density ease for quite a while, considering this was not a girls' dorm room. "Remember she's got the O_2 controls for you and all us!" Sorensen admonished Webster.

April 4, 2013
0215 Hrs
Naval Air Station Key West
Key West, FL

The wheezing air conditioner in the shabby conference room was doing an admirable job of injecting molds into the air. The room smelled heavily of the sweat and fear of the men who had been conferring there most of the previous day and throughout the night.

"Remind me again, Lieutenant Commander Costello, just why we have this woman in here?" Captain DeLucca demanded from his end of the table.

Costello took one slow breath to allow himself to answer with the same level of patience he had used the previous two times he had been asked that question since his and Stella's late-night arrival in this room. "Because, Sir, even though I am the Senior Operational Diving Officer at NEDU, and I do have SAT dive experience, you said you needed ultra-deep and hydrogen diving capability for this mission. There is only one person qualified today to answer detailed questions about ultra-deep hydrogen diving, and that is Dr. Curtis."

"That's still the answer you're sticking with, even though she's giving me nothing more than a typical scientist's pant-load about 'maybe' and 'under certain conditions' and 'with more research'? Just answer me yes or no now! Can your team run this mission? Or are you NEDU clowns so soaked in test and evaluation crap that you can't be called on to actually do anything useful in the real world?" shouted Captain DeLucca, angrily pounding the table before him as he glowered from Costello to Stella and back. His gray brush cut was sticking in sweaty spikes across the top of his head, and his face was the unhealthy shade of red it had far too often assumed since he had taken command of the Navy's National Security Operations in Key West.

Stella threw her hands up in frustration. "How can I give you a yes or no if you won't give me any of the information I need on which to base my answer? Depth? Water conditions? Operation? Time window? Need for accelerated compression and decompression? I need more information than 'really deep' and 'right now' and 'that's classified' to give you a sensible answer," she responded as calmly as she could. Her eyes darted to Lieutenant Commander Costello's face beside her, but she found nothing useful there. He looked as frustrated and confused as she felt.

"DeLucca, she's right," said the weary voice over the speakerphone. "Give her the express security clearance, and let's get her briefed."

"Admiral?" asked Captain DeLucca warily, staring at the phone before him. The other officers at the table glanced at each other wordlessly, eyebrows raised.

"Yeah, you know, the special, expedited security clearance. Get Lieutenant Kratz to handle it. We've all been working on this for hours without any progress on this issue; we need to move faster than this," said the voice.

All Key West-based eyes in the room turned to Captain DeLucca in stunned silence. "Yes Sir, Admiral. Give us a couple of minutes here, please. Kratz?" Captain DeLucca beckoned to his adjutant, a broad-chested and rather pudding-faced young man who was seated farther down the table, across from Stella and Costello. In civilian terms, *adjutant* simply means "administrative assistant to a senior officer." It does not have to translate to "dirty work-loving, boot-licking minion-slash-hooligan," but in Kratz's case it did. After a brief, quiet exchange, Lieutenant Kratz turned to Stella. With a polite "Dr. Curtis, if you would accompany me, please?" he ushered Stella before him into the dimly lighted corridor.

Five steps later Stella was astounded to feel one hand grabbing her hair and another hand grabbing her by the throat and lifting her off her feet. Her back was slammed into the nearest wall. Kratz's breath was hot in her face. "If you ever even *think* about telling *anyone anything* about what you will be told in that room, or what you will learn about on this mission, just think about your brains being splattered all over this wall, which is the nicest thing that will happen to you. Do you understand?"

Stella's head was held in a grip far too tight for her to nod or move her jaw. She managed to blink her assent. The big man dropped her and stepped back, surveying her sagging form and ragged breathing with disgust. "You have sixty seconds to pull yourself together and get back in that room," he snapped. He stepped over her legs with calculated uncare and strode, or more accurately swaggered, toward the conference room door.

Forty-seven seconds later (according to everyone's watches), Dr. Stella Curtis strode through the conference room door and returned to her seat next to Lieutenant Commander Costello. "What do I need to know, gentlemen?" she asked, her hard, dark eyes scanning the sweating faces around the table. Only the red marks at her throat gave any indication of the recent events in the hallway. Costello, whose arrival within the previous hour from Panama City with Stella made him as much a stranger to Kratz as she was, looked shocked at the obvious signs of her abuse. Costello's malevolent glance at Kratz was noted by the young man, who returned the look with an insolent smirk.

"Here's the rundown," Captain DeLucca told the two NEDU newcomers. "At approximately 0800 hours this—I mean *yesterday* morning, a US Navy submarine operating in the Straits of Florida was attacked by a small underwater craft of enemy origin. The sub is now lying on the bottom in approximately seventeen hundred feet of water, essentially upright. Ballast tanks have been damaged, so she cannot surface. Nuclear power system is down for lack of adequate flow of cooling water. The sub is now running on battery power alone.

"The length of time that the life support systems can keep operating, and it's a miracle they're running now, is reduced to about seven days. That's our time window for getting those men out. Assuming that the damaged hull does not crush sooner than that. Almost all the men, and there are over a hundred of them, are in the forward compartments, which were not significantly damaged in the attack. Due to the flooding issues in the mid and rear sections, the forward hatch is our only viable point of access. The hatch is designed to mate with a rescue module, which is a component of a full submarine rescue and decompression system. That system is already being mobilized for transit from San Diego. All the components will arrive by plane over the next few hours, to be placed on a vessel here in Key West. It's anticipated that the rescue system will be operational within approximately seventy-two hours."

Captain DeLucca leaned across the table toward Stella and Costello. "There is one major obstacle to conducting this rescue mission. The enemy craft that attacked the sub is now lying as an exploded pile of debris covering the forward hatch and pinned against the sail, tangled in SEPIRB."

Stella raised a fingertip. "Sorry, Captain, but I'm a little Navy acronym-challenged. Sea burp?"

Captain DeLucca shrugged. "SEPIRB. It's just like an EPIRB, but the *S* at the beginning makes it specific to submarines."

Stella shook her head.

"Awferchris...oookay," the Captain huffed wearily, wincing again at the wall clock. "Submarine Emergency Position-Indicating Radio Beacon. It's a fiber-optic cable with a float on the end that a submarine deploys in emergencies to send out a distress signal. The DISSUB...can I say *that* to you?" he asked her irritably.

Stella nodded. "Disabled submarine, yes Sir, I know that one."

"Good. The DISSUB sent up one such cable, which the enemy vessel fouled on, and so they had to deploy another SEPIRB to call for help. Clear?" he asked Stella exasperatedly.

Stella nodded.

"We had the DISSUB reconned by—um, well, we had it looked at right away by a small submersible whose eyes we trust that was operating nearby when the attack happened. Based on that evaluation, we sent an ADS2000 yesterday afternoon to clear the hatch." This time the Captain ignored the blank look in Stella's eyes and her slow head shake.

"That operation was able to cut some of the SEPIRB cable and pull away enough of the debris to take a look at the hatch and its surrounding area. They saw that the rescue seat, a kind of metal flange that's the docking site for the rescue vehicle over a hatch, is too damaged for the vehicle to make a pressure-tight seal with the hatch. There's nothing further we can do with robotics or manned submersibles within our time window to conduct this rescue. We need divers to go down with torches, cut up and remove the rest of the debris, and weld on a new rescue seat. We've got a replacement seat being custom made for us in Groton right now. They're predicting it'll be done within twelve to twenty-four hours, so it ought to be here well within the time needed for everything else to come together. If this were all taking place in five hundred feet of seawater or shallower, you would not be in this room. Since it is in seventeen hundred feet of seawater and we need it now, we have to ask you the same question we started on an hour ago—namely, can this mission be run with hydrogen biochemical decompression?"

Stella closed her eyes for a moment. "No," she said firmly. The men in the room erupted with angry disbelief. The voice on the speakerphone sputtered, "Wrong answer, Dr. Curtis!"

"Wrong question, Admiral Schremp," she said, one finger raised defensively. "The question was originally phrased to me in the form of 'can the Hydrogen Team run this mission?' The answer to that question is absolutely yes; the Team is not only the best but the only team ready to dive on this mission. If you need them to go that deep and that fast, then for reasons I assume are obvious to everyone here, you must have the divers breathing a hydrogen-containing mix. My Team has the only current US Navy experience with hydreliox, *on chamber dives to 1000 feet.*"

42

Costello nodded vigorously. "They all have extensive underwater construction and demolition experience, dating from their years of operational diving before they were assigned to their current tours of duty as test subjects at NEDU. MDSU-1, MDSU-2, EOD, SIMA, ARS…"

Stella listened to him pour out his Navy alphabet soup of diving tours of duty to which the Team, and he as well, had been assigned. She noted it was having the intended effect of making listeners look suitably impressed.

"So cutting up metal debris not larger than a mini-sub and welding on a new part should be well within their capabilities, with the only challenges coming from the issues of working at that depth," Costello concluded.

"But the depth is the problem. Optimal service of all your needs for a dive profile that deep go way beyond what we have current expertise to cover, which is why my upcoming funding cycle was going to work on that," Stella explained.

"Were you planning to get to your point any time today, Doctor?" The speakerphone crackled with Admiral Shremp's irritation. Captain DeLucca nodded a curt agreement to his own lack of patience.

Stella continued without responding to the Admiral's needling or the Captain's rumblings. "Nobody yet, at least in this room, has field experience at seventeen hundred feet with the gas mix we think for theoretical reasons is what is really needed, which is the quadmix of hydrogen-helium-nitrogen-oxygen. Everybody here knows why we want a considerable percentage of hydrogen in the heliox. But you also know it is dangerous to use too much hydrogen. There are those who think that if you blend in some percentage of nitrogen in order to get some nitrogen narcosis to counteract the hydrogen narcosis, you are better off yet. Hence the need for these elaborate quad mixes. That was something the Office of Naval Research specifically mandated me to study."

"Dr. Curtis! This is not a classroom for you to be lecturing us in, like some damned professor! You are not the only person in your room with deep diving experience, you know. Now. Get. To. The. Point. Do you expect to be able to support this mission to seventeen hundred feet? And don't give me some runaround on what gas mix you'll use!" The speakerphone erupted again with Admiral Schremp's indignation. "And why did you tell me 'no', but still keep talking?"

Stella took a deep breath to suppress her own growing frustration with the discussion. "First of all, yes, gentlemen," she said, looking first at the speakerphone and then individually to the officers sitting around the conference table, "I am aware I am talking to a room full of experienced ultra-deep diving people. The lives of the Team are depending on it!" she exclaimed with rather more heat than she would have preferred. Struggling for control of her voice, she continued. "The Team has plenty of experience on chamber presses between three hundred and one thousand feet on hydreliox. We know how to manage those issues as well as anybody does, and with slow presses under controlled lab conditions, we have never had any problems. So far we have seen no need to make things more complicated by adding nitrogen at these depths. But pressing on down to seventeen hundred feet rapidly enough to respond to an emergency field need is a whole new world. My experience in this is confined to writing one grant proposal, and that is still more than most people in the diving industry can claim. I need to let you all know what my thinking is, given the...what, fifteen minutes or so of time you've allowed me to plan my mission strategy...in order to get your buy-in to the approach I propose to use. If you don't like it, tell me *now* what else you think we need to consider while we still have the opportunity to modify our action plan."

She stared at one face after the next. No man at the table could hold her gaze for long. The silence around the table and on the speakerphone encouraged her to gulp for air and continue.

"My Team, I am positive, will do whatever it takes to respond to this emergency. We were planning, in our next funding cycle, to spend a couple of years and a couple million bucks to instrument people and work our way slowly from one thousand to two thousand feet in a chamber, testing what the best blend of gases should be to optimize the responses we want and minimize the ones we do not want. But we've got to go now, and so I'm telling you as quickly as I can that we cannot offer you operational guarantees that we know best practices. I think our safest bet is to rely on what has been known to work in the past, optimal or not."

She scanned the room, looking for reactions. She was hard-pressed to detect any. Gulping for air, she plunged on. "Experience of decades past from COMEX in France and from Duke University suggests that if you need to press rapidly for operational reasons such as the current mission, High Pressure Neurologic Syndrome, articular pains, and hydrogen narcosis could all be bigger problems than they would have been on a slower press. This has led us to the theoretical recommendation to add nitrogen to the gas mix as a supplemental narcotic. But I do not recommend we experiment on this mission with the added complexity and uncertainty of blending in nitrogen. I was planning on lab testing the addition of five percent to ten percent nitrogen in small increments, with the expectation that the optimal value would be somewhere in the middle of that range. The logic is that five percent nitrogen at sixty atmospheres would be equivalent to the negligible nitrogen narcosis of a little under one hundred feet of sea water breathing air, and ten percent at sixty atmospheres would be more like being potentially dangerously nitrogen narcotized at just over two hundred feet. But we do not know if these narcotic properties scale at these super-high pressures and unusual gas mixes the way we are familiar with in shallower water breathing air. And you can see we are getting into some very high-precision gas mixing here, best done in pre-mixed gases, not bleeding into a chamber one gas at a time while operational concerns may also need managing."

Another quick scan of the room did show a few sad nods and shrugs around the table in response, but she received no interruptions. Taking encouragement where she could, she continued. "Admiral, I am not trying to quibble or pick nits with you here. This is important. We can use hydrogen; in fact we *must* use hydrogen in the heliox breathing mix. But it is not trivial to decide how much hydrogen is our limit or whether we can add yet another gas to our mix. If we bleed in too little nitrogen, we've increased the divers' breathing resistance with a denser gas mix for no benefit to them and a possible source of confusion for us. But far worse, if we bleed in too much nitrogen, we're risking having divers basically drunk and stoned simultaneously. I am hoping for input here on how you all think this should be managed."

One of the sweaty faces around the table jerked to attention.

46

"What about oxygen? You haven't said one word about how you're going to manage your oxygen. OTUs! On a SAT dive you're going to have to manage those OTUs!"

Stella leveled her gaze on the man for a long moment while the rest of the group checked their note pages. "Point five," she responded calmly.

"Point five what?" came the admiral's voice from the speakerphone. "What the hell is she talking about?"

Stella studied the back wall of the conference room for a moment and slowly pumped her palms in frustration. "If I had known what I was being summoned to Key West for tonight while I was still in PC, I could have brought my grant proposal with me, and then I'd have better numbers for you faster. You could simply read my dive profile and gas switches, and then you could study those as you wished, and I would not have to babble gibberish at you. As it is I have to answer your very legitimate concerns with numbers off the top of my head," she explained.

"Will using some other part of your head make this any faster?" came the sarcastic voice from the speakerphone.

"Sorry," Stella replied. "I did some math calculations and gave you the answer without giving you the logic. I meant point five atmospheres of oxygen pressure will be the highest that will be used for the dive. For safety reasons when working with mixes of oxygen in hydrogen, we must never work with more than two percent oxygen, balance hydrogen. That constrains how we start our press and thus what PO_2 values we can work with. But as you said, when divers are breathing elevated pressures of oxygen for days, there are also oxygen tolerance units to consider. When we

47

balance the constraints of explosivity and oxygen tolerance simultaneously, it turns out that your OTUs will win out and limit us to using point five atmospheres for our maximum PO_2. At that level, we should not have to worry about cumulative toxic effects of oxygen exposure as computed in OTUs."

Throughout her calculations and discussion, the officer who had posed the question sat glowering and fidgeting. When she finished, he muttered, "Point forty-eight atmospheres. We never go above point forty-eight atmospheres of oxygen for long SAT operations. And point forty-six would be even better!"

Stella was silent for another few moments. By then most of the men present understood that her wordless stare was just an indication of her mental calculator in action, and they watched her with growing interest. "I assume, Sir, that your saturation dives are at two hundred or maybe as deep as five hundred feet, and that you pre-mix all your gases to a high precision?" Stella asked him.

The officer growled his assent.

"I understand your concerns, but at our operational depth of seventeen hundred feet, which is just over fifty-two atmospheres, we will have to let the percentage of oxygen drop to around one percent to be at point five atmospheres of oxygen, which gets a little scary to manage operationally. I am not sure we can guarantee gas-mixing precision as high as we would have to use to say we were at exactly point forty-six or point forty-eight atmospheres of oxygen instead of approximately point five atmospheres. But we'll do the best we can. No matter how carefully we meter the oxygen, we still cannot guarantee that the Team will have no pulmonary issues from oxidative damage. But as far as we know, that should be self-limiting and self-repairing. Did that answer your questions? Are we in agreement here?" she asked the officer.

The officer continued to look irritated. "I'm not a mind reader. You needed to tell us that sooner. I'm just saying you shouldn't ignore the oxygen. It's important. And too much oxygen has consequences. Consequences!"

"Yes, you are right. Thank you for weighing in on this. I really appreciate getting some feedback here," she said with a sincerity that made him duck his head back into his own notes. "But are we all in agreement that we take our clues from the literature that a maximum partial pressure of hydrogen should be kept below twenty-four atmospheres and that any potential added benefits of supplementing with nitrogen should be set aside in favor of keeping the gas mixing simpler for this operation?"

Stella waited through a full ten seconds of resounding silence. "Hearing no objections, I'll take that as a yes on the trimix." She watched as muscles stiffened around the room, but still no man spoke. Costello, aware everyone was watching him as well as her, had to work hard to keep a noncommittal face while thinking, *Hoo-yah, Stella!*

"Now for my next point. What I am objecting to, which made for that original 'no', Admiral, is the use of hydrogen biochemical decompression on this mission. My chamber dives of the past year at one thousand feet support the original animal research, indicating that biochemical decompression should work to accelerate the decompression and shorten decompression time by about half compared to a heliox dive to the same depth. But in continuing deeper, we were planning on troubleshooting problems by means of physiological monitoring and having the medical backup of the lab. We did not plan to start at seventeen hundred feet of open water. The hydrogen biodec bugs cannot directly touch the helium, so the more helium is in the gas mix, the less we know about accelerating decompression rates. I have a theory about what may happen to the helium in a biodec diver, but that's another story.

"You've given me plenty of reasons why you need divers to get down there and complete this mission as quickly as possible but no reasons why the divers need to decompress rapidly. Just let the Team run your mission as a saturation dive on a hydrogen-helium-oxygen trimix, bring them in the saturation chamber back to Key West, and then decompress them on a standard heliox schedule dockside. The French did their hydreliox dives like that for years. It'll take over three weeks to run a heliox schedule decompression from seventeen hundred feet, but who cares? And putting the Team on a standard decompression schedule will all but guarantee that your diving medical officers can spend all their time taking care of the disabled sub crew, who may have bends, with or without controlled decompression, or other injuries of their own to worry about."

The men around the table shot surprised looks at each other. They slowly nodded and muttered grudging assent. It suddenly occurred to Stella that their silence and evident negativity all this time was not to the various aspects of the gas mixing during compression as she had laid them out but to what they had assumed was the obligation she would impose on using hydrogen biochemical decompression to complete the dive. She was well aware there was no love in this room, or most other Navy rooms, for this edgy technology. Once she made it clear to them she was taking

50

hydrogen biodec off the table, they were mollified and even showing signs of growing enthusiasm.

"Good points, Dr. Curtis," Captain DeLucca acknowledged gruffly. "We'll take this under consideration. Do you have anything else to ask Dr. Curtis right now, Admiral?" he asked the speakerphone.

"No, not at the moment, but have her to stay close by until after we've spoken more. Keep Lieutenant Commander Costello in the room; we will need more from him. Thanks, Queenie," responded the Admiral.

Stella's usually unreadable expression turned into a tense half smile at the speakerphone. "You're welcome, Admiral. We'll do our best."

Captain DeLucca turned to his adjutant. "Lieutenant Kratz, take Dr. Curtis to the coffee room and make her comfortable until we need her again."

"Yes Sir, Captain." The young man rose and ushered Stella through the conference room door. Lieutenant Commander Costello watched her departure with her brute escort uneasily.

February 14, 2013
2100 Hrs
Operations Facilities, Navy Experimental Diving Unit
Panama City, FL

As the four men in the chamber and the lone woman outside the chamber settled back down, Soaps turned pensive again. "You know, Doc Stella, sometimes people can surprise you and come around to being not so bad. You want my worst Valentine's Day ever story, sure, I can give you one, but in my case it has a happy ending."

Stella adjusted her perch on the stool and urged him to continue.

"Before Teresa and I were married, she had a hard time telling her folks she was seeing a Black man. Her daddy especially. They're Miami Cubanos originally, and he was fixing to find her some nice Cubano husband. She was living in this apartment near the base, to be close to work, and her folks were up there in Destin. So when she finally decided it was time she introduced me to them and get the yelling over with, she invited them down to her place for a barbeque. We didn't notice at the time that she had picked Valentine's Day for this thing, or we'd have done something on our own and called them some other time. So her folks pull up in front of her place, and I come walking out to meet them at the curb. Her daddy flips out. Refuses to get out of the car. Her mama, she's a real sweetie, she gets right out, gives me a nice little hug, and walks straight on into the apartment. Teresa keeps trying to talk her daddy out of the car, but I tell her to just let him be and go on in.

"Mind you, even though it's February, it's pretty hot out there in that car in the sun. So I make small talk with

Teresa's mama, give her some of my barbecued shrimp—best damn shrimp on the Redneck Riviera, if I do say so—but I'm keeping my eye on my watch. About an hour later, I walk out to that old man in that hot car with a couple of cold beers in hand. You bet he's ready for one. And I sit down on the grass next to the car while he works on that beer, and I tell him how much I love Teresa and how good I'll be to her, and what fine people I come from. And you know what? That old man starts coming around and agrees to go inside. Course, the fact that my daddy and my uncle are the S and S of S&S Automotive Parts—biggest family owned car parts chain in Florida," he added with pride, "did seem to help some of that turnaround. That and the fifteen percent family discount they give. And the beer filling up that old bladder.

"Yup, I know what I'm doing," Soaps concluded with satisfaction. "So there you have it, Doc Stella. Not a romantic Valentine's Day, like I know all you ladies like, and not a whole lot of fun at the time. But her daddy walked her down the aisle at our wedding, and that was going on five years ago now, and her daddy comes over to barbecue with me pretty often. He says my Key lime pie—you know I make mine old school, with baked meringue on top, not whipped cream—is the best he's ever had."

"God bless, man. Ya got a lotta grace," said Sorensen, reflecting what they all thought.

April 4, 2013
0330 Hrs
Naval Air Station Key West
Key West, FL

Kratz turned on the light in the tiny coffee room, sending palmetto bugs scuttling in every direction. "Have a seat, please, if you don't mind the critters too much. I'll nuke us a coupla coffees," he said, reaching for a cold pot of some dark and evil-looking liquid and two not impressively clean mugs.

Stella deftly scooped up a palmetto bug in her hand and studied it scuttling across her palm as she sat at the battered table.

Kratz peered at her uncomfortably. "Found a new pet?"

"Bugs were some of my favorite toys as a kid," she responded. "They kept me entertained while I watched my Grandma's sheep graze."

"Hmmm. If you say so. Boy, I sure was not following much of that whole conversation back there," he admitted with an uncomfortable chuckle. "Mind filling me in?"

"Do you know anything about diving?" she asked him.

"Sure! I took a cert course around here last year. Been out on a reef with buddies a couple of times already. I got the part about you being worried over how much of what gases your guys should breathe and how to keep them from getting the bends. The bends are like when you shake up a can of soda and then open it fast," Kratz said proudly, his hands illustrating his words with a final flourish of twiddling fingers. "But I got bogged down in the details after that."

"I see," she responded, still watching the bug explore first one hand and then the other. "Maybe we'd better take this from the top. You know that as a scuba diver, your tank is usually filled with air, right?"

Kratz nodded brightly.

"And how deep can you dive on air, and what problem do you have if you go too deep with your air tank?" she asked patiently.

"My cert has me rated to dive to a hundred and thirty feet. If I go deeper, Martini's Law says every extra foot deeper is like I drank another martini. I think that's the same thing as—whaddya call it—rapture of the deep!" he finished excitedly. "The only thing I'm not sure I get is why with an advanced cert, I can dive deeper without getting drunk."

"You're on the right track, although your one-foot rule is a little harsh," she corrected politely. "The point of limiting a diver with a basic certification to a hundred and thirty feet is for two good reasons. One is that at deeper depths, the number of minutes you can spend on the bottom without requiring obligatory decompression stops on the way up is very short and easy to overshoot. The other is to avoid nitrogen narcosis, the rapture of the deep you mentioned. As you breathe higher and higher pressures of nitrogen, it becomes increasingly narcotic. We won't bother for present purposes with why, nor am I even certain I can fully explain the why. The point of the hundred and thirty foot rule is not because there is no narcosis shallower than a hundred and thirty feet or that at one hundred and thirty-one feet you are blind drunk. In fact when we measure people carefully enough, it can be shown that you are slightly off your fastest reflex times even in less than one hundred feet of water.

"As with alcohol consumption, there is individual variation in susceptibility to nitrogen narcosis. Certifying agencies chose one hundred and thirty feet as a compromise on giving beginning divers lots of ocean to dive in while keeping them reasonably far away from what for most people would be really debilitating levels of nitrogen narcosis. Think about beginning car drivers; you tell them to turn off the radio and minimize other distractions to keep all their attention focused on their driving, which takes a lot of brain power for a new driver. With increasing experience in driving a car, you can sing along to the radio, chat with friends in the backseat, and so on, with less and less likelihood of a wreck. Usually. In the same way, with years of scuba diving experience plus advanced certifications over time, the milder effects of nitrogen narcosis aren't as devastating to the safety of your dive as they would be to a less experienced diver. It's also possible that experience and prior exposures build up some amount of resistance to the narcotic effects. But just as with alcohol, past a certain blood level everyone is totally wasted, no point denying it or insisting you can handle it. For most people that's around two hundred feet, plus-minus about twenty or thirty feet."

"But your mission is going to be at seventeen hundred feet!" Kratz exclaimed. He suddenly remembered the coffees he had left in the microwave. He hopped to his feet and sashayed to retrieve the two mugs. Stella accepted hers, fortunately for him, with no visible reaction to his dance performance.

"Yes. That gets into the part about mixed gases you probably found so confusing. Don't worry; the subjects we were discussing would not have been covered in your basic certification class or even in most advanced sport divers' classes," she assured him.

"So then you switch to nitrox? I have a buddy who just took a nitrox class," Kratz told her.

"No, oxygen-enriched nitrox is not for our purposes. But thinking about nitrox issues will get you into the ballpark of what we are facing with ultra-deep mixed-gas diving. The reason your buddy wants to dive nitrox should be that the lower nitrogen content of his breathing gas will significantly extend his safe bottom time at depths in the fifty- to one-hundred-foot range. That's something you want. The bad news is that you also get something you don't want with nitrox. The nitrogen is diluted with extra oxygen, and past a certain oxygen pressure for a long enough time, oxygen induces seizures," she clarified. "If you wanted to go to depths greater than about two hundred feet, there is no mix of only nitrogen and oxygen that would be safe to breathe for more than a very short time. What we usually do at the two-hundred-foot point is to replace the nitrogen with helium. Helium does not have the narcotic properties of nitrogen. And as you go deeper on heliox, you'd need to continually dilute the oxygen with increasing percentages of helium to keep the oxygen pressure in a range that is safe from seizures but enough for life support. We generally aim for operating between point four and one point five atmospheres of oxygen at any depth."

"How many OTUs does that make?" Kratz asked her with a wink.

"Ah, then you were following some of the conversation." Not having noticed his wink, Stella mentally upgraded Kratz from pond scum to mosquito larva. The improved rating would not hold for much longer. "That officer had something important to ask, and he had a right to be concerned about the answer. I appreciated that. What I was describing to you as an operational range between point four and one point five atmospheres of oxygen is the exposure we can give divers on one or a few relatively short dives. That is very different from the exposure we are allowed on a multiday saturation dive, due to cumulative effects of oxidative damage to lung tissue."

Kratz grinned. "I know you think I'm just some muscle-bound hunk." Mistaking her head shake for a compliment, he flexed a bicep, intending to enhance her admiration. "But I've got some brains"—he pointed to the bicep—"to go along with all my muscles." He tapped his skull and snorted at his own little joke.

Stella did not respond. Back to pond scum rating for Kratz.

Even Kratz could see his charm was not working on her. Yet. Not quite ready to admit permanent defeat, he cleared his throat nervously and struggled for new footing on this slippery slope. "Helium, huh? Oh, helium is what makes the Donald Duck voice thing I've seen on some TV specials?" he asked.

Stella debated momentarily whether to speak to this lunk further or not. She decided it was politically necessary to retain some civility as best she could. "Right. Helium's low density causes the vocal cords to vibrate faster than they would in air. We have electronic unscrambling devices that help translate the voices back to nearer their normal range to reduce the problems with communications," Stella assured him. "But now we're getting to the complicated part. An additional advantage to replacing nitrogen with helium is that a helium molecule is smaller than a nitrogen molecule. As pressure increases, gas density increases, and it becomes harder for divers to ventilate their lungs with the dense gases. The smaller size of helium molecules makes a less dense gas than a comparable pressure of nitrogen."

Stella took a cautious sip of her coffee. It tasted the way it looked. She set the mug down. "Now is where we need to make this even more complicated by introducing another gas: hydrogen. Somewhere between one thousand and two thousand feet, even a helium-oxygen gas mixture becomes so dense it is hard for divers to ventilate their lungs with it. The only solution to that problem is to replace the helium with an even smaller molecule, and there is only one molecule smaller than helium."

"Ah! That's what the hydrogen is all about! But isn't hydrogen explosive when it's mixed with oxygen?" Kratz asked, impressed with himself for remembering so much high-school chemistry.

"Yes, it can be," Stella assured him, "but not at all relative mixtures of the two gases. We work in a range that is too oxygen-poor to be combustible. But molecular size is not the only issue with hydrogen. There are two problems unique to ultra-deep diving that we need to deal with. One is called High Pressure Neurologic Syndrome, or HPNS. We think it's caused by the ultra-high pressure interfering with nerve conduction, especially at synapses. It manifests as tremors at least and psychosis at worst. The other problem is called High Pressure Articular Syndrome, or HPAS, which causes joint pains in divers compressed too rapidly to great depth. The divers usually call that 'No Joint-Juice Syndrome' because they say it feels like their joint bones are grinding against each other without any lubrication.

"One would normally try to reduce the risk of HPNS and HPAS with a slow compression, but in this emergency situation we don't have the luxury of time. So now we get to where we want to add hydrogen to the gas mix. Hyperbaric hydrogen has been found to induce a narcosis of its own. There is reason to think that a touch of hydrogen narcosis suppresses both HPNS and HPAS and thus allows a deep press to go a little faster without hurting the divers. So breathing hydrogen on an ultra-deep dive is mostly a good thing. But past some tipping point, and it remains controversial as to exactly where that is, the hydrogen narcosis wins out, and you have a real mess of psychotic divers who are risks to themselves and to their mission. The only other option, and that's what you heard me asking those officers about, is to also add some amount of nitrogen into the mix, to have its depressant narcotic properties slightly counteract some of the excitatory effects of the hydrogen. The problem is that for the moment, nobody knows what amount of nitrogen to add."

"Oh, that's the drunk and stoned thing you were talking about—mixing your uppers with your downers!" Kratz said with so much excitement he sloshed some coffee onto the table. He took his first taste of the coffee remaining in his mug. "This stuff is nasty." He winced. He reached far across the table for a bowl with its lid askew and pulled it into Stella's reach. "Sugar? I think your little pal and all his buddies have been tap-dancing in the sugar bowl, but that may not bother you."

"It doesn't, but no thanks." She set the bug on the table, still holding it carefully by the back edge of its shell, and offered it a few crystals of the sugar. When she finally released it, it

60

shot away.

"Maybe now you can appreciate that we are talking about some very complex gas mixing, with very small increments being quite important, and with huge penalties for getting anything wrong," Stella said. They both swirled the coffee in their respective mugs, to give themselves something better to look at than the rest of the room and to give themselves something to do with the coffee other than drink it.

"So just how deep can you dive? Can you keep switching or adding gases and go to three or four thousand feet?" he asked.

Stella shook her head. "All the physiological and technical problems become so great that to date no dive has been conducted at much beyond two thousand feet. I doubt such dives ever will be made. In fact..." Stella looked startled at her thought. "Those dives to two thousand feet, as far as I would know, were all conducted in chambers. This operation will be one of the deepest open-water dives in the world. It certainly could be the US Navy's deepest."

"Wow!" Kratz looked impressed. He seemed lost in more thoughts than she expected him to be capable of having for over thirty seconds. He shifted in his seat and looked up at her again. "Now tell me about this chemistry stuff Captain DeLucca was talking about. What is that anyway?" Kratz asked her.

"Hydrogen biochemical decompression," she corrected. "Originally designed in the mid-nineties by researchers working for the Navy in Bethesda, Maryland. Let's go back to that shaken soda of yours. Not really an accurate image of all the biological events taking place in decompression sickness, but for the purposes of this conversation, it will do. When you learned to dive, did you use a dive computer?"

He nodded. "Sure."

"You know the computer was keeping track of how much time you spent at various depths, in order to estimate how much nitrogen you were absorbing and thus advise you when you needed to end your dive in order to minimize those soda bubbles and the risk of decompression sickness?" she asked.

He nodded again.

"So a diver is in the water, filling up with gas that has to come out under controlled conditions or the diver may get hurt when he returns to the surface. Biochemical decompression is a way to scrub some of the gas out of the diver from the inside. We give our divers big capsules full of freeze-dried microbes that are like bacteria, about twelve hours before they are going to start their decompression. That gives the capsules enough time to travel to the large intestine and break open, releasing the microbes. The microbes are specially chosen to be of a kind that can safely live in the essentially oxygen-free conditions inside the large intestine, where they will consume some of the gas that the divers have been breathing. In our case, the gas the microbes consume is hydrogen. They combine the hydrogen with carbon dioxide that is made by the diver's own respiration.

"This chemical combination makes water and methane, or what you might know as natural gas. Basically, we are taking the hydrogen, which your body cannot use in its own cells but will absorb in large quantities during an ultra-deep dive with it, and by means of microbes we are converting a small but critically important portion of that hydrogen load primarily into a harmless liquid—water—and a smaller quantity of another gas—methane.

"We can't hope to scrub out all the hydrogen as fast as it comes into the diver through his lungs. But we don't have to. We only have to take out a few percent of the total load per unit time during the decompression phase of the dive because if we keep removing these small increments of hydrogen from the inside, in addition to what is normally coming out across the lungs, we can safely decompress divers in significantly less time than it would take with decompression across the lungs alone." Stella checked Kratz's face for signs of comprehension. He actually looked as if he were listening and thinking.

"You said something about helium in the gas mix messing up your calculations on hydrogen decompression?" Kratz asked.

"Yes. That's something we were just starting to get into, in our lab research at NEDU," she told him. "The microorganisms that metabolize hydrogen cannot metabolize helium. In fact nothing on Earth can make some other molecule using helium. So you would think the hydrogen-helium-oxygen trimix we are working with at NEDU would give us a slower safe decompression rate than what the Bethesda researchers got with their animal research using nearly pure hydrogen-oxygen mixtures. But so far that has not been the case. We know part of the answer to that: we have gotten bacteriologists to give us more metabolically active bugs that give us more hydrogen-scrubbing power than the Bethesda researchers had. The other part, and this is still my pure speculation, is that by pulling out hydrogen from the tissues and making methane and water in the intestine, we are creating a greater gradient for the helium to move out of the tissues and into the intestine of the diver as well."

"What happens to the water and the methane?" Kratz asked.

"The water gets absorbed in small enough quantities to be of no medical concern. The methane leaves the intestine the same way any other gas leaves the intestine. Which is good news for us, because we can monitor the whole reaction process by sampling the chamber gases for methane release rate from the divers."

Kratz looked at Stella in disbelief. "So you're telling me what you really do is make these divers, er, uh…" He hesitated, stifling a laugh.

"Yes. Only one word for it: they fart off the methane. And it's our job to measure their farting rate to be sure we are safely on track with the decompression. In the Bethesda days of this research, it was a hard sell to the Navy Brass that measuring rat and pig farts was a respectable thing to spend Navy funding on. Whole rooms full of admirals would laugh till they cried. Funding got very shaky and even evaporated for years. But the results were impressive enough, and the Navy need for this technology became great enough—you know, increased terrorism from nasty places with deep coastlines—that they eventually pushed it through anyway. I still get laughed at rather often, but that doesn't bother me."

"I guess you know Admiral Schremp pretty well?" he fished.

"No," she said helpfully.

"But he called you Queenie."

"Yes. A running joke of the hydrogen biodec program. It was a title that was originally bestowed on my predecessor, Dr. Parker, the woman who took it on the chin with all the rat and pig diving. The Admiral met her a few times, back when he was a Captain at BUMED. The people who liked Dr. Parker meant the title to be affectionate, and the people who didn't meant it as an insult. In Admiral Schremp's case, it's generally the latter."

"Queenie? I don't get the joke."

"It's what she and I are the Queen of that makes it a joke. It'll come to you," she said dryly.

He stared at her a moment. "You're the Queen of Farts! Now that is funny!" He gave another of those annoying laughs through his nose. "Oh, man, is this ironic," he said when he had more breath.

"Ironic?"

"You aren't the only member of that royal family. Your kingdom also has a King," he informed her.

"Who—some other scientist?"

"A college professor somewhere. Miami, maybe? Kind of a cross between a chemical engineer and a computer geek, I guess you'd call him. But you didn't hear this from me," he added quickly. "He who knows does not say, and he who says does not know," Kratz intoned with what was supposed to pass for wisdom. "This guy I didn't mention ain't called the King for nothing," Kratz confided, voice lowered despite the fact that Stella and he were in a closed room after working hours.

For the first time that evening, Stella smiled.

"I guess you do look a little royal," Kratz said, trying on his favorite I-might-get-lucky teeth-baring expression. "What are you—five-eight, five-ten maybe? A hundred thirty or forty pounds?" He pantomimed hoisting her to guess her weight. "Actually, that was the most fun I ever had with a security clearance," he smirked, with far less charm than he thought. "I kinda like ya, somehow. So—if you don't get hauled off to join the rescue mission tomorrow, do you think you'd like a little tour of Key West? I know some really good bars. Well, maybe *good* isn't quite the right word…" Again he produced that honking laugh.

Stella did not respond.

"You have a kinda Sig Freud thing going on that I'm starting to get the hang of," he announced. He incorrectly interpreted the look she shot him as incomprehension. "That's French, and it means 'cold blood'."

Stella did not respond. She seemed suddenly deeply absorbed with something on the table before her. Kratz peered over her coffee cup. She had neatly removed the head of one of the numerous dead palmetto bugs on the table and was carefully removing each leg, lining them up in a perfectly spaced row.

Kratz was irritating, and obviously not as bright as he thought he was, but neither was he completely stupid, competency in foreign languages, or even English, excepted. "OK…Maybe I'd better go check on the Captain." Kratz hastily left the coffee room. As he hurried down the hall, he shook his head. He could not clear his mind of the image of

Stella, that look of detached concentration in her eyes, neatly dismembering and lining up his bones.

February 14, 2013
2115 Hrs
Operations Facilities, Navy Experimental Diving Unit
Panama City, FL

Bill Murphy rolled over in his narrow bunk to rest on his elbow and spoke up. "If that's the kind of story you want to hear, yeah, I got a bad Valentine's Day that turned out good story for you. Shoot! I thought you wanted stories like how your old girlfriend showed up while you was wining and dining your new girlfriend."

They all asked, "Got a story like that?"

Murphy's verbal response was thankfully unintelligible outside the chamber, although the manual response was unmistakable. "So this was six years ago, when I was still with Ida, that LA girl," he began. "You know what we mean here on the Redneck Riviera by LA, right, Doc Stella?"

She nodded. "Lower Alabama."

Murphy continued, "Ida had some good about her. I liked her, I guess. Still do. But I got to admit I was mostly married to her to have somebody waiting on me whenever I was back on shore in PC and wanted some company, which was only once in a blue moon in those days. I signed up for a lot of deployments back then, and I guess maybe I wasn't the best husband. She was always a pretty big girl. But seemed like every time I come home, she was even bigger and flew off the handle at every little everything faster. So then came February fourteenth, and I knew it was Valentine's Day, so I called her and told her I'd be home that night and I'd take her out someplace nice. She started crying and making this big fuss, and I got worried. So I came home and found her in the bedroom. Blood everywhere." Murphy paused and shifted in his bunk, still shaken by that memory.

"She'd only scream and cry if I tried to touch her to see where all the blood was coming from, and she wouldn't tell me nothing. So I called 911 and got an ambulance to take her to the ER. I stayed behind at the house to wash some blood off me before going over to the hospital to see what was what. When I walked into the bathroom, I heard some funny noise, like a kitten mewing. We didn't have a cat. The noise seemed to be coming from the laundry hamper. I lifted the lid, pulled out a few dirty towels, and there it was. A baby boy. Still all bloody and slimy, and had its umbilical cord dangling. I grabbed him up in one of them dirty towels, ran to my car, raced to the hospital. The doctors kept him a while and then said he was OK, and with some rest and IV fluids, Ida was OK too. So on Valentine's Day, I got a son," he concluded simply.

"My Billy Boy, he's a great little kid. Ida...well...about then she started serious drinking and doing oxy. Last I saw her, she looked like she was rode hard and put up wet. So it was pretty clear to everybody that the boy couldn't stay with her. He lives with Ida's folks, over there in Something-Frenchie-Name, Alabama. My folks, they keep telling me to check and see if he's really even mine. But don't matter to me. I guess I just want a son. I try to send over money for him whenever I can and send him something special on his birthday, which is today. I'll have to remember to send something soon's we're out. When he's big enough, I want him to come live with his old man in PC, or wherever I'm deployed by then. I wanna teach him to dive, take him deep-sea fishing, go to the shooting ranges..." Murphy's monologue trailed away.

None of the four listeners could think of anything to say.

April 4, 2013
0400 Hrs
Naval Air Station Key West
Key West, FL

Lieutenant Kratz hastily pushed the door to the coffee room wide open. "Dr. Curtis, Captain DeLucca is ready to speak to you again. Come this way, please."

Stella rose quickly and followed the adjutant down the dim hall to the conference room. Its smell had not improved since she had left it.

"Dr. Curtis, thank you for joining us tonight. You may be excused, and the US Navy thanks you for your efforts," he informed her. "Lieutenant Kratz will escort you to the Lodge and see to it that you have a return flight to Panama City in the morning."

"Excused? But Captain DeLucca—I am going on this mission, aren't I?" Stella asked incredulously.

"Pah! Certainly not! Lieutenant Commander Costello is the officer in charge of the Hydrogen Team. But since he seems to feel he could use some backup on this mission, we'll decide which of us"—DeLucca waved a weary hand around the conference table at the sweaty faces collected there— "will assist in managing the gas mixes and switches you discussed at such very, *very* great length." He leaned back in his chair, aching and tired. "Why would we want a civilian scientist onboard for a classified mission when we are not planning to use your fancy bio stuff anyway?" he asked the ceiling, hands folded behind his head.

"I would never dispute Lieutenant Commander Costello's

leadership. But I think you need me along for at least two reasons, Captain. One is that there are only three people qualified to run the hydrogen dive chamber system: that would be our technicians Hank Johnson and Art Moore and me. You'll want three shifts of people to tend it round the clock. And the other is an old Navajo saying: shit happens," she finished.

"That old Navajo of yours sure gets around," Captain DeLucca said wryly. He hesitated, thinking. "You make a persuasive case. Gentlemen? What do you think?" Grumbles and shrugs were as coherent an answer as he received. "Very well. Lieutenant Kratz, please escort Dr. Curtis to the Lodge. Dr. Curtis, please stay in your quarters in the Lodge. We will call for you to board ship when we need you."

Stella nodded solemnly to Captain DeLucca, Lieutenant Commander Costello, and each of the other men in turn. She rose and walked swiftly toward the conference room door.

Kratz was waiting at the door. He opened the door for Stella and found himself needing to scurry at a rather undignified pace to try to catch up with her as she headed for the front door of the building. Outside, Kratz managed to get ahead of her and open the passenger door to the Captain's jeep. She strode past him without a glance, her cowboy boots softly thumping on the ground as she headed toward the Lodge. Kratz stood frozen by the jeep until even he felt foolish. He sighed softly as he watched her jeans retreating into the darkness.

February 14, 2013
2130 Hrs
Operations Facilities, Navy Experimental Diving Unit
Panama City, FL

"So I guess you want my lousy Valentine's Day story now," Jake Webster said with a resigned shrug. "Yeah, I got one of those too. Also involves my boy, but he'd been safely born in a hospital about four years earlier. Barb decided it was time to get him baptized. We were all three living in PC at the time, which was its own headache with a girl like Barb. She made me take leave and go up to Boston to her family's church for the ceremony. The February-fourteenth part was coincidental, but she liked the 'my little cherub' touch when she noticed it.

"In the church I attended as a kid, we baptized babies too small to have anything to say about it one way or another. But for some reason, Jacob Junior was walking and talking when we took him to the church. He had seemed oddly quiet and anxious in the car on the way over. We were halfway down the aisle for the ceremony when he suddenly started screaming his little head off, kicking and fighting and shrieking something about how he didn't want us all to be eaten. Barb was jerking on his poor little arm so hard, I was worried she was going to break it. So I scooped him up, waved to everybody that we'd be right back, and hustled him outside."

Jake shook his head in irritated amazement. "You know what was bugging that poor little guy? In his understanding of the day's events, as told to him by his mother, he was going to be 'appetized,' and then the minister and his wife would have us all for dinner, which to him meant he'd be rubbed with spices, and then we'd all be spitted, roasted, and eaten by them."

The three men in the chamber and the woman listening outside the chamber were all simultaneously laughing and moaning in sympathy.

"I was able to straighten things out with him, but he was shivering with cold-sweated terror for a pretty long while, given that a church full of people were all waiting. Once he was calm and warm enough, we went in and did the deed. But as soon as we were in private, I talked to Barb about why poor little JJ was so freaked out. She said she knew he was saying for the last couple of days that he didn't want to be 'appetized' or 'had for dinner,' but she thought it sounded so cute she didn't bother to correct or explain. I told her that was a pretty cruel way to treat a small child, and her jerking on his arm like that was inexcusably abusive. We got into it pretty hard then, and all kinds of things that were wrong between us started flying. It became clear to me that whenever she was mad at me, she took it out on little JJ. So that's when I left to come back to PC alone, while she and JJ stayed in Boston," Webster concluded.

Sad headshakes all around summed up the responses from the listeners. They were all pensive for some time.

"Well, Chief Sorensen," Jake Webster said, lifting his hand high enough from his bunk to tug the dangling arm of his friend. "You're awfully quiet up there. We have yet to hear your tale of love's woe on this day devoted to romance."

"We've all told our tales, now it's your turn!" urged Chief Byron Soaps from his bunk.

Cal Sorensen scrutinized the chamber ceiling. "Nothin'," he

effused.

"Aw, come on, dude! Spill!" urged Petty Officer Bill Murphy.

Sorensen rolled onto his side, the better to look down on his buddies. "It's true!" he insisted. "I married the only girl I ever loved, we have two bee-utiful little girls look just like their mama, and every Valentine's Day there's cake and ice cream for all us. Nothing bad to tell ya," he concluded. He rolled back and resumed his quiet contemplation of the chamber ceiling.

From outside the chamber, Stella commented, "You're a lucky man, Cal. I'm happy for you that you have such a good life." Murmurs of agreement came from the various bunks.

"Not lucky, blessed!" Sorensen quickly corrected her. "I'm grateful ever day for my many blessings." He rolled to put his back to his buddies and the dim chamber lights.

He had never told anyone in the Navy, not even these best friends of his, of the dear baby boy who went from playing peek-a-boo with his daddy one evening to being found dead in his crib the next morning, a victim of that punt of a diagnosis, Sudden Infant Death Syndrome. And why should he mention it now? Hardly relevant to the current topic of conversation. His son had become their own little angel on a February 15, anyway.

April 4, 2013
1845 Hrs
Navy Lodge, Naval Air Station Key West
Key West, FL

Stella channel surfed on the television in her room, unable to find anything sufficiently engaging to take her mind off of her confinement and the impending challenges of the mission. She had slept badly that short night and awakened nervous and restless before sunrise. A call she had made to Art early that morning had succeeded in reaching him. But for hours today, phones belonging to Art and the Team seemed to be turned off. Not knowing how any of the preparations were going was the worst part. She paced. She stared at the clock, begging it to move its numbers faster. She paced some more. And this had gone on all day. As in all day. The whole miserable blankety-blanked day. She was at her wits' end. A shave-and-a-haircut knock made her jump. She sprang to open the door.

Senior Chief Jacob Webster stood in the doorway, with a grease-spotted box in his hands and the handles of a plastic bag slung over his forearm. "Special delivery for Dr. Stella Curtis! One medium pizza with every topping they have *except* pineapple," he cheerfully intoned.

Stella quickly sorted through her head for some clever retort but was too excited over seeing Jake and getting some actual news and a break from her boring confinement to quarters. "Get in here!" was all she could come up with.

"Yes Ma'am!" he responded, marching briskly to the little table along the wall. He deposited the pizza on it along with the plastic bag. The contents of the bag made an appealingly slushy sound in the process.

"So?" Stella asked eagerly. "How is everything going? Any more news from the sub? Is our equipment here from NEDU yet? Anything installed and recalibrated yet? Gas supplies in yet? Is the Team starting a press soon?"

Jake laughed. He reached for the bag he had set on the table and pulled it toward himself. "Looks like we don't need any more caffeinated beverages in this room."

"Aw, duuuude!" she remonstrated, with more cultural fidelity than erudition. A brief and friendly tug-of-war over the bag ensued until Jake accidentally kicked a waste basket by the table. The clatter of empty soda cans in the basket made them both stop and stare. With a nervous giggle, Stella reluctantly relinquished her grasp on the bag. "You may have a point," she acknowledged sheepishly.

"Everything is going fine," Jake assured her. "We got everyone mustered and working at your favorite time this morning."

Stella groaned softly. "Another 0-dark:30 joke. Oh, great."

Jake grinned. "Yes indeed, another Navy cliché."

"Meaning you've had too little sleep and probably nothing to eat in far too long?" she asked, worried.

Jake shrugged. "We're doing well enough on both counts. We know how to catch a few zees here and there. On the plane. Trading off with each other for an hour or two. Everyone here at the Air Station has been super helpful, so that makes the work go much more quickly and smoothly and has given us time for snacks. And of course there's always your favorite strategy for replacing both food and sleep: caffeine!"

"You know what I always say," Stella responded with her first real smile of the day, "a yawn is just—"

"A silent scream for coffee!" they said in unison, sharing a laugh as well.

"Anyway," Jake continued, "the gas mixing and analysis systems are safely aboard. Hank and Art are busy getting them up and calibrated. Whenever I ask Hank how they are progressing and if they need our help, he just says, 'Not my first rodeo!' in that slathered-on-extra-thick good ol' boy drawl he sometimes uses. You should see Art's face whenever he does that."

"I have," Stella responded with a knowing nod.

"For a change there's a cliché that's more your idiom than Navy. You've actually participated in some rodeos, I imagine?" he asked her.

"I've been in a few barrel races in Rez rodeos," she acknowledged.

"Who won? You or the barrel?" he quipped.

Stella directed her inner gaze toward her current choice of deity, soliciting it for forbearance. "I suppose you think that's the first time I've heard that joke."

"No?" he asked innocently.

"No." She stepped closer to the table. "Would you like some

of this pizza?"

"I can't stay long, but I'd love a quick slice, now that you're offering," Jake responded, grabbing for the box and digging out a piece of the oily pie like a starving man. "Lieutenant Commander Costello is getting all the dive gear and the cutting and welding equipment and supplies ready, and he needs help with that. We're in the process of inerting the tubes we'll be using for our hydrogen, so I've got to get back to the Team ASAP. The breathing-grade hydrogen we need had to be ordered in from Miami, and the tube truck for that can't get onto the Overseas Highway until traffic gets light tonight. HAZMAT requirements, you know. We expect to be able to cascade the hydrogen into our banks overnight, when it's a few degrees cooler. Helium got loaded a couple of hours ago. Oxygen also onboard. Our chamber was rescrubbed and checked out this morning. So things are looking pretty good!" he finished with a cheerful flourish and a new mouthful of pizza.

"Wow! You have been pretty busy, I see. Or, rather, I hear," she added with a sad look around her room. "Watching TV and cruising the vending machines while what might be the biggest mission of our lives is in play is not as much fun as you might think," she informed him.

Jake nodded sympathetically. "Art said he picked up that duffel of personal stuff you asked him to round up at your apartment. It'll be onboard when you get there. Oh, and also the case from the lab you wanted," he added.

"Good! I'll be happy for a clean T-shirt by then, whenever 'then' actually is. Oh, for heaven's sake! How could I forget? I have something for Lieutenant Commander Costello." Stella grabbed a piece of paper from the top of a nearby dresser and thrust it at Jake. "I've been working on the dive profile. What do you think?"

Jake scanned the piece of paper quickly. "Looks like a pretty aggressive run to the bottom, but what the heck. I think we can do that."

"I know I promised the Team you'd be playing around with some nitrogen narcosis on the next depths, but I've left the nitrogen out of this profile as one too many things to be fooling with. Part of a deal I struck for us last night. It doesn't take the sharpest knife in the chandelier, as you would say, to put this together. But I figured the Lieutenant Commander and Art and Hank would all have their hands full right now with equipment setup and would be pressed for time to generate this. It's fine if they want to tweak the stop lengths or depths. After all, they're the ones with the operational experience here, not I. The best-laid plans of mice and women may go awry no matter what we choose, but at least this is a starting point for us."

Jake grinned and pushed the plastic bag with the extra-large cup of soda in it back toward her across the tabletop. "I was wrong. Keep up the caffeination, Doc! And don't worry; lots of people think of you as a sharp knife in the chandelier." Jake received the friendly smack in the shoulder he had been hoping for since she had opened the door. He folded the paper neatly and put it into a pocket, which he patted to confirm its security. Then he glanced at his watch. "Gotta go! The Team will be needing me to help finish prepping for that incoming load of hydrogen." He turned and headed toward the door.

"Hey, Einstein!" Stella taunted. "How do you spell HAZMAT?"

Jake turned back to face her. With a touch of conjurer's drama, he pulled his cap from a hip pocket and, with a very well-practiced hand, secured it on his head at its most boyishly rakish angle. "S-T-E..."

"Go!" she commanded with a laugh. He went.

Depth	G	Press	Time	Comments
0–300 fsw 1–10 ATA	He	30 fsw/min	0 h 10 min	PO_2 kept at 0.2 ATA as % O_2 drops from 20% to 2%, safe to add H_2
300–500 fsw 10–16 ATA	H_2	20 fsw/min	0 h 10 min	Make up O_2 consumed. Aim for PO_2 at or below 0.5 ATA for limiting OTUs
500 fsw 16 ATA	H_2	Rest	1 h 10 min	1.5 h elapsed
500–750 fsw 16–24 ATA	H_2	10 fsw/min	0 h 25 min	
750 fsw 24 ATA	H_2	Rest	1 h 5 min	3 h elapsed
750–1000 fsw 24–31 ATA	H_2	10 fsw/min	0 h 25 min	
1000 fsw 31 ATA	H_2	Rest	7 h 35 min	11 h elapsed
1000–1100 fsw 31-34 ATA	H_2	10 fsw/min	0 h 10 min	
1100–1250 fsw 34–38.5 ATA	He	5 fsw/min	0 h 30 min	Switch to He press at PH_2 max
1250 fsw 38.5 ATA	He	Rest	1 h 20 min	13 h elapsed
1250–1500 fsw 38.5–46 ATA	He	5 fsw/min	0 h 50 min	
1500 fsw 46 ATA	He	Rest	2 h 10 min	16 h elapsed
1500–1700 fsw 46–52.1 ATA	He	2 fsw/min	1 h 40 min	Consult divers to decide He/H_2
1700 fsw 52.1 ATA	He	Rest	1 h	Consult divers to decide He/H_2 and rest length
Total			18 h 40 min	

Operation SECOND STARFISH

Depth (fsw)	ATA	PO_2	% O_2	PN_2	%N_2	PHe	% He	PH_2	%H_2
0	1	0.2	21.0	0.8	79.0	0.0	0.0	0.0	0.0
300	10.0	0.2	2.1	0.8	7.9	9.0	90.0	0.0	0.0
500	16.0	0.3	2.1	0.8	4.9	9.0	56.2	5.9	36.7
750	23.5	0.4	1.7	0.8	3.4	9.0	38.3	13.3	56.6
1000	31.0	0.5	1.6	0.8	2.5	9.0	29.0	20.7	66.8
1100	34.0	0.5	1.5	0.8	2.3	9.0	26.4	23.7	69.7
1250	38.5	0.5	1.3	0.8	2.0	13.5	35.0	23.7	61.5
1500	46.0	0.5	1.1	0.8	1.7	21.0	45.6	23.7	51.5
1700	52.1	0.5	1.0	0.8	1.5	27.0	51.9	23.7	45.5

Susan R. Kayar

February 25, 2013
0200 Hrs
Experimental Dive Chamber, Navy Experimental Diving Unit
Panama City, FL

He saw her form in front of him, a soft curve in the dim bluish light. He reached out to touch her. Warm, smooth, and utterly yielding to his touch, he drew her to him in the narrow, hard bunk. Yes, this is how he had always imagined it would be to take her in his arms, to draw her close, to hold her. So warm. So soft. He slid a thigh over her hips. Her body molded itself perfectly to his. Yes, this is how it should be. These are the curves of her body just as he had always imagined they would feel. His hunger to take her and make her his darling, his very own, grew. So yielding, so warm, yes. "Oh, Stella!" he breathed ecstatically.

He could feel her sweet breath on his shoulder. Her lips approached his ear. She said, "Dude! Dude! If ya wanna get busy on a pillow, use yer own!"

"Whaaa?" Jake Webster said thickly. He struggled to hold on to the warm form that was being unceremoniously ripped from his tender embrace.

"You pulled my pillow off the edge of my bunk, and judging from your sound effects, lover boy, you were going to make a mess on it any minute now," Cal Sorensen murmured with uncharacteristically careful enunciation and slightly irritated amusement.

"Whaaa?" Webster said, with no discernible increase in mentation.

84

Sorensen whispered as loudly and distinctly as he dared without waking Soaps and Murphy in the next pair of bunks in the narrow test chamber. "Dude, you were having a dream. She's not here. This is my pillow," he explained as he successfully wrestled the pillow free and tossed it up onto his own bunk. He stared down at his buddy, whose arms were still flailing helplessly after the dear mirage, his sleep-dulled eyes barely visible.

"Aw, fer cryin' out loud," Sorensen mumbled. "Here, dude." He yanked the pillow from under Webster's head and stuffed it into his eager arms before clambering back up into his own high bunk.

"Y'all OK over there?" said a sleepy voice.

"Yeah, Soap. Chamber dreams. S'all good," said Sorensen.

"Uuuh-huh! Reeeal good, sounds like!" agreed Byron Soaps with a deep chuckle. "Bone appétit," he added for his private amusement.

"We'll all be breathin' fresh air in a coupla hours an' sleepin' like babes in our own beds tomorrow night," Sorensen said reassuringly.

April 5, 2013
1800 Hrs
Aboard *Whatever*, Naval Air Station Key West
Key West, FL

Stella and Captain Gilchrist stood together on the bridge as their vessel sat in harbor. The crew was scrambling around them, loading and making preparations. If all continued to go this well, they would sail tomorrow to the site of the disabled submarine, or DISSUB, as everyone but Stella would say. Stella had just been permitted to come aboard, and she recognized the need to introduce herself to the Captain Officer in Charge of the Operation. They chatted pleasantly about Key West for a few preliminary minutes.

"Is anyone ever going to tell me where we're going or how long we'll be underway?" Stella asked.

Captain Gilchrist surveyed her carefully out of the corner of one eye, under guise of wiping his smooth skull with one hand as he adjusted his cover with the other hand. He was still considering whether he liked this tall, sturdy, rather alien-looking woman as part of his operation. He decided to give her the answer he usually gave his young granddaughter on Sunday afternoon sailboat trips. Seconds later Stella strode angrily away from the bridge.

Art Moore found her shortly thereafter along a stretch of railing, her usually impassive face twisted with anger. "What the hell, Stella?" he asked in wonderment. "What in the world is eating at you already? You can't get this wrapped around the axle before we even clear the dock, or you'll have nothing left for the tough times ahead."

Stella turned to stare at him. "They do not trust me! I am

burdened with the shared responsibility for the safety of the Hydrogen Team and therefore the safety of the submariners we are supposed to go out and bring back. But nobody trusts me enough to tell me the simplest details! I have been kept a virtual prisoner in my hotel room for the last day and a half while you prepped everything. Do you have any idea how brain frying that kind of confinement is right now? I do not know where the Team is. I do not know what any of this equipment is," she said with a sweep of her hand across the deck. "It is so…so…disorienting to not know so much as the names of things or where or why we're looking for them."

"Stella, you know many of those details are classified. None of us can be told anything more than what you've heard. But you shouldn't let that spin you up," Art responded soothingly.

"Captain Gilchrist thinks I can be spoken to like a child!" she spat out.

"What did he say?" Art asked.

"Yes, I know the exact location of this mission is classified. I do not need to know latitude and longitude so I can call my evil spy buddies and rat us all out before we even get there, or whatever scenario people are imagining here. When I asked him where we were headed and how long it will take us to get there, what I am really wondering about is… well…I'm not much of a sailor, so I'm worried about how rough the water is going to get the farther we go offshore and how long I may have to stay seasick. But instead of giving me some general answer fit for an adult with an authorized job here, he gives me a child's bedtime story answer of 'heading toward the second starfish to the right and straight on till morning,'" she said indignantly.

Art looked puzzled.

"That's a nautical version of Peter Pan's heading when he flies to Neverland," she translated with an irritated flourish of hands.

Art smiled at the deck briefly before composing his face enough to look again at her smoking eyes. "Don't you think a US Navy Captain could have given you a much harsher answer than that one, in response to a civilian asking him for what under these circumstances qualifies as classified information, if he didn't like you?"

Art studied her face for another long moment as she grew more quiet. It dawned on him that he recognized the strange appearance of her coloring, unquiet eyes, sweaty forehead, and bluish lips. "How can you be seasick when we haven't even cast off yet?" he asked her.

Stella shrugged. "I have been this susceptible to really bad seasickness all my life. All I have to do is watch those nasty waves rolling our way out there, and over the side goes my lunch."

"Ah. Then don't watch the nasty waves rolling our way," he suggested quite reasonably. "Have you tried taking any anti-motion-sickness meds?" The dark clouds moving rapidly toward them and the rising chop did not bode well for a landlubber of this sensitivity.

Stella nodded. "I've tried every medication there is, and none help except to make me groggy, which I cannot afford right now. I suppose I know I should not look at the moving water, but it is a little hard not to. The waves are rather fascinating. I have been known to get motion sick sitting in a movie theater if the camera swings around too wildly or if the image moves too quickly past a stationary camera."

"So you can understand that you may be letting your eyes fool your stomach and then letting your stomach overwhelm your brain in this situation?" he proposed. "OK, I get it that you felt isolated in your hotel room at what for the rest of us was a frantically busy time. I get it that you find many aspects of this mission disorienting, but it doesn't have to stay like that. Lots of things you want to know you can figure out for yourself. And then there are probably things you really won't want to know at all."

Stella shot him a look of disbelief and confusion but was clearly listening intently to him.

"What do you want to know first?" he asked her calmly.

"Where is the Team?" she demanded, immediately regretting her harsh tone with a friend clearly trying to help her. "Sorry. Where are they?" she repeated in a quieter voice.

"They're right over there, in that chamber." He pointed across the deck. "They're fine. Press started at two o'clock this afternoon. Hank's in charge of it right now. We three will be taking eight-hour shifts, with whatever overlap we think we need as things progress. Your shift will be from noon to eight p.m., mine will be from eight p.m. to four a.m., and Hank's will be from four a.m. to noon. Same shifts we do at home, to keep things simple. The Team just got to their thousand-foot rest stop about a half an hour ago, so hopefully they're getting some sleep while they can. We'll go look in on them in a bit."

"If the press started at two o'clock, why was I not permitted to board until now? You and Hank had to split up my shift today, right?" she asked him, her fists firmly on her hips.

Art studied the deck briefly before responding carefully. "Hank didn't want—"

"Oh," she groaned, her hands sagging limply to her sides.

"No, I mean Hank was convinced he and I knew this first stage of the press to one thousand feet so well that we didn't need to drag you out of a comfortable hotel room just yet," he said unconvincingly.

"*Comfortable* hotel room? It had everything short of padded walls and a straitjacket for me! Translation: Hank did not want me around until he starts to be unsure he can manage things himself," she said. "Not my first time to note Hank's antipathy for me." Stella shook her head in irritation. "Oh, and where is Lieutenant Commander Costello? Did he get my dive profile? What profile are you using now?" she asked him in rapid fire.

"One question at a time, please," he reminded her. "Lieutenant Commander Costello is still rounding up and prepping the cutting and welding equipment and the other heavy gear. He's around here somewhere. Yes, he did get your dive profile and passed it on to Hank and me. Well done, by the way. It's what we've been going by today. Which, between you and me, may have fueled Hank's wish not to have you onboard when we started using the profile," Art admitted.

"We are facing—literally!—matters of life and death here, and this man wants to play 'whose profile is this?' games?"

Stella asked hotly.

"My world, and welcome to it." Art sighed. They both blew out some irritation onto the warm sea breeze. "So, enough of him. Back to you. What else do you need to know to feel oriented?"

"What's the name of this ship?" she enquired.

"Oh, come on! It's written right there," he said, pointing to neat black lettering on a nearby lifeboat.

"I saw that, but I didn't think it could be the name of this ship. That name doesn't sound at all Navy. Isn't this the USS whatever? Some dead president or a state or a city?" Stella asked.

"No, this is the Good Ship *Whatever*. It doesn't belong to the Navy, so it's not the USS anything. The Navy has contracted it out for this use. This is a Vessel of Opportunity, as they say. Everyone but you, given your very un-DOD-like attitude toward acronyms, will refer to it as a VOO. You may also hear people calling it a dynamically positioned ship, meaning once we get on-site, it will stay there very precisely without anchoring, by means of sensors and compasses that feed information to computer-driven propellers and thrusters. It has great deck space for all the major heavy equipment we need. The Navy doesn't maintain its own fleet of vessels like this one, so it contracts these out as needed. Same way the Navy contracts out for civilians like you," he reminded her. "Did you ever read about the Civil War ironclad ship, the *Monitor*? First ship with a revolving gun turret, funny-looking thing with a freeboard as low as a sub's on the surface. Some call it the Navy's first modern warship."

Stella nodded. "Sure, I know the Navy was involved in the recovery of the turret of the *Monitor* off Cape Hatteras. I read all about that. Back in maybe 2003 or so?"

"It was 2001 to 2002," he corrected her. "That salvage mission, and a helluva fine job it was, by the way, is important to us because it got the Navy back into the business of doing saturation diving. There was a long time, which you probably don't even know about, during those years between your dad's time and yours, in which the Navy was out of SAT diving for operational purposes. The Navy still trained SAT divers to maintain the skill base and for experimental work like yours. There were two ships, the USS *Pigeon* and the USS *Ortolan*, that were designed for submarine rescue missions and carried SAT systems, but I don't know how much field use they saw. It became harder and harder to keep those systems certified until the ships were decommissioned in the early or mid-nineties. It took a Navy policy pendulum swing to relearn what passes for obvious to you: that keeping divers compressed and therefore saturated with their diving gases between long working dives saves hours of decompression time per day, even in a couple hundred or so feet of water, not to mention that SAT diving is the *only* way for us to do ultra-deep diving. Because of the infrastructure used in the *Monitor* mission, that's why we have this contracted ship—"

"Vessel of Opportunity," she pronounced carefully.

"Yeah, very good, this Vessel of Opportunity prepared to be tricked out rapidly with everything we need for a SAT dive mission. All the equipment was flown in yesterday morning and locked into dedicated sites on deck. This system, all new, is called a SAT FADS, a Saturation Fly-Away Diving

System. It's amazing! That big chamber there"—he pointed with his chin across the deck—"is where the Team is right now, and the bell they will ride up and down in is there." He pointed again. "We had to request a special chamber and bell to get the depth and hydrogen rating we need, but every other element of the SAT FADS system is standardized. The mechanism for bringing the bell up and down is there. Compressors and all the other control equipment are in those vans." His hands waggled over the relevant areas. "Everything containerized and ready to go. All we had to do, once the SAT FADS arrived, was mod for our gas mixing and gas analysis systems and load up the tanks with our own supply of gases."

"Who are all these people?" she asked, sidestepping every few seconds to let someone move quickly past her.

Art glanced around, dodging people on his own. "Some of them are divers from other commands, probably from Mobile Diving and Salvage Units..."

"Mud Sues?" Stella asked.

"Very good!" Art congratulated her. "MDSU divers who will be responsible for things like running our gas farm, bringing the diving bell up and down, docking and undocking it with the main chamber, managing the welding and cutting equipment and any other underwater construction tools the Team will need, things like that. Lieutenant Commander Costello will be our Diving Officer, but there will also be a Master Diver and a Chief Warrant Officer, who are probably also from a MDSU. Other people are seamen here to run the ship. It takes a lot of people to manage an operation and a vessel the size and complexity of this one," he informed her.

He turned himself and angled Stella with a gentle press on the shoulder to look at the ship next to theirs at the dock. "Now you need to look over there at the equipment for the sub rescue."

"That ship is a voo too?" she asked him.

"Yes, it is. The *Voo2* is even more loaded with real things of beauty than the *Whatever* is. The entire sub rescue system was flown in as modules, just like our SAT FADS. This equipment is brand new also, probably being used for the first time in anything but practice. The system is collectively known as the Submarine Rescue Diving and Recompression System, or the SRDRS, as you would never say. Those four big chambers over there are components of the SDS—the Submarine Decompression System—the decompression chambers they'll be bringing the submariners up into. Those big box-car pieces—those are the units that contain the generator, the environmental controls for the chambers, the freshwater pressurization system, and all the ancillary parts to make this system run, all designed to be modular and brought into Key West from San Diego by air. It's that modularity that allowed everything to be dropped in and assembled so quickly for the SRDRS and for our SAT FADS.

"All the equipment will be completely installed in about seventy-two hours, which will be by tomorrow noon or early afternoon. That's lickety-split by the standards of only a few years ago, for operations with far fewer capabilities," he assured her. "In decades past, a conventional SAT system alone would have taken weeks to assemble, and nothing like the SRDRS has ever existed before. There are untold numbers of battles that needed to be fought to get all this specialized and sophisticated equipment commissioned and certified. And heaven only knows how long we'll be allowed to keep it, given the Navy's history of adding systems and then letting them go if they don't see much use. Not that anyone wants to see lots of subs needing rescue. But right now you, my dear, are looking at one amazing collection of state-of-the-art saturation diving and sub rescue equipment, such as few people today, and none before you, have ever seen."

Stella surveyed the scene before her, interested and impressed.

Art shot her a quick smile. "Here's a fun fact you'll enjoy. The motivation to build this much infrastructure to decompress crew from a DISSUB came from work on decompression sickness risk in submarine rescue scenarios modeled by colleagues of your dad's, back in the Bethesda Navy lab. Heck, there may even be some of his test dives and modeling work that was used."

Stella's eyebrows shot up. "Hoo-yah!" she murmured. "And, by the way, that would mean *your* contributions as well."

Art tilted his head in modest acknowledgment. "Those were the days, or rather decades, of some excellent work, some of it still sitting on library shelves and some of it turning into things like this," he said with an expansive gesture at the decks before them. They both let their eyes roam the scene for a while, letting the concept of patient lab work and mathematical modeling slowly transforming into tons of equipment and life-saving strategies sink in.

Stella shook and pulled herself back to the events of today. "Do we know how high the air spaces in the sub have become pressurized?"

"Not yet, no, but that will be known before they start bringing the crew up. You can be sure the pressure will be enough to worry about bending the crew if they don't have chambers for them. Luckily for us, that part's not our job. The *Voo2* has a Chief of Dive Operations, Master Diver, and all those other dive managers and chamber tenders who'll compute their deco schedules and all of that."

Art pointed farther down the deck railing of the *Voo2*. "We're not done with the new equipment yet. That vehicle hanging there in its cradle with that big crane, that's the Pressurized Rescue Module, which you'll hear everyone else calling the PRM. It's the next generation of submersible after the DSRV, the Disabled Sub Rescue Vehicle of your dad's day. It'll carry sixteen men at a run. When the operators know what the air pressure gauges are reading in the DISSUB, they will match that air pressure in the PRM and also up here in the SDS chambers. Once the Team clears away the rest of the debris and welds on that new rescue seat, the PRM will mate with the DISSUB, pick up sixteen guys, transport them to the surface, and mate with an SDS chamber to offload the crew, all without any change in air pressure for them. The PRM then returns to the DISSUB, picks up another sixteen guys, and adds them to the SDS chamber. Then once a whole load of thirty-two men is safely inside an SDS chamber, the chamber can be decompressed to one atmosphere at the controlled rate needed to prevent bending anyone for their particular air pressure conditions. And of course while that's happening, the PRM is busy bringing up men into the other SDS chambers. Pretty slick, huh?" he ask her hopefully.

"Huh," Stella responded, her enthusiasm taking a hit from

her still-growing queasiness. "But what about the decompression load of the pilot of the—what did you call that rescue vehicle?"

"It's called the PRM, and it's piloted remotely by a tether. See it there?" Art responded. "But it does contain a crew of two men who control things like the opening of the hatches and adjusting the trim as men board it. Yes, the deco of those two crewmembers will have to be managed at the end, just like the rescued men."

"Tethered? Doesn't that considerably limit its mobility?" she asked.

"Yeah, but what it loses in mobility it gains by being on continuous power instead of running on battery power that needs recharging between bottom runs. The tethering also keeps it under the control of the vessel, so it can't get lost, regardless of currents or sea states," Art said.

Art turned to face Stella directly. "There's one more part of this whole new submarine rescue system, and it's already been instrumental on this mission. But you don't see it here. It's a one-man hard suit that stays at an internal pressure of one atmosphere."

"Really?" Stella looked surprised. "Everything else here is new, but a hard suit is last-century technology. I thought those weren't rated for the depth we need."

"You're right about the last-century part but wrong about the depth rating. The Navy has commissioned four suits rated to dive to two thousand feet. The suit is called the ADS2000, with ADS standing for Atmospheric Diving System. You remember Captain DeLucca telling you they sent a mission on the first day to start clearing the hatch, and in that process they discovered that the rescue seat was damaged, and they would need a new seat welded on to make the hatch operable again?"

Stella nodded. "The Captain rattled off some alphanumeric like that, which I didn't get at the time."

"Well, that was the work of an ADS2000. They were designed with the expectation that they would clear away any crapola on hatches in scenarios just like this one. It was a godsend to the mission that one could be deployed so quickly, which I guess means there was one already in Key West. It started clearing debris and surveying the site as closely as only the pilot in such a suit could do. But one of the few things an ADS cannot do is handle a flame torch, out of concern for melting a hole in the suit and, to some extent, as a matter of dexterity. So once the realization hit that welding was essential, that's when the Michelin Man had to clean up what he could, take some still photos and videos of the scene, call for a pull, and head for home. It's a real lifesaver here that it was possible to make the determination that another approach was needed while there was still time to redirect the efforts."

Stella nodded again, with lights clearly going on in her head as pieces of information fell into place.

"Enter the Hydrogen Team, capably led by Stella Nellie Curtis Comma P-H-D and company," he added with a sardonic bow.

"Uhhhhhhh" was about all Art got out of Stella's initial response, her head in her slightly trembling hands. She collected herself and lifted her sad eyes to his. "This old fight rears its ugly head again. How many times was the funding for the Hydrogen Project on the cutting board as the Navy debated using in-water divers versus robotics or submersibles for deep missions?"

"Lots," Art stated with indisputable accuracy. "And here is the day when we show them yet again that robotics and vehicles are great for many things, in fact probably most things, and unarguably safer when applicable, but we still need to keep people ready to deploy for times when only people can do the job." They both stared at the harbor for some time.

"I have a nasty question," Stella asked cautiously. "Do we have any certainty that when the Team cuts away the rest of what you so technically called the crapola around the sub hatch and welds on a new flange, they will find a properly functioning hatch that can be opened to admit the crew into the whatchamacallit—the PDQ Mobile?"

"Pressurized Rescue Module...actually, never mind, I like PDQ Mobile better. No. We know the sub hatch is not damaged enough to be leaking, but nobody knows if it can still be opened," Art responded. More mutual harbor staring ensued.

"I know you like these memorable nicknames of stuff instead of all the gobbledygook of acronyms, so how about this?" Art asked. "The stationary hyperbaric chamber with the Team in it is known fondly by all as the Big Dipper. The diving bell, or PTC, which stands for Personal Transfer Capsule, they call the Little Dipper. How about that?" he asked her with a faint attempt at cheer.

"I like it." Stella was quiet for a moment before asking,

"Now, what about the disabled submarine? Or, as you would say, the DISSUB. Yes, I know, I know, the details are classified," she said quickly, anticipating Art's objections. "I have no interest in its official name or even its class. What am I supposed to call it besides *it*?"

Art stared at the ocean briefly. "What would the nearest thing to *submarine* be in Navajo? Not that there are that many on the Rez."

"Well, a boat in Navajo would be a *tsin naa'ee*[th,] and 'boat that swims under the water' would be a *tsin naa'ee*[th] *tá*[th]*t*[th]*'ááh naagháhigii*," she said in phonetics virtually impossible to render properly in a Latin alphabet.

"Easy for you to say!" Art marveled. "Can we maybe shorten that down to the first part that sounded kinda like you were saying 'skinny eel'?"

Stella looked puzzled. "You heard 'skinny eel' in that? Not sure anyone on the Rez would agree. That last sound should be a little more like a *th* than an *el*." Then she smiled for an all too fleeting moment. "At least you're trying. And the imagery is great. Sure. The *Skinny Eel*. Yeah, I like that."

"Oh! Got one more for you," Art told her with a friendly poke in her shoulder. "Captain Gilchrist says the enemy sub has been dubbed the *Mad Cat*. Claims he picked that up from conversations with the Captain of the *Skinny Eel*. Some kind of joke about the way its wreckage was tangled in comms cable, like a cat in a ball of yarn. Getting rid of a big bunch of that mess of cable was one of the jobs the ADS2000 was able to do during its working time on the bottom. The Team will be glad for that."

Stella nodded. "Sea burp," she said crisply.

Art looked confused for a moment. "Oh! SEPIRB! Well, at least you're trying. And I like the imagery." They both chuckled.

"Anything else still sticking in that craw of yours, while we're clearing the air?" Art asked Stella, glad to see her sense of humor slowly warming up.

Stella mulled the question briefly. "Since I can't ask where we're going, may I at least ask how long I am going to have to stay seasick?"

"That's on the list of things you can figure out for yourself. Once we get underway, you'll see our heading on your own compass." He pointed to her heavy black sport watch. "You can get a clue as to how long we can be underway even before that," he said. "Did you bring your i-whatsit with you?"

Stella reached into her hip pocket and procured a small device with a screen. "Do we get Internet reception here? Yes, looks like we do. What do you want me to look up?" she inquired.

"You were told the sub went down in the Straits of Florida. Not the Gulf of Mexico, not the Caribbean, not the Atlantic. That's a big limit on our travel time right there. See if you can pull up a NOAA chart of the Straits of Florida."

Stella tapped for a while on her device. "Will chart 11420 do what you want?"

Art adjusted his glasses to squint at the screen she angled

toward him. "Sure, that one. Now tell me what really big thing is across the Straits from Key West."

"By 'really big thing,' I assume you mean 'large land mass'?" Stella asked, her edge of irritation still bubbling nearer the surface than Art had calculated.

"OK, yes, the very large land mass right there," he said patiently as he pointed at the screen.

"Cuba."

"And how far away is Cuba from Key West, in round numbers?" he asked. "You can calculate that from a nautical chart by using the degrees of—"

"Yes, yes, I know this part. I may have the stomach of a landlubber, but I'm not an idiot. Grandpa Curtis took me sailing around Cape Cod, as far as my vestibular limitations permitted. He taught me to read a nautical chart well enough for me know that one minute of latitude or longitude is approximately one nautical mile, with a correction for your location on the globe." She studied the screen for a while, sliding the image back and forth across its surface as she mumbled to herself. "About ninety to a hundred miles?"

"Yeah, like that. Now, do you see a dashed line in the Straits, about halfway between Key West and Cuba? What's it labeled?" he asked.

"It marks the boundary of the territorial waters of the US versus Cuba."

"Do you think that a US Navy sub was operating anywhere south of that dotted line, got into trouble, and now we're sending in an entire US Navy operation the size of this one to go and get it back? The answer of course is 'oh hell no,' meaning that...?" he led.

"Meaning that we cannot travel offshore for more than forty or fifty miles due south without starting an international incident viewed as an act of war?" Stella asked hesitantly. "So it depends then on how far east or west we also need to go to get there."

"Good! Now you're waking up," Art said encouragingly. "Back to your chart there. You know our mission is in seventeen hundred feet of water. Where in the Straits of Florida are there depths like that? Remember that the depths are marked in—"

"I know. Fathoms. Multiply the chart numbers by six to get feet." She scanned the chart for a while. "Wow. The Florida Straits can get super deep. There's a pretty narrow band along here, falling off the edge of a sort of shelf, running parallel to the Lower Keys, that's in the two hundred eighty to two hundred ninety fathom range, and it's only about twenty or thirty miles from shore. Assuming we don't have to go too far either east or west along that line, then we may really be going only forty or fifty miles maximum. At our speed, which is...?"

"Let's say eight knots for a vessel like this," Art proposed.

"We can expect to be underway not more than five or six hours. I think I can survive that!" she said with a sad smile.

"Getting to the site is not likely to be a big deal. Staying onsite for probably a couple of days with that blowing our way," he gestured toward the dark sky, "could be

103

challenging for you."

Stella had stopped listening to him but was staring hard again at her small screen. "Wait. Oh crap. Prohibited area? Naval Operational Training Area? Explosives dumping area? And what are all these zigzag lines?" she asked with alarm.

"The zigzags are underwater communications cables. If you'll follow them, you'll see they're almost all going to Havana. Nobody is going to waste their time messing with deep underwater phone cables if you could just pull up a bar stool in Havana to eavesdrop on the calls. Sure, some of the cables probably go to the other end of Cuba, to Guantanamo Bay, and those calls might be of interest to somebody we don't want listening in. Some of those prohibited areas are marine sanctuaries, and they are off limits to big ships to avoid hitting reefs and such. Those areas will cause us to pick our route carefully to stay in deep channels. But I would think it's really the Naval Operational Training Area and the explosives dumping areas that should scare the 'oh crap' out of you," he said. "They scare me. No way for us to know right now if those factor into our issues or not."

More companionable silence ensued. "OK, Dick Tracy. Now tell me what we can surmise the *Skinny Eel* was doing down there, and why did it get into trouble?" Stella asked Art softly, without taking her eyes off of the harbor.

Art shifted his weight a few times. "Well. Let's see what we can put together. The sub was operating in a narrow band of coastal water before you get to really deep water leading to Cuba. No matter what they say about the Cold War being over by decades and relations improving with Cuba, do you think they're our buddies? No. Who are they buddies with? Guys we like even less than we like Cubans? Yeah. So if you were the US Navy, what would you have a sub doing in that location?"

Stella mused on this. "Surveillance?" she proposed. "And while they were watching out for bad guys, they found some?"

"Yeah. Like that." Art nodded solemnly. "Since you and the average modern American eight-year-old can find hairy information like what you just saw within a few seconds of Innieweb search, what else do you think there might be out here that NOAA doesn't publish?"

"So while the *Skinny Eel* was doing surveillance, they found some bad guys, and those bad guys could have been going through our old ordnance trash piles or watching Navy operational training as only a couple of who knows how many possibilities of...of...?" Her question trailed off.

"I think the word you're looking for is either *espionage* or *terrorism*," Art informed her. "Welcome to the wonderful world of black ops. Happy you know now what some of the choices are for what—how about Operation SECOND STARFISH may be about? Still want to know every detail?" he enquired with raised eyebrows.

Stella pondered the question then slowly shook her head.

After another long shared silence, Art spoke up again softly. "Sure, I know what you've been wanting here. You want what everyone wants. Respect. Respect for your skills and abilities and your place in this shared effort." He carefully turned her so they stood closely face to face. "You have the respect of everyone whose respect you really need, starting of course with Lieutenant Commander Costello. I'll grant you, you have your detractors out there. But only a high-school cheerleader expects everyone to admire her. You, Stella Nellie Curtis Comma P-H-D, are the one who cowboyed up, as you would say, and came out here to help run Operation SECOND STARFISH—yeah, I'm liking that name, you?" Stella nodded ever so slightly. "And your detractors are *not* here." He finished with soft-voiced gusto and stepped back to survey her fully.

Stella lifted her chin and pointed pursed lips discretely toward the bridge. "What about the guy with the four stripes over there?" she murmured.

"Who do you think asked me to come looking for you and see why you walked away from him so mad and hoped I might be able to say something to put you at ease?" he asked her pointedly.

She took a few deep breaths. "Part of me feels better, with the disorientation of not knowing anything taken away. And part of me feels worse for knowing, or at least guessing, just how scary-bad this could be. Art, buddy, you're a real friend," she said warmly, placing a palm on his forearm. "And I think I know something I need to do right away: go and apologize to Captain Gilchrist for stomping off in a snit-fit. That was childish and inappropriate. I know, I know," she said, waving a hand to stop Art's alarmed look. "I won't say word one about what we've been discussing or our speculations. I'll just tell him I'm sorry I misunderstood his kindness in a situation he found awkward, and I'll promise to try not to ask him any more classified questions. I should probably even tell him we're dubbing this effort Operation SECOND STARFISH in his honor. And no, I won't tell him we're calling his command the Good Ship *Whatever*. I don't think he would be as amused as we are about that one. He's also not likely to enjoy our *Voo2* joke at the expense of the other ship either. But there's something I need to do before that."

"Go have a cup of coffee with me?" Art asked hopefully.

"Oh God, no!" She leaned over the rail and barfed.

February 26, 2013
0830 Hrs
Cafeteria, Navy Experimental Diving Unit
Panama City, FL

Chief Byron Soaps, Chief Calvin Sorensen, and Petty Officer William Murphy strutted as best they could without spilling breakfast trays and sloshing coffees, in an elaborate mini-parade formation through the NEDU dining hall. Their trademarked red bandana do-rags and "If you aren't diving hydrogen" T-shirts had long since ceased to get them any more than passing glances of irritation from most of the other diners on most days. But today was special, even to the most blasé of the other divers in the aptly named mess hall. It was the Team's first full day back after release from their thousand-foot hydrogen test dive. "Hoo-yah!" and "welcome home!" were called out from various corners of the room. The marching men tossed their chins in gruff but proud acknowledgment of the greetings.

The three friends installed themselves in their usual chairs at their usual table in the back right corner of the hall and got busy with their breakfast trays. Senior Chief Jacob Webster trailed in late, wiping a blue-gray eye socket with a limp paw as he steadied a mug of black coffee gingerly in the other hand.

Soaps greeted him with a smirk. "Gooood moanin', Lova Boy," he drawled. "Still dreamin' those special dreams?"

Webster kept his eyes downcast as he struggled into his chair next to Sorensen. Soaps was not yet done having his fun. He grabbed an air partner in a rough embrace, sashayed her, and gave her a big dip off the edge of the worn table. "Oooh

Barbie Doll! Oooh, ooooh oooooooooh!" he crooned in rising falsetto.

Murphy looked puzzled. "Wazzuuup? Did I miss something? Other than of course getting out of the can yesterday? And how cool is that?" he asked with elaborate high fives all around. "Best—hot—shower—ever!" Heads nodded vigorously as hands drummed the tabletop.

Sorensen sighed. "S'nothin' big, Murph. All us have had a uhh...personal dream er three in the chamber or in the barracks, erwat? Give a dude a break, will ya?"

"Ah," said Murphy wisely.

Webster silently sipped his harsh, hot coffee with a wince. He darted a quick look at Sorensen and noticed his buddy's subtle twist of fingertips at lips.

As he picked at his bland eggs, Soaps shook his head and chuckled at a memory. "I ever tell y'all about the day I met Doc Stella? Now *that* was embarrassing!"

Sorensen and Webster exchanged looks and snorts. "Duuuuude. You cannot possibly have had an introduction more embarrassing than mine. But go ahead. Love to hear your story," Webster urged him with a magnanimous wave.

Soaps settled himself further into his hard plastic chair. "I had just been assigned to the Hydrogen Project and was really pleased, so I wanted to go right away and find this scientist who was supposed to be the head of it. I walked all over the ops area, asking for Dr. Curtis. Wouldn't you think somebody would have thought to mention it was a Dr. Stella Curtis, or she-something, or 'that lady,' or would in some way indicate it was a woman I was looking for? Nooooo. Everywhere I ask, they just point to some other place until someone suggests Dr. Curtis might be in the gas farm. So I go out there and poke around among the bottles for a moment until I see some guy who asks if he can help me.

"I figure I should be all cool in this plum assignment, you know, so I tell him, 'I've just been assigned to the Hydrogen Project Team, and I'm looking for my Main Man.' From out of nowhere, Doc Stella jumps up like she was a jack-in-the-box. She says, 'That would be me.' I started babbling: 'No, Ma'am, I was looking...er...um, I didn't mean...'" She says, 'I believe you are looking for the Main...um...Mama in charge of the Hydrogen Project, and that would be me. I'm Stella Curtis. Most people around here just call me Doc Stella. Pleased to meet you...?'

"I gave her my name. We shook hands. We leaned against the nearest wall and chatted. And that was that. I was sooo embarrassed and afraid I'd given her a bad impression from the get-go of me being some sexist jerk, assuming the head scientist had to be a man, but she brushed it right off," he finished with a deep chuckle.

Webster waved a dismissive hand. "No worries, man. Doc Stella wouldn't hold some small gender confusion thing like that against you. It happens all the time to her, I'm sure. I imagine if anything, she was impressed you had the sense to realize you might have caused offense."

Murphy started waggling in his seat. "Oh, oh, I can top that one for embarrassing! I was Duty Diver one night, sleeping on that cot in sick bay, and I thought I heard footsteps. Must have been about ten o'clock. Couldn't imagine why anyone would be messing around at night down there.

"I got up and snuck out onto the ops deck and headed over to the light switch on the far wall, hoping I could catch the guy red-handed. So there I was, groping in the dark, wondering who was out there, when I felt this hand on my chest. I heard this woman's yelp about three inches from my face. I might have let out a bit of a yell myself, I was so startled. I found the light switch and flipped it on, and it was this tall lady I'd never seen before. She was wearing an EDU badge, so I figured she wasn't a thief or nothing. She was staring at me, kind of up and down, and it dawned on me that I hadn't put on my T-shirt, and my UDTs were looser than usual because I'd been sleeping that way. I started sort of putting a hand over my chest, my fly, back to my chest, not sure where to put it, so those big eyes would stop sliding around all over me like that. She was real flustered too. She started babbling something about how she was looking for 'the Do...the Doodoo...the Doodee Doodoo Di Di...for the k...the k...the k...'

"I started to catch on, so I asked her, 'Are you looking for the Duty Diver to get the key?' 'Ya. Ya-yah' was about all she could get out. She wanted to do some late-night work in her office and needed the master key from me to get into her building wing."

The three listeners laughed for quite a while. "She came and found me the next day and said she was so sorry, she had no idea I was already asleep, or she wouldn't have bothered me. I just told her I'd turned in a little early, and no biggie. The Duty Diver expects to be on call for any needs, handing out keys after hours included. I didn't know for another couple of weeks I'd be assigned to work with her. Glad I was," he concluded, unnecessarily for this audience.

Soaps looked appraisingly at Webster and Sorensen, who seemed to be sharing a private joke. "You boys have something you want to tell us?" he asked.

Sorensen poked Webster with a friendly paw and said, "Go on, dude. May's well!"

"OK, OK." Webster needed another pull of coffee to summon his narrative courage. "My bud here and I were working in the machine shop, using that monster of a grinder on something or other, can't even remember what it was anymore. The grinder kept kicking out on me in all directions, and I was really fighting it. All of a sudden, I looked up for a moment, and there stood this tall, amazing woman, staring at me with those big brown eyes. And then that damned grinder kicked, and I felt a flash of pain. I dropped the grinder and looked down. There was a gash across the bottom of the fly of my UDTs, and then a dark stain started to show."

Soaps and Murphy were wincing and bending forward. Webster needed more caffeine fortification as well as the assurance of sympathy to continue his tale. "I was, to say the obvious, horrified. Some woman standing there or not, I had to know, right there, right then, if I was still a man. I turned away from her a little and asked Dr. Sorensen here," he jerked a thumb accordingly, "to please tell me how bad it was. He and I managed to get my shorts a little down on my hips so Cal could look, and he said, 'It's not too bad. Just your scrotum is cut on the right side. A doctor will have to check it out and tell you anything else.'"

"*Just* your right nut sac?" Soaps and Murphy chorused, laughing. "Yeah, well, under the circumstances, it could have been a lot worse," they agreed.

"And now comes the *really* embarrassing part," Webster informed them to their greatest amusement yet. "This tall lady hadn't walked away or turned her back or anything. And when she heard Cal say he wasn't sure how bad the cut was, she said, 'I'm a sheep rancher. Let me evaluate that for you.' And without waiting to be invited, she came over, knelt down in front of me, and yanked my shorts to the ground so she could get a really good look."

"At your junk? And you hadn't even bought her a beer or nothing yet?" Murphy hooted.

Webster nodded slowly, his eyes squeezed tight in humiliated recollection. "She used a corner of my T-shirt tail to dab at the blood, and then she took her fingers and very carefully tugged a little here and a little there as she looked inside the cut. Then she got up, and in this super-businesslike voice she told me, 'The testicle is uninvolved, the epididymus appears intact, major blood vessels have not been severed, and with proper suturing and prophylactic antibiotics, there should be no sequelae.' Or at least that's what the roaring in my ears let through," Webster concluded.

"I concur," Sorensen added with mock dignity.

"I was so embarrassed. I wasn't sure whether I wanted to have her disappear from this Earth so I would never have to face her again or whether I was grateful to her for some quick medical advice that really did take away the worst of the scare. But by then the pain was really getting to be something else, so she and Cal helped get my shorts on well enough for him to steer me over to the clinic."

Sorensen leaned across the table toward the all-ears listeners.

113

"Wait till ya hear the next bit."

"There's *more*?" Murphy and Soaps chorused, aghast.

"Oh, yeah," Webster assured them ruefully. "The clinic doc took a look and pretty much agreed with what Doc Stella had said about everything inside being intact, just the skin cut along with superficial blood vessels. But he said he was worried about all the grit and dirt left by the grinder and that if he didn't clean it all up really well, I might get a serious infection that would jeopardize that testicle anyway. Then he pulled out a bottle of hydrogen peroxide and a *wire brush* and started scrubbing."

Two male faces hit the table in sympathetic agony.

Webster was relentless in his tale. "Oh yeeeah. That pegged the hurt needle. I cloaked. Old Cal here had to keep me from falling off the table."

"I was wonderin' who was gonna hold *me* up!" Sorensen added.

Webster continued. "It took me some hours before I could think through the Vicodins about everything that had happened, and it sank in what that lady—and I still didn't know her name yet—meant by 'I'm a sheep rancher.' Not 'I'm a doctor,' 'I'm a nurse,' 'I'm an EMT.' But 'I'm a sheep rancher.'"

Soaps, who had been looking puzzled, lit up. "Oh, good Lord, good Lord, good Lord. Now I get it! She's got her nose in your sac and evaluating what's left to snip if you were a sheep, so you'd be singing soprano in the sheep choir." He rocked and slapped his ribs as he laughed.

Murph pursed his lips and blew out some skepticism. "I did a lot of cutting on bull calves in my day, and I never gave no never mind to that much of what was inside those swinging steaks, as we called 'em at the dinner table. Doc Stella must have been playing doctor from way back if she took the time to see all that stuff and know part by part. Me, I just yanked, slashed, and tossed 'em into a bucket."

"Man, that must hurt like hell," Soaps ventured as he wiped the laughter tears from his eyes with the back of a hand.

"Oh no. Not if you keep your fingers back far enough from the knife," Murph deadpanned. "That's a stock joke, you know. Stock. Get it?"

After he received his drubbing, Murph turned to Webster. "So when you saw Doc Stella the next time, as your boss, did she ask you, 'How they hanging?'"

"Nope. She just said, 'Hi', and has never mentioned a word on the subject since," Webster assured them all with genuine relief.

All four Hydrogen Team members, their breakfast trays and mugs now as empty as they were going to be, kept glancing at their dive watches as they gazed out the wall of glass just past the end of their table. A messy tangle of sea grapes and palmettos ran up almost to the window and lined the edge of the narrow beach. The morning sun was bright on the calm sea beyond. The running path that threaded through the plants had already lost most of its morning commuters. Then the runner they were waiting for came into view, or at least into view if you knew where to sit in their back corner of the room.

Stella was kicking it in her last yards. Her golden-brown legs flashed amazingly long, smooth strides. Her thick black rope of braided hair swung over her tiny green running shorts like a pendulum. A small towel that had been tucked into the waistband of her shorts on the back of a hip counter-swung with the braid. The effect was hypnotic.

With a final toss of her head, she coasted to a nervous walk as she circled the beach shower. Her tank top was soaked with sweat and glued askew to her sport bra. She bent from the waist in a few pumping stretches, then reached for the fluffy clouds and arched backward. She tugged the towel loose from her hip and tossed it over a sea grape. Yanking off her running shoes and setting them primly aside, she stepped onto the concrete platform of the shower. Utterly unselfconsciously, she enjoyed the cool water pouring over her, dancing a happy jig in her enthusiasm. Finally satisfied that she was cool enough, she shook like a puppy before reaching for the inadequately small towel to pat herself somewhat dry and reclaim her shoes.

By the time she was in the dining hall, the Team had already bought her the orange she ate each morning and had pulled up a chair at the end of their table. They rose and drummed excitedly on the tabletop at her approach.

"Ladies, gentlemen, and United States Navy Divers: Now appearing for the first time in public since their grand tour of one thousand feet of hydreliox—the best all-hot-air rock band *in the world*—it's Stellvis and the H-Bombs!" intoned Byron Soaps in his richest announcer voice. All five jumped into their air-band poses, strumming and drumming opening chords to five different songs.

If eye rolling were an Olympic event, there would have been several medalists around the mess hall that day.

April 6, 2013
0115 Hrs
Aboard *Whatever*, Naval Air Station Key West
Key West, FL

Art leaned over Stella's outstretched figure in her narrow bunk and gently but insistently tapped her shoulder. "Stella, wake up, please. Something weird is going on with Soapy, and we need you to help figure out what it is. Doc Balinski and Lieutenant Commander Costello are working on it, but they want you to weigh in with them."

Webster, Sorensen, Soaps, and Murphy had been lying on their narrow bunks in the deck-secured pressure chamber known to all as the Big Dipper. In the dimly lighted confines of the chamber, with the odd sounds of the chamber compressor, mixed noises from the ship, pre-mission jitters, and all the eerie sensations associated with ultra-high pressurization, especially with hydrogen, a nighttime of deep sleep would be impossible. But brain fog at any hour in rest mode was inevitable. As the chamber pressure gauge edged past thirty-four atmospheres, a pressure equivalent to a depth of around eleven hundred feet of seawater, a literally unnerving situation turned bizarre.

First came weird noises. The strange sound-transmitting properties of hyperbaric hydreliox, coupled with the echoes within metal walls, made the sounds defy accurate description other than *vaguely barnyard* and point of origin impossible to determine. After some minutes of squeaky moos, quacks, and oinks, the origin became all too apparent. Chief Soaps had abandoned his upper bunk for the minimal chamber floor space and was cavorting on varying numbers of limbs from one to four, in vague synchrony of posture with critter noises.

118

Bill Murphy roused first. "Soapy! Stop horsing around!" he urged. In response Soaps reared on his knees, struck out with hoof-shaped fists, and whinnied loudly. Then he clumped on his knees the extra steps needed to reach Murphy's face, which he began showering with big wet licks, whimpers, and puppy pantings.

Cal Sorensen, as Medical Corpsman and thus the closest thing to a doctor they had, was the first to be genuinely alarmed by this display. He dropped down from his bunk behind Soaps and started tugging the determined man away from the flailing Murphy.

"Soapy! Wake up! Dude!" Sorensen urged repeatedly as he increased the pressure and extent of his embrace on Soaps. Suddenly Soaps spun around in his arms.

"Maaaa maaaaa!" Soaps wailed plaintively. He curled into a fetal ball in the arms of the astonished Corpsman and burst into tears.

Sorensen looked over at the opposite lower bunk and was relieved to see some gleam of alertness in the open eyes of Webster. "Dude! Send somebody to get Doc Stella on the line. See if she can handle this, or have her call for the DMO!" Sorensen urged. "I think we got ourselves some kinna psych hit here. I need help." Webster managed to slide his body out around the two men sprawled in the aisle to reach the comms system.

Sorensen stroked Soaps's forehead and felt it drenched in sweat. "Soapy, dude, you're burning up!" he exclaimed. "Let's getcha into a nice cool shower and see if that makes ya feel any better," he offered. Soaps, thumb in mouth, continued to cry as he rocked in Sorensen's arms.

"Murph, gimme a hand?" Sorensen asked. Murphy, who had finally managed to wipe off the slobber, both real and imagined, mumbled an assent as he slid his body around to rise and help lift Soaps onto his feet. Together in the tight space, they inched Soaps toward the chamber corner with the marine toilet and shower.

"OK, dude, let's ditch those shorts," Sorensen said in his most soothing croon, if Donald Duck could be thought to croon. He reached with one hand to try to tug off Soaps's UDT shorts.

Suddenly Murphy and Sorensen found themselves wrestling a man gone wild. Shrieks of "No! No! No!" reverberated in the chamber as Soaps fought to retain his own grip on his shorts.

"OK, OK, have it your way, dude, take it easy," Sorensen tried. "Keep your shorts on if ya want. We'll get ya some dry ones later." Together Sorensen and Murphy edged the shaking Soaps onto the wastewater management box and turned on the water in the shower wand. "Theeerrrre ya go! Nice cooool shower!" Sorensen murmured as he began running water down Soaps's head and shoulders.

For a moment Soaps stopped struggling and shouting, in evident confusion over this new sensation. That was when things turned truly ugly.

"Get it off me! Get it off me! Get it off me!" he screamed. He batted away the shower wand, hitting Murphy with a painful whack on the nose. Soaps's hands flailed wildly, grabbing and pulling on his hair, his ears, and his nose in rapid succession. Sorensen and Murphy struggled to wrench the shaking hands loose without doing more harm yet. But each time they freed his hands from one body part, the frantic Soaps found another to grab.

As Soaps trained his fury onto his fingers, his wedding ring caught his attention. The more he yanked on the ring, the less likely it was to come off. He was at risk of pulling that finger out of joint. The pain made him scream even louder but increased his furious tugging. And then, as his soggy shorts started slipping down, other items of greater interest to a married man than his ring finger came in for their own turn at abuse. The sound effects from that assault were genuinely deafening.

"Cal, take one step to your right," Jake Webster suddenly enunciated clearly into Sorensen's ear. As Sorensen complied, he managed to look down and see the syringe in Jake's hand, taking careful aim at Soaps's glistening, round brown gluteus.

As Soaps sagged and his hands loosened their terrible grip, the three other men groaned their relief. Together they dabbed him dry with a towel and eased him back to a bunk. Sorensen trained a professional eye on his friend's battered body as the other two men looked away in modesty and empathetic discomfort.

"Everything still there, but he's gonna be sore," Sorensen predicted. "What did ya shoot him with?" he asked Webster.

"I did what Doc Balinski told me to do. Got it out of the first aid box there," Webster told him.

"Good call," Sorensen responded, scrutinizing the bottle's

label. "Thanks for the backup," he said, addressing the collection of anxious faces that were pressed against the chamber's portholes, eerily lighted on and off with strokes of lightning. "Now what?" he enquired.

Diving Medical Officer Ron Balinski brushed Stella aside at the porthole to give himself more space to confer with the shaken men. Dr. Balinski, in his mid-thirties, had more experience in hot and ugly situations than one would expect from his calm and pleasantly boyish face and wispy blond hair. Stella had always gotten along well with him. "He'll be out for a while on what narcotic he has onboard, and it's anybody's guess how long 'a while' is at this pressure and gas mix, and with psychosis manifesting. Let me put heads together with Doc Stella and Lieutenant Commander Costello, and we'll let you know what else we can do."

Balinski took a few steps away from the Big Dipper and rejoined Stella and the Lieutenant Commander. A half dozen other concerned men pressed forward to listen as well. "So what do you think?" Stella asked him anxiously. "Is this the psychosis of a hit of High Pressure Neurologic Syndrome, in which case we add more hydrogen, or the psychosis of hydrogen, in which case we take away some hydrogen?" She looked seriously from one man to the other.

Costello shook his head and looked pointedly at the physician. Balinski shrugged. "It's one of those two things for sure. At least the list is short. You think Chief Soaps would have told us if he had noticed any onset of tremors or other symptoms of HPNS before they got to this stage? Or maybe another Team member would have noticed and told us?"

Stella nodded vigorously. "We've been through this many

times in the lab. They know they have to be observant and a hundred percent honest with me for our work to make sense."

Hank Johnson, who had been rallied from his own unrestful bunk, was hovering nearby and listening. He snorted derisively. "Did you remember to tell the Team not to mess around in there and make stupid jokes?" he asked Stella.

Stella, Costello, and Balinski all looked startled at Hank. "What do you mean by that?" Costello asked him.

"We were only around three, maybe three and a half hours into the press, not even to the thousand-foot stop when Soaps got onto the comms and crabbed about my hitting the outside of the chamber with some big chains, and please stop making so much racket. When nobody, including the rest of the Team in there with him, knew what chain sounds he was talking about, he just said it was a joke, and never mind."

Stella looked horrified at Hank. "About three and a half hours...you mean around eight or nine hundred feet? Soapy was having auditory hallucinations at a depth that corresponds with HPNS, and you didn't tell anyone until now? You said nothing to the Senior Dive Officer?" she demanded with an emphatic gesture toward Lieutenant Commander Costello. "You did not call for the Diving Medical Officer to evaluate?" she said with another emphatic point at Dr. Balinski. "And of course we know why you did not call me! You did not see fit to have me permitted onboard for maybe as much as another hour after that!"

"Hold on a moment!" Costello interjected. "You were not onboard when the press started? And it's because no one sent word to you that you were permitted to come onboard?"

123

He turned from looking surprised at Stella to irate at Hank. "You were assigned to call her over here in the morning. I asked you where Dr. Curtis was this afternoon when you started the press, and you gave me some baloney about 'she's around' when you knew she was still in the Lodge? That is totally unacceptable!"

On hearing voices rising, Art had stepped away from the control panel of the gas system to join the cluster and was now adding his own glare at Hank.

Hank shrugged uncomfortably. "We didn't need her to start the press, so why bother to drag her onboard to get her seasick any faster than she already was? And Soapy said he was just kidding, and nothing came of it, so what was I supposed to say to anyone about him?"

"I chose the team for this op with good reasons. I need a Diving Medical Officer, and I need a scientist with hydrogen diving experience. Yes, certainly, I also need experienced hydrogen chamber operators like you and Moore. But it was not your call to undermine any other action or member of this team. That stops *now*," he finished, keeping his anger in check as best he could.

Hank stood tall and unflinching but uncharacteristically silent through his reprimand.

Dr. Balinski, who had stepped back into the group of onlookers to give Costello room to express himself, stepped forward again. "Can we get back to the medical matter at hand, please?" he asked politely.

With a resigned shake of his head, Lieutenant Commander Costello pulled a piece of paper from his pocket and silently handed it over to the DMO, deliberately turning his back on Hank. Dr. Balinski briefly studied the dive profile in Stella's neat handwriting. "Let's call that auditory hallucination at nine hundred feet or so a mild manifestation of HPNS. There was that long thousand-foot rest stop soon after that. The rest stop might have been enough to fix that problem, since Chief Soaps could easily be talked out of the hallucination and said nothing further until now. Given the timing of this new and much more severe psychotic episode, near the high point of hydrogen pressure, I'm going to guess what we have now is hydrogen narcosis. Sound right to you?" he asked Stella.

Stella nodded solemnly. "According to the literature, a low pressure of hydrogen should suppress HPNS, so it's odd that Soapy was manifesting HPNS at a depth one can expect on heliox. But then again, HPNS can manifest as early as five hundred or six hundred feet on heliox, so maybe the hydrogen did delay the onset of mild HPNS for him. I don't know how HPNS is expected to interact with hydrogen narcosis at higher pressures of hydrogen. And I don't know if susceptibility to either one of those two conditions predicts a subsequent susceptibility to the other."

"That goes beyond anything I've read myself," Balinski agreed. "I'll look through what I have in sick bay for antipsychotics and take a shot at prescribing something. I can still have someone run over to the hospital to grab me something else if I don't have anything good onboard. It's also anybody's guess how long he might need to be drugged before his brain adjusts, if it's going to."

Stella nodded again. "In earlier experimental dives to this depth that I've read about, when someone took a psych hit this bad, they just brought the chamber up and waited for the lower gas pressure to relieve the problem. We don't have that luxury. We can only manipulate the partial pressure of the hydrogen and keep going. If we act as if it's hydrogen narcosis, drop the hydrogen pressure by maybe as much as an atmosphere, and then continue the press on helium, but the problem does not resolve, then we'll know what to do on the second pass: add back more hydrogen into a slower press."

Costello nodded as well. "With a conservative approach like that, it seems we cannot go too far wrong here," he concurred. He stepped to the comms switch for the Big Dipper. "Consensus out here from the science and medicine team is to decompress you thirty feet and go back to the last partial pressure of hydrogen before Chief Soaps took his psych hit. Then we'll return to the press with helium, so the hydrogen pressure doesn't rise to that danger level again. We'll re-evaluate that strategy if the Chief does not improve in—what, a couple of hours?" Costello said into the comms with a glance back at the doctor.

Dr. Balinski stepped within speaking range of the comms. "Yes. We should know within a couple of hours if Chief Soaps is improving. As a guaranteed strategy, the best thing we can do for now is to restrain Chief Soaps with meds."

Cal Sorensen posed the question they were all reluctant to ask. "We can knock 'im out when we're here, if we gotta. But what if he wakes up psycho later, while we're all on the bottom working?"

Dr. Balinski hesitated before answering. "Worst case scenario: if he does not show signs of stabilization before you all head out into the water, you may have to restrain him yourselves with ropes or sheets and take it one hour at a time. But let's hope it doesn't come to that and that the Chief adjusts to the pressure and gas mix and anti-psych meds in time to let you dive without worrying about him."

Costello leaned in again to the comms. "You men will have to plan on running this mission with three divers instead of four. Do you think you can do that?"

"We'll do whatever it takes," Senior Chief Jake Webster responded without hesitation. The two remaining coherent heads in the chamber nodded silently.

Balinski conferred briefly again with Stella and Lieutenant Commander Costello before leaving the makeshift rain shelter in front of the Big Dipper and heading carefully across the rain-slick deck toward the sick bay, with instructions for someone to send for him immediately if anything else seemed problematic before his return. The Lieutenant Commander likewise gave some more looks around and instructions to Art before disappearing himself.

As the impromptu crowd broke up, their corner of the deck fell quiet except for the sound of the rain on the roof of their shelter. Stella had always found that sound soothing. She stood there silently, willing herself back into peace. But suddenly she heard a voice unnecessarily close to her ear. "Not even off the dock, barely halfway to target depth, and you're already one man down. Are you glad you're here, and thinking you're running this show, Little Miss Hydrogen Diver?" Hank drawled.

Stella stepped back so suddenly, she had to put a hand out to the chamber to keep from falling. "What the hell, Hank? Are you blaming me for this?" she demanded, startled and confused.

127

"Too fast a press can do these things, both the HPNS, if it really was that, and a hydrogen narc, if it really is that either. Like you would actually know," he added with a sneer. "It's *your* dive profile. You know I never was onboard with this hydrogen crap anyway. If it was up to me, anything that divers couldn't do with heliox would be done with submersibles and robotics, case closed. And I certainly would not have dragged a seasick girl along to be underfoot," Hank concluded with even more than his usual scorn.

Stella stood dumbfounded.

"Hank, get your stupid ass over here and do your job, and let everyone else do the jobs they were ordered to do," Art barked from his station a short distance away at the control panel. Hank gave Stella a final "harrumph" of contempt before helping Art with the mandated chamber gas switches.

"Do you remember that Stella was hired to work on hydrogen diving and biodec, with neither of those things her invention?" Art demanded in a tone as low as his anger would permit. "How about the part where Lieutenant Commander Costello and you and I were all given the opportunity to adjust the dive profile as we thought best but *chose* not to because we have no more actual experience with hydrogen narcosis or HPNS than she does? You sure switched mighty fast from saying Stella wasn't needed out here to saying Stella is to blame at the first sign of trouble. Do you remember the part about how you'd be 'right-sized' out of a job if Stella didn't have a successfully funded grant program? Most importantly, how about the part where we are all out here to rescue over a hundred guys, as quickly as we can, using the approach a bunch of Navy Brass thinks is the most likely to work?"

128

Hank's "pshhhht!" and accompanying waving hand held about as much intellectual content as Art expected for a response. Within an hour the chamber pressure had been decreased by a little less than an atmosphere, and the press was back in progress on helium. Doc Balinski had delivered to them an antipsychotic medication and a sedative to be pressure locked into the Big Dipper and used as needed. Once everything was on track again, as best they could tell, Hank stalked toward his quarters through the rain and left Art by his controls and Stella standing alone by the Big Dipper. All was quiet with the Team inside.

Stella sagged to a sitting position on the deck with her back against the Big Dipper and tried to take some slow, deep breaths to clear her head. She felt a shoulder slide down next to hers. Lieutenant Commander Costello had materialized again out of the dark and crouched near her, waiting for her to be willing to speak to him.

"That whole thing was a rude awakening," she finally said to him. "In every sense of the expression. I guess I had no right to expect everything would work perfectly on this mission, but a team member down for the count before we even sail? It sounds like that HPNS hit earlier today was not as bad as it might have been, but we don't know if that predisposed Soapy to taking a hydrogen narc. If we had known about the HPNS, maybe a slower press after the thousand-foot stop would have been safer. The literature says both an HPNS hit and a hydrogen narc are completely reversible, but they sure are scary. That was so little more hydrogen pressure than we've already used in the lab with nothing like this happening. It's even a little less than what COMEX said was the range to be wary of. It must have been too fast a press, just like Hank said. It certainly was a faster press than anything we ever tried in the lab, when there was nothing to rush for. I think I'll just sit here a while longer, if you don't mind." Stella tipped her head back against the Big Dipper and closed her eyes.

"I heard that rant from Johnson," Costello told her gently. "That was out of line. I'd have stopped him myself, but your buddy over there at the controls jumped on Johnson even before I could, and he was doing such a thorough job, I thought I'd let him keep going. I've known Johnson for years, so I know he has skills and abilities we need. But I can see now he has personal insecurities I was not aware of. Johnson's the kind of man who, if I keep reprimanding him in front of you, will just look for more ways to take it out on you behind my back. We cannot afford to turn an operation of this magnitude into a playground brawl.

"But I can speak to you as an adult. Please consider that Johnson lashed out at you to cover his embarrassment at having been caught lying to me. Much worse, he's embarrassed at having missed something important during the press, which he realizes now he should have understood and acted on. Neither Dr. Balinski nor I think Chief Soap's hydrogen psych hit should in any way be blamed on you. Who knows if it should or should not be blamed on Johnson? I would guess not. We are all sailing in new territory here. As you said, we have every reason to think Chief Soaps will come out of this unharmed. The only real regret is that his abrupt exit means we are one diver shorter than we were a couple of hours ago. That's unfortunate but probably not fatal to the mission," Costello assured her. "The other men will have longer duty hours, obviously, but they can manage it. It's not like we just lost Murphy. We'd be down for the count if it had been Murphy."

Stella opened one eye to look puzzled at Costello. "Oh? How so?" she asked.

"Murphy is our welder. It's rare for divers assigned to NEDU to have underwater welding experience. It's a particularly hard qualification to earn and then to maintain, so we're incredibly fortunate to have him on the Team."

Stella moaned softly. "I did not know that! I did not know there was that much difference in the underwater construction and demolition skills. I thought all four had the same training and they could all weld. That's truly terrifying!" she concluded. Her head sagged.

Costello studied her profile in the dim light, trying to think of something reassuring to say to her. "I know you don't like Navy sayings tossed at you all the time instead of logic or science, but there is a Navy expression that seems to me appropriate to the situation: 'smooth seas never made skilled sailors.'"

Stella did not respond.

"There must be some old Navajo equivalent to that saying. Like maybe something about slow prey and good hunters? Or maybe slow sheep and good ropers?" he asked, hoping to get some grudging acknowledgment from her. He certainly got the grudging part.

Stella slowly opened one eye again and fixed him with it. "OK, you want me to match your old saying with another old saying? How about this one: 'experience is simply the name we give our mistakes.' Oscar Wilde," she specified. "That might sound like a good Navajo name to you, but I am pretty sure old Oscar was not one of my home boys." Her eye closed again. "But thanks, Bob. I appreciate your talking to me. You are very kind. And a good leader."

"Oh, one more thing," Costello said, "while we're on the subject of leadership. In the way the Navy expects to operate, an officer should be able to delegate a task to any man—or woman—and expect to be obeyed. Immediately and without challenge. But we're also in the real world and at an interface between Navy and civilian worlds. Johnson is retired military, so I expected him to obey accordingly. But I did not check up on him adequately. I can see now that if I had assigned your buddy Moore the job of calling for you at the Lodge, you would have been onboard hours before the start of the press. We needed you, as is now evident. And it must have been nerve-wracking for you, stuck alone in the Lodge so long, wondering what was happening out here. I'm sorry that happened. Rest assured, if I ever need to call for you again, I'll ask the right person to do it."

Stella smiled. The deck's lights were too low for Lieutenant Commander Costello to get the full effect of the smile, but he understood the warmth and gratitude it conveyed.

Costello settled down, seated flat on the deck with Stella for as long as his butt could remain comfortable and not too cold and wet. When he realized she was dozing, Costello asked a sailor on watch to find her a blanket. Then he got up, conferred briefly again with Art at the controls, glanced in at the Team, and left for his cabin. Only when Art's shift ended at 4:00 a.m. and Hank was scheduled to start his shift was Art able to persuade Stella to return to her cabin.

February 26, 2013
0845 Hrs
Cafeteria, Navy Experimental Diving Unit
Panama City, FL

Commander Lewis Richter, Commanding Officer of NEDU, was a bear of a man in his mid-fifties, with a graying chronic bed head. He was well enough liked among his fellow officers and respected by his subordinates. He came into the mess hall expecting and receiving a flurry of men jumping to attention around the room. "Sit-sit-sit," he said, waving them back into their seats informally.

He poured himself a cup of coffee from a dispenser, fished in his pocket for change to hand to the cashier, and surveyed the room. He spotted the table of Hydrogen Team divers and angled toward them for a brief greeting and congratulations. From the vantage point of their end of the room, he finally found, in the back corner on the left, the man he was looking for: his Executive Officer, Lieutenant Commander Bob Costello, already nursing his own coffee cup. The two men had worked closely together for years, and Richter thought of Costello as a rock-solid and sensible man. He also rather envied the younger man for his carriage in uniform.

"So here you are," he greeted Costello, with another wave of casual refusal of a stand to attention. He slid his bulk into a seat at the table. "Marcy said I might find you here. But why in the world would you pay to drink this dreck," he said with a careful flourish of his sludge-filled mug, "when you could drink her better stuff all day for free?"

"Oh, I guess I just like a change of view once in a while, Commander," Costello replied. His eyes were glued to the big wall of glass just beyond the Hydrogen Divers' table.

133

Commander Richter followed his XO's gaze. "God bless America!" the startled Commander breathed softly but fervently. "That's *her*? Stellvis? Good thing she wore that silly cape instead of those little green things for her Christmas party act, or we'd have had a riot on our hands. Swing low, sweet chariot!" he softly basso profundoed. "Oh, come on! She's taking a cold shower? Really? No." Richter looked nervously around him and began to rise. "This is totally wrong! We're the leaders here. We can't just sit here watching this like two dirty old men at a peep show!"

"Relax, boss," Costello responded softly. "Anyone else who can see *her*, which is only the red do-rag boys over there, or, as you would call them, the H-Bombs, is definitely not looking at us, and anyone who can see *us* cannot see *her* from this angle. We're just two guys—well, OK, two senior officer guys—sharing cups of coffee and looking out the window at the nice morning. Nobody in this room wants to be within discrete hearing distance of us anyway, for their own reasons."

Commander Richter inclined his head in grudging acknowledgment as he resettled into his seat. "You have this all really carefully figured out, don't you?"

"That's why you pay me the big bucks, boss."

As Stella finally walked briskly out of sight of the window, Commander Richter began to rise. "Well! That *was* a great cup of coffee after all. Ready to get back to work? We've got to finish up that program review and realignment."

"Wait, Sir. Worth your while, now that you're here, to stay a couple of minutes longer."

The CO looked quizzically at his XO but slowly retook his seat. The two old friends sat over their cooling coffee cups as Stella noisily joined her Team and grabbed for the proffered orange. "Wow. Fingernails *and* teeth? That's both oddly fascinating and a little disturbing to watch. Rather...*savage* might be the word."

"Sure."

"Anyone ever tell her you should peel an orange with a knife first?" the Commander asked in low tones.

"You wanna see that woman with a knife in her hands, boss?"

"Mmm. Guess not." The CO studied his XO in silence for a long moment. "Is it time to start finding a woman for you, Bob? Been how long now—almost three years?"

"Do we have to go there again, Sir?" he asked with a sigh. "It's been two years, ten months, and three days since Katie passed. I won't lie to you, Sir; my mind has drifted that way now and again. But I'm a simple man, with simple needs. My kids are definitely not ready for something like *that*," he said, subtly inclining his chin toward the other table. "One of these days, I'll be at the supermarket, my cart will roll into some nice-looking forty-something widow with a couple of half-grown kids of her own, we'll have a chat over coffee, we'll arrange a barbecue or a picnic for all the kids together, and before you know it, we'll be the next Partridge Family."

"I think you mean the Brady Bunch, but she sounds nice, your supermarket sweetie. Not that you have given the subject much thought. Yeah, it might take more energy than it's worth to out-gun Annie Oakley over there," Richter said, with the barest flick of fingers in Stella's direction. "You really do keep these things all thought through very well."

"Big bucks, boss" was all he chose to comment—but definitely not all he thought.

April 6, 2013
0900 Hrs
Aboard *Whatever*, Naval Air Station Key West
Key West, FL

Stella sat in the mess of the *Whatever* unenthusiastically pushing a fork around in a plateful of something alleged to be food. Lieutenant Commander Bob Costello had urged her to join him in a meeting here, in a setting where they would be less distracted than on the crowded deck, so he could pick her brain on some newly emerging technical matters.

Stella did not want to be away from the deck right now. Lieutenant Commander Costello, Hank, and Art had all told her there was really nothing she could do for the Team at this stage. Soaps was still asleep and not manifesting anything abnormal. The other Team members were awake and eating their breakfast. Her turn at managing the press would come at noon. They urged her to attend Costello's meeting.

To her chagrin, Hank Johnson had joined them for the meeting. Stella had tried hard to prevent Hank from trading duty time with Art, whose counsel, not to mention company, she vastly preferred. But Hank would have none of it. Costello, having witnessed Hank's bad behavior toward Stella the previous evening, was also not in favor of including Hank with Stella in a meeting. But Hank pulled the "I have seniority over Moore" card, so there he was. Hank wanted to be in on whatever new thing was being offered. He sat on the other side of their small table, wolfing down his chow like a starving man.

Costello was feeling re-energized that morning. "This is what I got into Navy diving to do!" he said enthusiastically.

137

"A lot of what an XO is required to do is pencil pushing and administrative floor mopping. But this! This mission is just like Swede Momsen's to save the crew of the USS *Squalus*! You know about him and just what cutting-edge stuff he did? He proved the usefulness of a new gas—helium—in diving, just like we're doing with hydrogen, and he saved a whole DISSUB crew. Just like we're going to do!"

Stella and Hank politely nodded, albeit with less excitement than Costello. Having one man on the Team already down had put a damper on their mood; the complexity and odds against a favorable outcome for this mission were weighing heavily on their minds. They struggled to match the optimism of their leader.

"My dad taught me about Momsen and the *Squalus* when I was a kid," Stella agreed. "Yes, I guess that factored into getting me here today too. And while we're talking about our heroes, let's have a 'hoo-yah' for Arne Zetterström of the Swedish Navy, who pioneered hydrogen diving. He did that when his country did not have good access to helium," she reminded them. She and Costello briefly clinked coffee mugs while Hank studiously looked somewhere else.

"So here's the deal I need your input on," Costello told them, his hands carefully cradling his coffee mug. "Captain Gilchrist has been talking to Cap—that is, the Captain of the—what do you call it? The *Silver Eel*? Sorry, Stella, I know this omission of proper names bugs you."

"*Skinny Eel*," Stella corrected him. "But *Silver* wouldn't be bad either."

"Anyway, the Captain says there's one more sailor alive on the DISSUB who is not in the forward section, and he's not accessible by the hatch the Team will clear. When the sub was attacked and sections started to flood, all hands were ordered to try to make it to the forward section. Most did. A few have not reported and are presumed drowned somewhere within the sub. But this one sailor barricaded himself inside the environmental systems control room because he realized someone needed to be sure the room didn't flood and the systems stayed in operation. If he hadn't done that, the controls probably would have shorted out, and the crew would have run out of oxygen or would have had respiratory failure from the buildup of CO_2 while waiting for us to get in to them. So he's really the hero of this whole rescue op. But we're at a loss to figure out how to get him out."

"You mean this one crew member has been isolated, without water or food, for the past three days?" Stella asked in alarm.

"They say he had a full hydration pack of water on him when he went in, and he found another pack of bug juice and a fist-full of granola bars stashed in various corners of the room by shipmates. So he's not in imminent danger of dying of thirst or starvation, although I dare say he's getting pretty hungry and thirsty by now," Costello clarified. "As for being alone, he's in voice contact with the forward compartments. The biggest problem is he's starting to catch on to the fact that current rescue plans don't include him. And you can imagine what thoughts of his fate are going through his mind."

Stella and Hank slowly shook their heads in sympathy.

Costello continued. "If this DISSUB scenario were in six hundred feet of water or less, and if this man had a dry path to an escape hatch, we'd have a solution to the problem. He would go to that hatch and don a bail-out suit, what they're calling an SEIE—a Submarine Escape Immersion Equipment suit. Then he'd seal himself in the lockout trunk, equalize with ambient pressure, inflate the suit, open the hatch to the water, and launch himself to the surface. The shorthand term for all that is to *blow and go*. But he's in seventeen hundred feet of water. That's far deeper than his suit is rated to handle. Plus his pathway through the sub to the nearest external hatch is flooded.

"Theoretically, I suppose he could put on the suit and open an air valve that would flood his chamber, and that would give him an all-water access to an escape route. But I imagine that flooding his room to fifty-two atmospheres of pressure will so thoroughly mess him up he won't be able to swim his way out. Just consider the oxygen issues alone: the air enclosed in his suit will be so horribly high in oxygen pressure it will make him seize pretty quickly and yet may be too small in volume to keep him breathing for as long as it will take him to get out of the sub and reach the surface. Forget about what that much nitrogen would do to his brain. We don't know if he'll still have a heartbeat when we find him or even how long we'll have to look for him on the surface after seventeen hundred vertical feet of ascent," Costello concluded with a sigh.

"So no more Steinke hoods?" Stella asked.

Hank snorted. "How many times do we gotta tell you that you're a generation behind in Navy submarine technology? No. No more Momsen lungs, since we've channeled Momsen into this conversation anyway. Those were two generations before now. No more 'stinky' hoods. Those earlier devices were not much more than trash bags to stick over your head compared to the new suits."

"Those trash bags saved some lives, as I recall," Stella reminded him pointedly. "Momsen and Steinke deserve more respect than that."

"Huh," Hank shot back brilliantly. "The current device is way more than any old one. It's what the Lieutenant Commander just said: an SEIE suit is a full-body container, kind of like a HAZMAT suit but with some insulation against the cold water. And it comes with its own one-man boat to bob around in on the surface waiting for a pickup. Assuming he has a beating heart and a functioning brain to deploy it," Hank said with a nod to Costello. "Which he won't have."

Costello nodded back. "And then of course there's the problem that even if we get Harris—oops, I wasn't supposed to give you his name, but oh well. Common enough name that it can't reveal much to you anyway. If Harris manages to get out of the DISSUB and to the surface without killing himself, he'll probably bend like a pretzel before we can get him into recompression, and even that can only be on the treatment table we're giving his crewmates. So what can we do for him?" he finished with a sad shrug.

"Is he somewhere on the *Skinny Eel* that one of the Team can swim into? Could Harris climb into his hazardous material suit, open that air valve, and flood the room to ocean pressure so our diver can access his chamber and carry Harris out? Then maybe the PDQ Mobile could bring him to the surface?" Stella asked slowly.

"PDQ Mobile?" Costello asked, puzzled.

"Woman can't remember three letters. She means the PRM,"

Hank translated with irritation. Costello remained looking puzzled.

"Pressurized Rescue Module, that submersible hanging from the edge of the deck," Stella clarified before Hank could.

"Oh! In that case I'd go with PDQ Mobile myself." Costello smiled at her. "Get a diver assist and then use that vehicle to bring up Harris? Hmmm." He looked impressed but thoughtful. Hank, as usual, looked scornful.

"I can get the Captain of the—OK, just for you, Stella—the *disabled submarine* to answer that question about where the environmental systems control room is relative to hatches and flooded sections. Maybe that would work if we had a hydrogen diver do the thinking and swimming parts of moving Harris out," Costello mused.

Hank made yet another indignant noise. He ticked off his objections one by one with irritated tugs on his fingers. "You're presuming Harris just happens to have an SEIE right there at hand. No, he doesn't. Those would be stored at the lockout trunk for his section."

Costello raised a hand. "Actually, he does have an SEIE. The Captain said when he ordered the evac of the rear sections, he instructed the crew members to pick up SEIEs for themselves on their way forward. That way if a blow and go proved to be possible, there would be enough suits to go around. Harris complied with that first instruction, but once he had his SEIE in hand, his sense of duty made him return to his station. The Navy needs guys like this one kept alive."

Hank seemed not to have noticed the correction to his list of objections. "You know we spend hours, not minutes, pressurizing the Team from the surface to seventeen hundred feet. The compression pains alone would be agonizing to this guy. You'll undoubtedly blow his eardrums into his brain in the first few seconds while flooding the room as fast as it's gonna flood, which should be about like watching Niagara Falls fill a teacup. And the currents of incoming water will fling him around like a leaf in a hurricane. Sure, he'll seize from the oxygen pressure and be narc'ed like you've never seen a narc on the nitrogen pressure. How's he supposed to suddenly inhale air that's fifty-two atmospheres dense? And the PRM is designed to carry people in air, not water. What do you plan to do? Strap him to the outside of the vehicle like a harpooned whale? And yeah, his dead body is gonna inflate like a football when it gets to the surface."

Stella did not respond. She stared vacantly at the tabletop. Slowly she tugged on her own fingers to respond to Hank's objections in sequence. "Blown eardrums are really painful but not fatal, and not even necessarily permanently deafening, right? Articular compression pains are bad but also not fatal. If Harris does not have to swim while having those pains, because one of the Team is carrying him, won't those pains diminish as he comes up? As for the oxygen-induced seizures—or do you need me to say *oxtox*?—they are also not fatal as long as the person doesn't inhale water, which I gather Harris won't while inside his full-body suit. Same for the nitrogen narcosis: ugly but not fatal.

"The fact that the full fifty-two atmospheres of air is too dense to ventilate the lungs with may be a good thing in terms of mitigating the toxic effects of excess oxygen and nitrogen. If he's not breathing at fifty-two atmospheres, then he's not loading his tissues with gases that would lead to the elevated risk of severe bending later. I imagine the water at seventeen hundred feet and for much of the ascent is going to be really cold, insulation in the suit notwithstanding, which should protect his brain from damage if he's without circulating blood, right? The hyperoxia while he is still breathing at something less than the total fifty-two atmospheres will be at least a small advantage in that regard also, won't it? Maybe the initial nitrogen narcosis could be neuroprotective. Who knows? At least being deeply narcotized could keep him from being panicked at all the other frightening and painful things happening. And yes, why not attach him one way or another to the outside of the PDQ Mobile? At least we'll know exactly where he is and how fast he ascends." Stella looked up at Costello, waiting for his response.

"Wow" was all Costello could muster for a first reaction. "There's a lot to take in from both of you. But by and large, I'd have to say Stella is making some pretty good points. That might be the right idea," he said, his voice rising in enthusiasm as his brain digested all it had been given.

Hank fidgeted with irritation. "Pssshhhht!" he said with a dismissive wave of a hand over his head. "Before you can think outside the box, first you have to know where the box is. None of what she says has ever been done before. She's one hundred percent guessing! She's gonna lead that poor boy on, thinking he's gonna make it, when even she knows it's cold-blooded murder! And by the way, Little Miss Know-It-All, you still haven't said how you're gonna manage the level of bending we know Harris is subject to, like everyone else on the DISSUB, after unloading him from the outside of the PRM on the surface and twiddling around getting him into a chamber, assuming there's anything left of him worth moving into a chamber." Hank sat back in his seat, puffing with self-satisfied indignation.

"Hey, take it easy, Johnson!" Costello admonished him. "If you've got better ideas, let's hear them. There are some guesses involved in this strategy, yes, but I'd put the percentage at less than one hundred. If the Navy expects sailors to blow and go in six hundred feet of water, that's already enough pressure to seize on the oxygen and narc on the nitrogen, without anyone speaking of murder. And even if Stella's ideas don't get Harris out alive, do you think Harris wants to suffocate alone in the dark, which is just what will happen if we do nothing? Do you want to be the one to tell him we plan to leave him there? Do you want to be the one to tell him our best plan is only a way to retrieve his corpse faster than they'll retrieve all the other corpses already down there? At least with Stella's approach, he'll have a chance, however slim. If it were your son down there—hell! If it were me down there, I'd ask for that chance!"

Stella did not respond. The two men turned dourly back to their cold plates, assuming the conversation was over. "Perfluorocarbon infusion," she said carefully.

"Holy cow! What an amazing idea!" and "Woman, you are so out of your effing mind!" were the two responses.

February 26, 2013
1600 Hrs
Office of the Commanding Officer, Navy Experimental Diving Unit
Panama City, FL

Commanding Officer Commander Lewis Richter settled into his office chair, his own soft groan matching that of the chair. "OK, Lieutenant Commander, have a seat, and let's get the last bits of this realignment done. I'm getting sick of working on this all day."

His Executive Officer, Lieutenant Commander Bob Costello, slid easily into the chair on the other side of the big desk. "Yeah, boss, let's do that," he concurred as he shuffled and scanned the waiting pile of pages before him.

Commander Richter studied his own sheets in silence. "So it looks like we're in agreement on everything but the R&D piece of this pie. Where have we heard this before?" the CO asked dully.

"Only every budget review," the XO agreed. "Looks like two point four mil is what we'll have left after all the other bills are paid this quarter. If we gave the thermal protection program, the antioxidants project, and the hydrogen biodec project the remainder of everything they each gave us budgets for last fall, we'd need two point seven mil. So something's gotta give."

"Mmmmm," Commander Richter said helpfully.

"Well, I think we need the full budgeted one point three mil for biodec, and that means we need to divvy up the remaining one point one mil between the other two, and I'd

146

say give six hundred K to thermal protection and five hundred K to antioxidants, " Costello concluded.

"That's pretty thin on those two programs. Those guys won't be happy. You sure your girlfriend over there needs all that money for farting?" Richter needled. "The biodec project is already the most expensive one we've ever run, with all those infrastructure costs."

"There's nothing personal in this, I promise you, Commander," Costello responded emphatically. "For one thing, when was the last time we got anything genuinely exciting out of thermal protection or antioxidants? Biodec has been our most reliable performer for the past couple of years. And the program is heading into a very expensive finish here, what with all the deep chamber testing coming up in the last quarter. I really believe this is an important project; we'll look back on it with considerable pride that we ran it on our watch," he assured his boss.

"I just dunno," Richter said with a shake of his messy gray head. "Seems to me like we're putting a lot of resources into a speculative project that even if it works is of value only in the once-in-a-blue-moon event there's some ultra-deep salvage mission. Back in early days, like eighteen hundreds early, the Navy farmed out salvage to private contractors instead of supporting all that infrastructure ourselves, which, when you think about it, makes a lot of sense. And hydrogen is just such a weird and dangerous thing to work with. Do we really need it at all?"

"We've watched this pendulum swing more than once, Sir," the XO responded. "We send our R&D money to colleges and private industry contractors to save ourselves the ups and downs of expensive and speculative efforts for a few years. Then the lead professor suddenly retires without finishing our product and nobody is prepared to fill his shoes, or we suddenly need something the contractors weren't working on because it is so Navy-specific, or what we need is too highly classified to farm out. And then we run from behind trying to create our own programs in-house again. I think we need to think bigger than just the hopefully rare ultra-deep salvage missions and bigger than thinking of hydrogen diving as just some novelty," Costello urged. "Remember this is only the beginning for biodec; if everything works with hydrogen biodec, then DARPA may pick up the tab for the really expensive and really cool DARPA-hard part: nitrogen biodec. That's worth all the support we can give it at this stage," he said with feeling.

"About that...I never did get the whole nitrogen biodec thing," Commander Richter said, picking idly at a scab on his forearm to help him think. "Nitrogen is an inert gas, so what's the deal with that?"

"Dr. Curtis can explain this better than I can. Actually the best explanation I ever heard was at a Navy emerging tech meeting. Some professor, from the University of Miami I think, had been reading Curtis's papers and wanted to talk about her work, but she wasn't there, so he cornered me. He wound up telling me more than I could tell him. Anyway, the point is that nitrogen is like hydrogen in that while they are both inert gases to us, there are bacteria and whatnot microorganisms that can eat these gases, combine them with other stuff they are eating, and turn them into new compounds. Some of those compounds are not gases, so the total load of excess inert gas drops faster in the diver than with just deco time.

"The bugs Dr. Curtis is using now turn hydrogen into water

and methane, and she can easily monitor the methane coming out in their farts and thus know how well the gas scrubbing is coming. But the bugs that eat nitrogen make different stuff, I think it's nitrates or nitrites or maybe both. The nitrogen products stay dissolved in body liquids in the diver's gut, where she can't measure them so easily, so she can't predict the course of the scrubbing action. And the bugs might not want to work the way we want them to, without some genetic engineering, because they're expected to make products that are already in abundant supply in poop. We use poop as plant fertilizer because it's always loaded with these nitrogen compounds, and nobody—not even a bug—likes to make expensive products you can get for free from your environment. And the final problem is that it might take a huge amount of these fancy engineered bugs to chew up a useful volume of nitrogen quickly enough to do the divers some real good," Costello explained.

"A butt-load perhaps?" Richter snorted derisively.

"Yeah, that would do it," said Costello with a slight smile. "All these complexities and uncertainties are why she's going to go for those DARPA bucks for funding that phase next year instead of depending on our usual funding lines for support. It's just too expensive and too speculative for us to do alone. But just think of it, if that all works: divers pop a capsule, or maybe a bunch of capsules, the night before a big air or nitrox dive; the bugs in the capsules come out in the intestines and do their gas scrubbing thing; and then we get to lengthen the dives or shave major time off the deco or lower the hit rate, or some combination of all those things! It would be a real game-changer for diving—more progress in manipulating dive profiles to better fit mission needs than we've seen since probabilistic modeling, and that was how many decades ago?" he concluded with more enthusiasm

149

than he had shown in a long time.

"And you really think Miss Green Shorts can deliver on all that?" Richter asked, the heat rising in his voice as well.

"I know it's a long shot. So does she. But given how far she's gotten with hydrogen, I think we'd be cowards not to try," Costello said, his fist gently thumping his boss's desktop.

Richter pursed his lips contemplatively for a long moment. He sighed. "Poop. Farts. Designer bugs. Pills to ward off DCS. Hmph. I just don't like the sound of any of this..." He sighed again, shaking his head sadly. He raised his eyes to meet the earnest gaze of his XO for another long moment. Finally, with a weary shrug of his hunched shoulders, he grabbed his pen and scribbled furiously on the pages before him. "OK. Fund the farts. Budget realignment done. Let's get the hell outta here." His pen hit the desktop, and two chairs scraped back simultaneously.

April 6, 2013
1300 Hrs
Aboard *Whatever*
Straits of Florida

The Team in the Big Dipper was hitting one of those lulls that was particularly difficult on nerves. They had reached the full operational pressure equivalent to seventeen hundred feet of seawater at about 10:00 a.m. The ship had finished loading its cargo of salvage equipment, including the replacement rescue seat that took hours longer to custom make than originally predicted. They had set sail an hour ago, but they were another four hours away from arriving on mission site.

The *Voo2* was still loading its sub rescue equipment at the dock in Key West and would soon follow the *Whatever*. The difference in sailing time of the two vessels was not a problem; the earlier arrival of the *Whatever* onsite would allow the divers more time to get started on their final hatch clearing and rescue seat welding. The problem was there was not one thing for the Team to do. It was not a reasonable hour or an appropriate psychological state for them to sleep, despite the fact that they knew they would be working all night. It was boring and frustrating, and it felt weird to be bored and frustrated while a mission the size of this one was in play.

Stella, performing her chamber-tending duties outside the Big Dipper, was in approximately the same mental state. She did have to watch the chamber controls to maintain constant total pressure and to maintain constant chamber oxygen pressure by replacing metabolized oxygen as needed and assure that carbon dioxide was adequately scrubbed out. But at her current experience level at managing a hyperbaric chamber, these tasks did not occupy much mental activity.

Senior Chief Jacob Webster decided to inject a little interest into their dead time. He flipped on the communications between the Team and Stella. "Yo, Doc Stella," he hailed her.

The voice startled Stella. She jumped on her seat by the control panel and leaned forward to where she could both look across at a porthole on the Big Dipper and still watch her bank of gauges. "Jake! What's going on?" she asked with a touch of alarm in her voice.

"We're bored in here. Talk to us, will you?" he asked.

Stella briefly smiled her relief. "Sure. What do you want to talk about?"

"Oh, I don't know…How about you tell us how you got to be the big Elvis fan you are?" Jake suggested. Sounds behind him seemed to be assents from the other Team members. Or at least the other fully aware ones; poor Chief Soaps was still too tranked out to emote that much. Each time he had come out a little from his sedatives, he had gotten too agitated at the thought of being dismissed from the operation. He did not seem to be suffering from HPNS or hydrogen narcosis per se, according to Doc Balinski's best guess, but he did seem too frantic to be trusted loose in the Big Dipper or certainly in the water. Consequently, he was being kept continuously in la-la land.

"That could wind up being a rather long story. Are you sure you want me to go into that?" she asked them.

Jake snorted, or at least that was how she interpreted the

sound she heard. "Not like we have anywhere else to go. Sure. Hit us with your longest story. It could not possibly be as boring as sitting here all afternoon."

"You have a point. OK, but don't say I didn't warn you," she admonished the men. She settled herself more comfortably on her stool. "The bottom line is that I inherited my Elvis fan status from my parents. When they were dating, one of their favorite things to do was to attend Rez rodeos, which always have a few musical and comedy acts for intermissions among the rodeo competitions. Back then, a popular act was a pair of guys who were both Elvis impersonators. They called themselves 'the Navajo Elvis and his brother, Elvis.' My parents were in that goofy stage of being in love in which all sorts of silly little things are just hilarious. That was one of the funniest to them. They both enjoyed Elvis music to begin with, but looking forward to seeing that act made them become totally obsessive Elvis fans. They bought every performance of his they could. That music rocked our house for years." Stella sighed and halted her monologue for a moment. "We were happy. I don't think I have ever met a couple as happily in love as they were. Even as a kid, I understood that."

The Team realized they had unwittingly hit a sensitive spot in Stella. They left her to her thoughts for a while. "Your dad was a doctor, right? How did your parents meet? Was your mother one of his patients?" Jake asked her.

Stella stirred a little on her stool. "It's a little more complicated than that," she told him. "I guess you know from hearing Art and me talking about my dad that he used to work for the Navy in Maryland, doing diving research, as payback service for the Navy supporting him through medical school. He had always had this rather romantic notion of wanting to live in the Wild West and practice medicine among Indians. That might even have made him choose an old Indian Motorcycle. Anyway, once his obligation to the Navy was over, he arranged an interview for a job as a physician in a Rez-adjacent hospital in Gallup, New Mexico. Then he climbed on *Red Chief* and headed west. He aced the interview, of course, and jumped in with both feet as an emergency room physician."

She felt something cool brush her forearm. It was a chilled bottle of her favorite flavor of sport drink, being offered to her by Lieutenant Commander Costello. She gratefully took it and lubricated her throat. "Hi, Bob," she greeted him with a smile.

"Mind if I eavesdrop on this story?" Costello asked her, his smile matching hers. Stella helped him pull up a stool. Before they were completely settled, they found they needed to round up another stool for Art. This pre-mission restlessness was clearly contagious.

"One afternoon, after my dad had been in this pretty hard job in the emergency room for about six months, a Navajo family came in. It was a father and four girls, ranging from a twenty-year old down to a six-year old. The father was carrying a small, bloody bundle in his arms, and he was frantically trying to get someone's attention. The three younger children were all screaming and in tears. Only the twenty-year old daughter was holding it together and trying to speak calmly and tell staffers that they needed a doctor. The admissions staff was doing that 'wait your turn and we'll get to you' thing. Somehow my dad intuited how bad the situation was. He came over and asked to see the bloody bundle. It was a three-year old boy with a crushed skull. He rushed the boy off to surgery, but it was far too late to save him."

She glanced in at the Team members. They were all staring at the floor and shaking their heads, clearly imagining how they, as fathers themselves, would feel if they were in the same situation.

Stella gulped some more sport drink and continued her story. "Emergency room staffers everywhere seem to have a sort of gallows humor. My dad never joined in, but at least he understood it as a form of emotionally distancing themselves from the horrifying realities they had to manage. The staff had their own name for what had happened to that three-year old: they called it 'Navajo head', and it was an injury they saw shockingly often. The father had been driving the family pickup on a dirt road way out on the Rez, with one little girl in the cab and two little girls and the boy all riding in the open back.

"The six-year-old girl was supposed to be holding on to the three-year-old boy, but the boy was famous for crawling out of anyone's grasp. 'Willy the Wiggle Worm,' they called him. The truck hit a pothole, and out bounced Willy, landing skull-first in the rocky dirt. The father scooped him up and drove as fast as he could into Gallup. He stopped only at a local elementary school to pick up the twenty-year old daughter for her help, since as a teacher her English was a lot better than his. But it still took a couple of hours to reach the hospital, and that was far too long for any possibility of help for the boy.

"The twenty-year old daughter became my mother," Stella explained simply. "My dad was so taken by her quiet dignity and her compassion toward all of her family members that day. And she was impressed with him as the only one in the hospital who actually tried to find out what her family's medical emergency was instead of asking them to sit and wait their turn while the staff filed papers on the people there ahead of them with sniffles and scratches. Oh, and also my mother's smile. My dad always said how much he loved her smile. He couldn't have seen it on that first meeting, but he claimed he lost his heart the first time he saw it."

"A strong woman with a good heart and a dazzling smile, huh? I can see a man falling pretty hard for that." Jake nodded knowingly. "So you take after your father, I presume?"

Costello and Art both understood the jibe before Stella did; they dropped their heads and groaned. Since Stella had naturally always considered a comparison to her father a great compliment, it took her a moment to understand the commotion that ensued in the chamber following Jake's smart remark. His pummeling from the men sharing his controlled environment was accompanied by their usual admonition not to poke the she-bear whose paws were on their oxygen valve. Stella gestured to Cal to put in a punch for her, which he gladly doubled.

Once order was restored, Jake took up the thread of their conversation with her again. "What did your grandparents think of their daughter dating a Paleface doctor? Upset about the Paleface part or thrilled over the doctor part?"

"A little of both, I think," Stella responded. "My *amá sáni*, that is, my grandma Nellie was mostly just happy her daughter was dating a sober guy with a solid day job. And once she realized my dad wanted kids who would be raised with a foot in each world, she was sold. My grandpa William, who was such a big guy he generally went by the name of Bull, was less excited, but he was not around that much longer. He was already trying to drink himself into an early grave before he lost his only son, and once Willie was gone, he tried that much harder until he succeeded. I never met him."

Stella took another few meditative swigs of her sport drink. "But to get back to the original subject of Elvis," she said, realizing she was killing everyone's mood by heaping one sad detail onto the next, "I think my parents really focused on their mutual Elvis interests as a way to block from memory their antithesis of meet-cute. They just told most people they fell for each other while singing along with Elvis. Why not? What's not to love about Elvis?"

"Was it really him or his brother, Elvis?" Jake quipped.

Stella smiled.

Art reached out and switched off the Big Dipper comms system. "How did you lose your mom?" he asked her gently. "Your dad stopped sending Christmas letters to me for a few years, and when I got him to start them up again, he just said she was gone and didn't want to explain. Do you mind if I ask you?"

"It's OK. You're a good enough friend I can tell you that," Stella assured him. "And you too, Bob," she shyly added, twisting a little uncomfortably on her stool as she included the other man at her side. "One Saturday afternoon my mother and dad and I were playing our usual rounds of Chinese checkers at the dining table. My mother wanted to serve us some cookies but noticed we were out of milk. She headed out the door to go to the convenience store near our house. A drunk driver ran her down. The police figured out

157

who the hit-and-run driver was because he had bloody milk all over his dented hood. I think my dad intuited what had happened because when we both heard the sounds of police cars and an ambulance in the neighborhood, he went white and bolted out the door."

"Oh my God! Are you saying your dad had to see your mother lying in the road?" Art asked, shocked.

Stella nodded slowly, her eyes squeezed tightly shut. "It took him a long time to be something like his old self, but I think he knew he had to try for my sake. And I had to try for his sake."

"How old were you?" Art asked her.

"Ten."

Art and Costello sat in stunned silence, shaking their heads. Finally Art reached over and switched back on the comms with the Big Dipper. They all made an effort to find pleasant new topics to discuss with the bored and antsy divers.

April 6, 2013
1745 Hrs
Aboard *Whatever*
Straits of Florida

Stella watched as the Team, minus Soaps, who was conscious but foggy from yet another prophylactic dose of tranquilizers, loaded into the Little Dipper and headed for the bottom. With nothing worse than Soapy's issues happening during their press and the other three Team members feeling well and rested, optimism was rising again that this mission would work.

That, of course, did not keep Stella from feeling anxious. She paced and fidgeted to the point that not just Hank but even Art and Lieutenant Commander Costello asked her to go somewhere else, out of the crowd of men needed to run the dive. It was understandable that she would want to know the Team's progress in their cutting and welding jobs, but their news would be updated to a level she could appreciate in increments of hours. And so much of what needed to be done now to keep track of two men in the water, to manage the Little Dipper with the reserve third diver in it, to manage their supplies of breathing gases and hot water for heating their suits via their umbilical cables, to promptly and correctly turn power on and off on demand to the cutting and welding tools in use, to manage the retrieval of the Little Dipper when the Team needed their rest and refueling breaks, and to keep an eye on the groggy man in the Big Dipper was considered more operationally intensive than anything for which Stella had the skills to assist.

So once again she was pushed to the sidelines. It was not a place she stayed in comfortably. She wandered in and out of the operational area like a zombie and finally just sat down

159

on the deck somewhere where she would be out from under the many feet and could overhear and watch the activities. The arrival of the *Voo2* at a little after 7:00 p.m. was a minimal distraction for her, despite its cargo of the most sophisticated SUBRESCUE equipment the US Navy had ever managed. It took all night for Art to think up the perfect small assignment for her.

April 7, 2013
0645 Hrs
Aboard *Whatever*
Straits of Florida

"Hello? Can you hear me? Harris?" Stella called into the microphone.

"Yes, Ma'am. I can hear you" came the reply.

"This is Dr. Stella Curtis. I'm the scientist working with the deep divers doing the rescue of your sub," Stella said as clearly as she could. "You can call me Doc Stella—everybody does," she assured him.

"Yes, Ma'am, Doc Stella," Harris dutifully replied.

"I hear you got yourself in a bit of jam there, huh, buddy?" Stella said, hoping to set a friendly tone with him.

"Oh yeah, Doc Stella, you sure could say that," he responded. "First time in my life I ever disobeyed an order, and this is what I get for it. Don't suppose there's anything to be done about it now?" He made a small coughing sound, which she took to be an attempt at laughter.

"That's what I want to talk to you about—what we can maybe do to get you out of there," she told him. "I hear you have a Submarine Escape Immersion Equipment bail-out suit there with you, is that right?"

"Yes, Ma'am. Captain ordered it. But soon's I got mine, I started thinking how much worse things would be for the whole sub if I left this room unsecured to flood and nobody to keep equipment in here running right, so I came back in

161

and…well…here I am," he finished.

"Wow! You certainly are one fast thinker," Stella said enthusiastically. "Do you know how to deploy your suit?"

"I practiced with it once. Wasn't my favorite day, gotta say, but right about now I'm thinking maybe that was a good day after all." Again came the sound of his strained laughter.

"Good! So you know a little of what's coming. But I have to tell you honestly, if you thought the practice with that suit was scary and uncomfortable, what we have in mind is going to be a lot more of both. Do you think you can hang in and do everything we need you to do?" she asked.

"Well, if my choice is between staying here alone until Doomsday cracks and doing a bunch of scary and painful stuff that might get me out, that call's pretty easy, Doc!" he said without hesitation or humor.

"Good. You made a brave decision when you stayed and secured the environmental controls, and that probably saved all your crewmates, so I know you're a tough, stand-up guy. We're going to do the best we can to pull you out of this mess. But you'll have to sit tight for maybe another day, OK? I guess you've heard we're already working on clearing and repairing the forward hatch so we can send the rescue vehicle down to pull up your crewmates. When that's done, then we'll send the rescue vehicle back for you," she explained.

"How do I get into it?" Harris asked. "All the passageways outside this room are flooded."

"That's the scary part," she said simply. "We know

162

passageways are flooded. That's how one of my Team will be able to get in to you. You'll need to climb into your escape suit and then open an air intake valve to flood your room. Once your room is full of water, my guy, who will be waiting outside your room, will open the hatch, swim in and grab you, and swim out with you. He'll take you to the rescue vehicle, and you'll ride on it to the surface."

"Gee, compared to starving and freezing and running out of air alone in the dark, that sounds not that scary at all!" he said with enthusiasm.

Stella hung her head, debating how much more of what lay ahead she should tell Harris. "I love your attitude! You'll do just fine," she settled on. "You just sit tight, don't do anything yet, and don't worry. I'll be back in touch when we're ready to come and get you."

"Doc Stella? God be with you and with those divers of yours. I'll be praying for you and for my crewmates."

Stella had a hard time pushing through the lump in her throat to respond, "God be with you too, Harris. You're a real hero."

April 7, 2013
0845 Hrs
Aboard *Whatever*
Straits of Florida

Stella awoke with a start in the stifling cabin, momentarily confused. She checked her watch. How could it already be nearly 9:00 a.m.? After spending all last night on deck, listening to the progress from the Team on the bottom at work, and watching them come and go from the few breaks they took, she felt wrung out. Her chat with Harris, however light she had tried to make it for him, was emotionally draining for her. As soon as she had finished that call, she had gone to her cabin and had meant to lie down for only a few minutes, hoping to ease some of her seasickness, but had slept fitfully for over an hour. Her sleep had been marred by disquieting dreams of sailors in the water, floundering and drowning, screaming for her help.

She quickly sniff tested her T-shirt and decided it flunked, so off it flew. She rooted around in her duffel and chose another T-shirt to yank on. Tennis shoes were tied with shaky fingers.

She stumbled onto the rolling deck and was momentarily startled to see the *Voo2* positioned so near to them, its decks a flurry of their own activities. She headed toward the Big Dipper and the comms station that linked them to the Team below. Rain was falling. Foaming waves were all around them. Something was wrong. The Team was expected to be working on the bottom for at least another hour before the Little Dipper dive bell returned them to the relative safety and comfort of the Big Dipper surface chamber for their next break and equipment servicing between work shifts. But a crowd of people was clustered under the makeshift awning around the portholes of the Big Dipper, staring at some activity inside. One of those people was the Diving Medical Officer, Lieutenant Commander Ronald Balinski. She closed her eyes for a moment and grabbed the nearest solid object for support. *Oh God! No!* was as much as she could think. She rushed forward.

As she approached the group of men at the chamber, an arm snaked out and grabbed her by the waist, arresting her progress and compressing her aching empty stomach. She struggled to break free. She heard the voice of Hank Johnson in her ear.

"Now, Stella, don't go freaking out," Hank admonished in a voice one would use to calm a petulant child. She struggled more wildly to shake off the painful and unwelcome grasp. Hank increased his man-handling.

"Let her go. Now," ordered Art Moore. After one more taunting squeeze, Hank released her. Art stepped in front of Stella and locked eyes with her but carefully avoided physical contact with her himself. "Stella, honey, there's been an accident. Doc Balinski has a handle on it, and he's going to take care of this," he said in as controlled a voice as he could manage.

"What happened? Who? What's wrong?" she demanded, dodging men until she could push her way to the nearest porthole.

Art snarled at Hank, "Don't you ever lay another hand on her again, you bastard!"

"Or what?" the taller and younger man sneered in return.

165

Art landed a very respectable punch into the surprised man's belly. "Or that," he explained. Hank doubled over, wheezing. Before he could catch his breath, he felt a second punch in the same spot. He craned his neck up to see Lieutenant Commander Costello glowering at him. Hank wisely decided to lower his head and take a few steps away.

Stella peered into the chamber, over Doc Balinski's shoulder. She saw Chief Calvin Sorensen bending over a man lying on a bunk, with his head and back propped up at a shallow angle. When Sorensen stepped aside, she saw it was Senior Chief Jacob Webster lying there, blood from his nose smeared across his face, and a collar around his neck. A patch of his hair had been shaved away from his forehead.

"Oh God! What happened?" she asked the doctor.

"Busy here," was all Balinski managed to tell her between instructions to Sorensen.

"Stella, hon, why don't you give Doc Balinski his elbow room there, and come over here to this porthole? I'll fill you in," Art assured her as he pressed her a few feet farther along the chamber. "We don't really know exactly what happened. All we know for sure is that Jake was cutting up debris from the *Mad Cat* while Murph was getting started on the welding of the rescue seat. There was an explosion coming from Jake's work area. The easiest way for that to happen in underwater cutting is for a pocket of bubbles generated by the torch to build up somewhere, which the torch ignites. And if there is anything oily or greasy in the same area as the gas bubbles, which there could easily be in a mess like they were working on, then the risks of combustion are even higher.

"Jake must have had his face right up close when it happened, and the explosion rocked his helmet hard enough to smack his head around inside the helmet. Murph checked him out right away, and Jake said he was OK. His nose got bloodied, which he said didn't bother him, so they both went back to work. Murph thinks they must have been working maybe thirty minutes longer before he looked over and saw Jake just hanging in the water, limp. Murph called for Cal, who was relief diver in the Little Dipper, to come and give him a hand, and the two of them rushed Jake back to the Little Dipper and called for a pull. When Cal got Jake's helmet off, there was a nasty bruise on Jake's forehead. Doc Balinski is evaluating what to do about that." Art finished simply.

Stella's eyes had been roving around inside the Big Dipper. "I don't see Murph. Where is he?"

"Working," Art responded.

"Working? Do you mean that Murph is in seventeen hundred feet of water working alone?" Stella asked, her voice rising with alarm. "I thought that was against Navy diving safety regulations."

Art nodded. "Yeah, well, it's also against Navy safety regs to blow holes in the sides of manned submarines in deep water. We know: leaving Murph down there alone is distinctly suboptimal, as you would say. Couldn't be helped. Got a mission to run, lives to save, precious time passing, like that. Once Cal and Jake were settled in the Big Dipper and it was clear Cal will be needed for his medical skills for quite a while up here, Murph insisted on going back down to keep on welding. And that was with Lieutenant Commander Costello's reluctant approval, since it's his head on the chopping block if anything goes wrong with Murph down there alone.

"A DISSUB emergency is considered a special circumstance during which the usual safety rules and regs can be stretched, but nobody likes to have to do that. It's easy for Monday morning quarterbacks to decide some lifting of a safety rule was not warranted, once something does go wrong. Murph knows what he's doing. He can go back and forth to the Little Dipper any time he needs a break, and we've got continuous voice comms with him," Art assured her.

Stella shrugged her lack of confidence in the sufficiency of these measures. Then she felt another man leaning toward her. She grudgingly gave some space at the porthole for Doc Balinski's medical corpsman assistant, Master Chief Tom White. He was a good corpsman and a good man. He wore his years of hard service, dating back to the Persian Gulf War, well on his short and muscular frame. But he had never learned how to interact comfortably with professional women. Or, let's face it, any women. "We've locked in some extra drugs and some tools for Doc Sorensen. This could get a little hard for you to watch," White warned her.

"Like what?" Stella demanded harshly, turning her face toward White's. She softened her tone and tried again. "Sorry. I mean, what's going to happen next?"

"Doc Balinski thinks when the Senior Chief hit his head inside his helmet, he caused a bleed to start in the outermost covering of the brain. That subdural hematoma is building up pressure in the Senior Chief's skull, and that's why he lost consciousness. The best solution is to relieve the pressure," White explained.

"Relieve the pressure? Meaning drill into his skull? And not in a sterile operating room but right here, right now, in the Big Dipper?" she asked with growing horror.

"Yes."

"What's the neck brace for?" she asked him, terrified to consider what his answer might be.

"Caution," White assured her quickly. "We don't know that anything is wrong with his neck. But in cases in which the skull was snapped back as hard as the Senior Chief's was, there's always a concern that the cervical vertebrae were injured. Until we can examine his neck properly, we can't risk damaging the spinal cord by letting his neck move around unsupported."

Stella returned her eyes to the scene inside the chamber. At first, from her vantage point, she could see only Cal's back and elbows as he worked. But when he shifted his stance a little, she had an excellent view. Boy howdy! Was Chief White ever right about this being hard to watch. In the usual abundance of caution when working in hyperbaria, not to mention hyperbaric hydrogen, a manual drill had been sent in rather than the electric drill normally used in hospitals. The drill was exactly what it looked like: something straight out of the machine shop, with only a stop to scrape off the big chunks and sterilize the drill bit on the way to the chamber lock-in. Cal had to apply a fair amount of pressure to keep the drill bit advancing through Jake's skull.

Stella closed her eyes and sagged forward against the chamber. She forced herself to pull up and look again. "Why is Cal drilling on the right side of Jake's head when I can see the bruise on his forehead over his left eye?"

169

"Ah, well," White said crisply, relieved to be talking about medical matters instead of thinking of ways to make a panicked woman calmer. "When a skull is hit hard, there are two ways the brain might be injured enough to bleed. One is by hitting the skull against the brain at the point of trauma, and the other is by the reverberation of the brain hitting the skull one hundred and eighty degrees away from the trauma point. The first of those is called a coup, and the second one is a contrecoup. If you have a coup, you make the burr hole through uninjured skin somewhere near the trauma point to drain the blood that's leaking nearby. When it's a contrecoup, you drill pretty much anywhere in the other brain hemisphere to drain the blood leaking from that opposing side."

"So how do you know whether you're working with a coup or a contrecoup?" Stella inquired, equally relieved to be steadying her nerves with facts.

"Easy!" responded White brightly. "Doc Sorensen looked into the Senior Chief's eyes and checked for pupil size and responsiveness to light. If the pupil is blown wide open and has reduced responsiveness to constricting to light on the side of the head where you can see the trauma, then it's a coup; if the other pupil is blown, then it's a contrecoup. When the pupils don't respond to changes in light at all, that's when you know things are really bad. As long as you can see your patient's eyes, you don't have to fool around drilling multiple holes. In the Senior Chief's case, his right pupil was wide, but it did close a little bit with light. His left eye had overactive reflexes to light. And there's other signs of pressure in the skull, like having the nerve that regulates the outward movement of an eye be overactive and make that eye twitch or slide outward. The Senior Chief has that in his right eye too."

Stella mumbled to herself briefly. "Cranial nerve number six, the abducens?"

"Right!" he responded. "Somebody was awake in anatomy class."

Stella gulped. "Now what?" she asked White.

"Once the pressure is relieved, he should regain consciousness pretty quickly. I've seen this work before," he assured her. "Guys in theater get skull whacks from IEDs pretty often, and many of the ones I've seen look a lot worse than this. The Senior Chief never did get as bad off as seizures, so Doc Balinski is pretty confident this will work. But we'll load him up with phenytoin, which will reduce his risk of developing post-traumatic seizures."

A dark trickle of blood suddenly began to pour across Jake's scalp from the base of the drill bit. Cal straightened up as he backed the drill bit out. He wiped his own sweat-dripping forehead on his sleeve as he reached for gauze to clean Jake's forehead. He neatly bandage the trephination site and wiped away the blood from Jake's nose. "There ya go! Good as new!" he crowed to the unconscious man, with as much confidence as he could summon.

Stella stared at Jake's face for what felt to her like about a thousand years, and White's watch registered as something closer to a half hour, before she began seeing his eyelids flutter and open. Everyone with a face at a porthole breathed a collective sigh of relief. But that spirit was short-lived.

"What, where, what, what, how, what?" Jake demanded,

171

flailing. Cal had his arms full trying to restrain him.

"Take it easy, dude," Cal told him. "Yer in the Big Dipper. 'Member hitting yer head down on the jobsite? I had to do a little work on ya, but Doc Balinski is right with us." Cal nodded his head toward the relevant porthole. "He says yer gonna be OK. But ya gotta calm down now!"

Jake froze for a moment, trying desperately to make sense of the situation, the thick collar on his neck, the explosive pain in his head, and his friend's words. Jake stared up at Cal. "I have to tell her! I'm going to die in here, and she doesn't know! I can't die without telling her…" he babbled thickly.

Cal looked perplexed. "Dude. You are not going to die," he said with the startling clarity he was capable of when needed, his face inches away from Jake's. "The procedure worked. I prayed on it. I know it. The Good Lord guided my hand. He wants you to stay with us. I just know it. Hear me?" he asked with a gentle press on Jake's shoulders.

Jake was shaking with tears. He thrashed on the narrow bunk. "I have to tell her—tell her—tell her…"

"Her who?" Cal asked him, struggling to keep Jake from falling off the bunk as he juggled bottles and needles one-handed. "You want me to tell your wife something?"

"No! No! Stel…Ste…St…" he babbled with increasing thickness as the new load of sedatives and analgesics Cal was administering began kicking in.

"Doc Stella? She's right here, dude, see? Look up there at the porthole." Cal pointed and tipped Jake's chin gently in the necessary direction. Cal pantomimed to Stella to switch on the nearest comms so she could hear and speak into the chamber. She quickly complied.

"Doc Stella, Jake wants to talk to ya. Wants to talk to ya real bad about somethin' important," Cal explained to her. "He's a little the worse for wear at the moment, though."

"Jake, buddy, I'm here!" she crooned.

Jake stared up toward her, the light from behind her haloing her head. His lips moved, but all that was audible was a soft, "Oh, Stella…" before he was obviously too sedated to continue. His half-closed eyes remained glassily fixed on her as his body slowed its thrashing.

An eerily beautiful sound began to fill the chamber. For all its distortions from the weird acoustics, it was oddly familiar.

> Down in the valley, the valley so low.
> Hang your head over, hear the wind blow.
> Hear the wind blow, dear, hear the wind blow.
> Hang your head over, hear the wind blow.
>
> Roses love sunshine, violets love dew.
> Angels in heaven know I love you.
> Know I love you, dear, know I love you.
> Angels in heaven know I love you.

Cal nodded enthusiastically to Stella to continue singing as he managed to release Jake's iron grip on his hand. Stella sang on and on, long after Jake's eyes completely closed.

Cal slid from the edge of Jake's bunk and found a free spot on Byron Soap's bunk. Poor zonked Soapy had been

173

completely forgotten for the past few hours in all the chaos. Cal sagged and dropped his face into his hands, with the enormity of all that had happened that day finally hitting him hard. Then he noticed a warm arm slipping around him and a familiar voice, despite the distortions from the chamber gases, in his ear. "You did good, man. You did real good. You just take it easy now. Gonna be all right," Soapy assured him.

"Welcome back, dude. We missed ya." And then Cal cried.

The two friends sat together for a long time, appreciating the crisis-free interlude. Cal stirred first.

"Ya know what Jake was all spun up about?" he asked Soapy in tones he hoped were too low to be heard outside the Big Dipper, in case the comms were still on. "He wanted to tell—"

"I know, bro," Soapy cut in, equally concerned that they might be overheard. "I've known for a while. Our chamber dive back home. I heard him, and it definitely wasn't 'Oh, Barb!' that night either."

"Do ya think she…" Cal asked hesitantly.

Soapy shook his head slowly. "I got enough trouble trying to understand what my own woman thinks."

Outside the Big Dipper, the crowd of anxious men began to dissipate as soon as it was clear Jake was sedated and as stable as he was going to be for the time being. Hank was seated back at his controls and alternated between staring at the panel before him and somewhere generally out to sea. From time to time, he exchanged words with Murph working alone in the depths.

Off to the side, out of the general traffic around the Big Dipper, two men had stood quietly throughout the impromptu concert. Now they stood staring at Stella as she leaned against the chamber, her tears visible on the porthole glass before her. It was slowly dawning on both of them that their staring was becoming noticeable to each other and inappropriate. Lieutenant Commander Costello and Art Moore shifted uneasily, not quite prepared to look each other in the eye.

"She's really…"

"Yeah, she is."

"I mean, of course, what's important here is Webster. This is bad—"

"Yeah, sure, of course."

"But to see a woman caring so much, it, well…makes a man think—"

"Yeah, it really does."

"I mean, that is, I'd never—"

"No, no, of course not! Me neither."

"Well, I guess I'd better go and uh…"

"Yeah, me too."

As the two men uncomfortably walked away from each other

in heaven only knows what directions, the primary difference in what each man was thinking was that one of them had to know that Stella thought of him strictly as a surrogate for her father. The other man was clueless on that score. But having to watch her tearfully sing a heart-achingly beautiful lullaby to another man did not make him optimistic.

March 3, 2013
1300 Hrs
Panama City, FL

It had taken a lot of polite persistence without seeming to push too hard to get this day to arrive, but it was finally happening. Stella had agreed to go for a Sunday afternoon motorcycle ride with Jake, out onto some country roads. Stella was the only other person Jake knew in all of Panama City who enjoyed being away from the hectic beach roads and taking leisurely rides through the pine and hardwood forests farther inland.

Truth be told, they made a handsome couple on bikes, him on his classic Vivid Black Harley-Davidson Electra Glide and her riding the magnificent vintage Indian Motorcycle *Red Chief*, paint and chrome sparkling in the Florida sunshine, man and woman in the prime of healthy lives. He loved riding with her, watching her shift those strange, old-fashioned gears by hand with long-practiced smoothness, seeing the look of concentration and determination in her face. Astride *Red Chief*, comparing her strong facial features to those of the war-bonneted face on the milky-white front fender tip light, with the word "Indian" emblazoned on the tank at her knees, non-Rez people clearly recognized her ethnicity. She was a Native American of the new millennium and a credit to ancestors from both sides of the Rio Grande. Jake thought she looked regal on her iron horse.

After a couple of hours of steady riding, they pulled their bikes into the parking lot of a roadside rest area with some picnic tables at one end. They dug into their saddle bags for snacks and ambled over to the tables.

Jake carefully popped the tab on his well-shaken soda.

Turning to face Stella, he raised his can high and toasted her. "To Big Chief Breaking Wind!" he said with solemnity.

"Sir Fartsalot!" she saluted gravely in return, lofting her own soda can. One full aluminum can tapping another did not a terribly festive sound make, but it was the thought that counted. They sipped in silence for some time.

Jake decided to start the conversation on a cheerfully neutral note. "You are so lucky your dad approves of your riding a motorcycle," he said. "My mom to this day freaks out whenever I mention going out on my bike. She used to be far worse when I first bought it. She would cry to Dad and her sisters and all her friends that I was going to die."

"Well, it's a true statement that two-wheeled riding has its dangers, and new riders are more at risk than experienced ones, but it's an exhilaration and an in-the-moment experience that car drivers will never understand," she responded.

"Actually, I'm not so sure she is picturing the risks of falling or colliding per se as much as she fears the image of her baby boy associating with disreputable people, present company excepted of course," he hastily added, to her amusement, "and participating in an intrinsically evil and dirty activity," Jake said pensively. "The loudest I ever heard her cry was the morning I called her from a road trip to wish her a happy birthday or Mother's Day or some such, and she asked what I had had that morning for breakfast. I said I just had a couple of those waxy little chocolate-covered doughnuts you get beside the cash register in a gas station convenience store and washed them down with a carton of milk while standing in the parking lot out front. That's what she thinks will kill me: the lifestyle of bad habits she thinks are associated with biking."

"Ah, the breakfast of Road Champions!" Stella said with good-humored recognition. "You do have to be careful what you tell parents about road trips, to be sure," she agreed with a nod. "My dad flipped out when I casually mentioned a road stop I made late one night, while I was on my Lewis and Clark Trail ride. I was in middle-of-nowhere Oregon, and no other motel was available for miles around. The place had obviously once been a rambling old house, added onto in bits and pieces over decades. The room I was shown to had a bed with only a pillow and a mattress. The pillow cover and mattress cover were worn to tatters from bleaching. I had to ask for a top sheet and a blanket, which turned out to be an old pink chenille bedspread. The only other furniture in the room was a lawn chair with some of the nylon straps hanging loose from it. There was a gray sink on one wall. Toilet was down the hall. I never did look for a shower, if ever there was one.

"The room had a window that was nailed shut and whitewashed, which obviously connected to the next room. The place creeped me out so badly, I bolted the door and pushed the lawn chair under the door handle. You can imagine how I used the sink. Mattress didn't seem to have bedbugs, so I laid down and tried to get some sleep. But the light kept coming on in the next room, which was bright enough to shine through the paint on the window and wake me up, at about one-hour intervals all night long."

At this point in her narrative, Jake began to moan and shake his head. "No, no, say it ain't so!"

"Oh yeah," she assured him. "By morning I caught on to the fact that I was the only guest who had stayed the entire night.

179

And alone. But hey!" she added brightly. "It was very affordable!"

Jake laughed long and hard. "I'll bet it was! For everyone. If you're not afraid of getting what you're paying for. If I had a story like that and I made the mistake of telling it to my mother, she would personally take a blow torch to my bike!" he assure her.

They let their laughter trail away as they worked on their snacks.

"So..." Jake began. He found his nerve in starting this part of the conversation, the real conversation he had been wanting to have with her, slipping from him now that she was actually beside him.

Stella did not respond.

"Soooo..." he began again. "I guess it's time for me to give some serious thought to my future, after the Hydrogen Diving Project is over, I mean..."

Stella did not respond. The silence between them grew long and awkward. Finally Stella said softly, "Jake, buddy, just say what you got me out here to say. I'm listening."

Jake ran his hand over his brushy head a few times, trying to remember the speech he had so carefully prepared. It was gone. He would just have to wing it.

"I've screwed up, Stella. Being around you these last couple of years, seeing what an intelligent person with a good plan and lots of determination can do with their life, makes me realize how much I'm wasting my own life. But a dozen or so years ago, I just didn't have a plan any bigger than not doing whatever my dad or Barb wanted me to do, which was to finish a long Harvard education, all the way through business school, and go work for Dad in Webster Marine Salvage. Everything about that plan just seemed too easy, too predictable. Have all my coworkers assume I was just my daddy's little lap dog? No. I wanted a challenge, but I didn't know what it should be. I think I have a plan now. And I wanted to run it by you," he finished.

"I'll listen," she said softly.

Jake swirled his soda meditatively, trying to decide how to proceed. "Rich kids like I was have two traps they can fall into: the 'I like money so I'll do nothing but spend it' trap and the 'I hate money so I'll reject it and anyone who tells me I need to earn it' trap. My dad kept me out of the first one by raising me well. But I fell into the second one all by myself. I dropped out of college before graduating. I enlisted in the Navy because I thought it would be this big test of my manhood to meet the challenges of becoming a Navy diver and get me into what I thought of as the real world, in a service job for very low pay."

Stella looked puzzled. Well? Not true?"

"Yes and no," he responded. "I weighed about a hundred and thirty-five pounds in college. Sure, it was harder than hell for me to bulk up and meet all the physical demands of passing the Navy diving test and being a real hoo-yah Navy Diver for all these years. I'll be forever proud that I accomplished those things. But that's the point: I've accomplished those things. It feels like it's time for a new challenge. And yes, of course, being a member of the Armed Forces is an honorable service to my country, and yes, enlisted people make low pay. But at least for me, with tons of other opportunities being thrown away in the process, it seems to me now that there was a kind of romantic fallacy in that line of thinking."

Jake shifted on his bench and was quiet for a long moment before continuing. "As I see it today, there is only one world. There isn't a real one for poor people and a fake one for rich people or some such division, and you don't add reality simply by subtracting money. Sure, there are some idle rich people who are disengaged from the needs and interests of working people, but there are also some idle poor people who are disengaged from the rest of life. It's who we are as decent human beings, how we treat our families and friends, how we face the adversities that can happen to anyone, and how we strive to engage and make ourselves useful in the world that make us worthy men or women, not what our weekly paycheck says."

Stella nodded in agreement but did not interrupt his musings, curious as to why he needed her opinion.

"My dad is a good man," Jake continued. "He has always been an honorable and hardworking businessman. Having your ship go down off Cape Cod is as real world a problem as anyone needs, and having guys come out—at great expense and often considerable personal danger—to salvage your ship is a service. My dad took his father's small company and grew it into a successful big one, with responsibilities to lots of employees as well as customers, which couldn't have been easy. I was mistaking the fact that it would be easy for me to get a job with Webster Salvage with it being easy for me to perform a good job for Webster Salvage."

"So your new plan is…?" Stella asked, hoping to understand

her role in this monologue.

"My current enlistment is ending not long after you're scheduled to end the biodec project this fall. So now is my big chance to push the reset button. I realize what I've liked best in diving is marine salvage. I'm ready now to get the education I was supposed to have finished roughly a decade ago, which I'll need to be a good salvage businessman, but with the perspective of this Navy background in doing the hands-on salvage part. I bugged out of Harvard ridiculously few credits shy of completing my bachelor's degree. I've been taking online classes with the University of Florida, and at the end of this semester I'll graduate with a bachelor's in business administration. Then I want to go on to get a graduate degree in business from UF and persuade Dad to open a branch of Webster Salvage somewhere here on the Gulf Coast, maybe even PC, with the plan for me to take over running the branch whenever he thinks I'm up to speed." Jake checked Stella's face to see if he could read her reaction so far. As usual, he could not.

"But you surely know that all biodec work does not end, as in really end, with this funding period in the fall, right? I'm working on getting really big DARPA bucks to try to make nitrogen biodec work. Don't you want to be part of the Team when we accomplish that?" Stella asked carefully.

"I love the Team!" he insisted quickly. "But time is not on my side. I'm not getting any younger here, but my son is getting older. There will always be great dive projects I'd love to participate in, so this could drag out forever. The nitrogen biodec work alone could take me to the end of a long Navy career if I let it. This base is loaded with divers who would kill to take my place on the Team, and you'd be happy to have them. And you have no idea how many divers have told me they'd give their left nut to have the personal opportunities I'm throwing away by being in the Navy when I could be with a successful private company."

Jake raised his eyes for a moment to look at Stella, who had slipped a hand over her mouth to unsuccessfully cover a smirk. "Ahhh, no," he protested, his head swinging widely. "I thought we had a tacit agreement never to talk about that."

Stella shrugged. "Talk about what? Your left one was not at risk, the one time I saw it."

The uncharacteristically girly smile of innocence she bestowed on him made him lose his train of thought for a moment. Recomposing himself for the serious ground to cover ahead, he continued. "Besides...if I stayed longer...there would be ethical restrictions on...what else I could do...personally...which would not have the same...limitations...if I were a college student." Jake ground to an uneasy halt.

Stella did not respond.

"UF is in Gainesville...That's not that far away from here, is it?" he fished nervously.

Stella studied the shapes of the clouds ahead for some time without speaking. Her right brain quickly rejected her left brain's urge to answer, "Gainesville is around two hundred and fifty miles, or about five hours away." Not the real question. Even her sense of the passage of time told her that her silence was growing painfully long, as sidelong darts of glances at Jake confirmed. But in addition to planning a serious answer to a serious question, she found herself distracted by other questions. How red could a man's ears turn? Would they burst into flame or merely melt off the sides of his head? What was this oddly pleasant sensation she had watching a grown man turn into a twitching blob of goo while waiting for her to speak? A more experienced woman than Stella might have called it feminine pride; others might less charitably have called it channeling her inner bitch.

Stella finally turned her head slowly to face Jake. "And where do your wife and son fit into these plans?" she asked.

Jake took a deep breath. This was getting to the hardest stuff of all. "That's the other aspect of my dad's manhood that I now admire and realize I've screwed up the worst. Dad was always a good husband to my mother and a great father to me. And he's being a better father to Jacob Junior than I've been. I have to fix this. I think it's as clear to Barb as it is to me that our marriage is a hopeless mess. We've fought too long and hard, and hurt each other too deeply, for there to be any going back there. I want a divorce as soon as I can get these plans going. But I'm worried about custody of my boy. JJ means the world to me. If I can show Barb, and my family and hers, that I have a responsible plan of action for myself, and one that will give my boy the life and the opportunities I had as a kid, I think I can persuade her to let me have joint custody of JJ. That way he can at least spend summers and vacations with me here in Florida for the next couple of years, maybe live with me full time when he's in high school, when a boy most needs a father. If I jump the gun on the divorce, I'm scared she'll demand full custody, and my boy will grow up without a father…or at least without me as his father," he finished sadly.

Stella did not respond.

"Soooo…" he started again uncomfortably. "What are your long-term plans, if I may ask?"

Stella shifted uneasily on her picnic bench before choosing careful words. "If the hydrogen biodec project continues to go well in these last months, I'm hopeful the Navy will convert me from a contractor to a civil servant. My odds on that go up if DARPA funds the deep hydrogen biodec project and the pilot project on nitrogen biodec. That will keep me busy here for at least four years, maybe longer if we get onto something big. And if I'm a civil servant, then I should be able to stay on one project or another in PC for basically as much of my career as I choose. I like it here. I'd like to stay," she concluded.

They sat in silence for a couple of centuries.

"You asked me what I thought of your plans," she said, turning again to face him squarely. "First of all, I don't think you need to worry that you've screwed up your life. You said yourself that service to your country and salvage diving experience are actions you are justifiably proud of, enjoyed acquiring, and will use to good advantage in this next chapter of your life. You've certainly made important contributions, smart and insightful ones, to my project, for which I'm grateful.

"I agree a real man is somebody like your dad and mine: a good husband and father. But the human heart is a complicated structure, and romantic love is something that doesn't always work out the way we hope it will. There are ethical and legal aspects that need to be respected in resolving a failed marriage, but there are plenty of people who have had to face divorce and gotten through it. If it's all done humanely, divorced men and women can go on to

186

make happier matches later. Your son will always be your son, even if your wife is not always your wife, so I'd say your priorities there are where they belong. If your plans— all your plans," she interjected with emphasis, "work out as you hope they will, then…yes…I think you'll have made some great choices and opened up important new opportunities for you to have a good life, with a chance that it will include everything you're wishing for."

Jake hoped like hell she meant those last words the way he wanted her to mean them: that there was a chance for him to share a future with her. He had gotten the message plenty clearly that he needed to be divorced before she would consider a serious relationship with him. The two sat quietly together on the picnic bench, lost in their own thoughts. He really, really wanted to slide over and put an arm around her, draw her to him, feel her warmth and strength. He glanced toward her, hoping to see some sign that she might accept such a bold move from him. Instead he saw that she had turned away from him and was preparing to stand up and walk away. His heart sank.

As she walked briskly across the parking lot, it began to register with him that there had been for some time an odd hammering noise that had steadily increased in loudness and frequency. The sound was coming from a horse trailer hooked to a rusty pickup truck at the far end of the parking lot. A horse inside the trailer had become frustrated and claustrophobic and was kicking repeatedly at the trailer gate. Stella strode toward the barred window of the trailer, to where she and the horse could see each other.

At the distance separating Jake from the trailer, he could not make out Stella's exact words, beyond her "*yá'at'ééh* there, buddy!" greeting, but he did hear her babbling something that included a lot of "goooood horsey! Niiiiice horsey! Preeeetty horsey!" as well as a gentle rain of phonetics he correctly guessed were equivalent phrases in Navajo. The effect on the horse was evident; its eyes were glued on her, its ears were erect and aimed toward her, and the kicking went from a constant pounding to sporadic to completely stopped in under a minute.

Jake leaned forward and listened carefully. Yes! Stella was softly singing. Singing to a horse in a parking lot. He listened again and realized he recognized the old folk tune.

> Down in the valley, the valley so low.
> Hang your head over, hear the wind blow.
> Hear the wind blow, dear, hear the wind blow.
> Hang your head over, hear the wind blow.

And then to his even greater amazement, she began to slowly step and turn in one-two-three time to the lovely old waltz tune. Both beast and horse were mesmerized.

Stella felt a gentle tap on her shoulder and looked around. Jake had doffed his cap in a gallant bow and was assuming his best grade-school waltz posture, left hand elegantly extended aloft to her, right arm swept out and ready to enfold her waist. She daintily plucked up the hems of her air skirts and, flourishing them in a grand sashay, curtsied deeply before accepting his waiting arms. She launched happily into the second verse of her song as they began their dance together.

> Roses love sunshine, violets love dew.
> Angels in heaven know I love you.
> Know I love you, dear, know I love you.
> Angels in heaven know I love you.

Oh my God, thought Jake. *The woman of my dreams is swaying and twirling in my arms and singing of her love for me. Can life ever get any better than this?*

No. Not for Jacob Henderson Webster.

Suddenly Stella was pulling away from him, a look of disgust and embarrassment in those magic eyes, which moments before had been so close to his and so full of contentment. He realized she was staring at something behind him. Jake turned to find a grimy little man stumbling toward them. He was evidently the driver of the pickup trailering the horse, and his bloodshot eyes made it clear why he had pulled off the road for so long that the horse was annoyed. "Hey, baby, can I cut in?" he leered at Stella.

Red Chief was firing up before Jake could even cross the parking lot.

April 7, 2013
1000 Hrs
Aboard *Whatever*
Straits of Florida

Stella finally eased her aching back muscles, too long hunched at the porthole of the Big Dipper. She slumped to the deck and sat, her back against the wall of the chamber, and stared ahead at nothing.

Hank Johnson left the section of bulkhead he had been holding up for a while and sidled toward Stella. He had been eyeing her carefully for some time while keeping another eye out for Art Moore and Lieutenant Commander Costello. Art was taking a split shift at the controls of the Big Dipper, but he observed Hank's movements warily. Costello was nowhere in view.

"Wouldn't do no good, you know," Hank said languidly to Stella. She continued staring ahead, with neither interest nor comprehension. "That Webster was a dirty dog. You were wasting your time there, darlin'," he drawled.

"What the hell, Hank?" she finally asked him, with no particular interest in the answer.

"I got second sight," he told her with a wink and a tap on his forehead. "I can see it all. That Webster would of promised you the sun, moon and stars, but in the end he'd a just run back to his rich wife and his rich life, and that would of been that for you," he assured her with a smirk.

"Why are you using the past tense for a living man? Not to mention what BS are you talking? Go away and leave me alone," Stella said with tired finality, unable to muster the proper level of indignation even to raise her eyes to him.

"How come you left out the most important verses of your song?" Hank needled her. Stella did not rise to the bait. Hank cleared his throat. In a passable tenor that mildly surprised Stella, he began to sing.

> If you don't love me, love whom you please.
> Put your arms round me. Give my heart ease.
> Give my heart ease, dear. Give my heart ease.
> Put your arms round me. Give my heart ease.
>
> Build me a tower forty feet high,
> So I can see her as she walks by.
> As she walks by, dear, as she walks by.
> So I can see her as she walks by.
>
> Write me a letter. Send it by mail.
> Send it addressed to the Birmingham jail.
> Birmingham jail, dear, Birmingham jail.
> Send it addressed to the Birmingham jail.

"What the hell, Hank?" she asked with growing irritation and confusion, finally tilting her head back to look up at him. "In all the times I've heard that song, I've never heard anything about other loves or towers or jails. It's a lullaby. It's about wind in a valley. Violets. Angels. My Grandma Curtis rocked me to sleep with it. Where did you get crap like that?"

Hank shrugged, still smirking. "Old song, not mah doin', darlin'," he continued, the affected drawl getting thicker by the moment. "Don't you get it? Her man doesn't love her, but another, and so she asks to have a watchtower built to get a good bead on the other woman and fully expects to spend the rest of her life in prison for blowing the brains out of her rival."

Stella's head waggled painfully on her tired neck. "I am sick of you and your bullshit. Go away. Leave me alone."

The rain had finally stopped, but the wind over the sea was chilly. She shivered in her damp clothing as she pulled her knees in toward her chest. Her glower at Hank was momentarily blocked by a wall of soft gray. She looked up to gratefully accept the fleece blanket dangled down at her by Lieutenant Commander Costello. As she wrapped herself in its much-needed warmth, Costello mouthed something to Hank that was more to the point than merely "go away." Hank did as instructed. By Costello.

April 7, 2013
2300 Hrs
Aboard *Whatever*
Straits of Florida

Shhhhhh thup thup thup thup. Shhhhhh thup thup thup thup. Shhhhhh thup thup thup thup. Stella was slowly awakening in Grandma Nellie's hogan, to the soothing sounds of Grandma at work at her tall weaving loom just outside the hogan's entrance. Soon Grandma would be calling to her to wake up from her nap and take the sheep back out to pasture for their late afternoon feeding. But for now it felt so good to just lie there, pull the soft, old blanket closer under her chin, and smell the rich aroma of strong black coffee on the wood stove. Her dad would never let her, at twelve years old, drink coffee at home. But Grandma Nellie gave her adult responsibilities and let her fill her mug from the coffee pot ever brewing on the back of her stove.

Life was so simple and so good here. Full of the rhythms of the sun and the moon setting their days, marking the times to eat their own fresh produce, to drive the sheep out to pasture and keep watch over them, to admire the stately upward march of Grandma's rug on the loom. Each return she made from the rocky pastures revealed some surprising new design element in the nascent rug. Ah, how she loved these long summer days in the hogan.

"Stella. Stella, wake up, please."

"Soon, *amá sáni*, I promise! Just another couple minutes, OK?" she wheedled hopefully.

Lieutenant Commander Costello twisted his body to look back at Art as he knelt on the deck in front of Stella's curled

193

form, a steaming coffee mug in one of his extended hands. "What's she babbling about?" he asked Art.

"I got this," Art assured him. He leaned over Costello's back and gently tapped Stella on the shoulder. "No, Stella, I'm sorry, but your grandma's not here. We need you now. Here's some coffee for you. You have to wake up and help us right now."

Stella stretched languidly and pried a reluctant eye open. "Oh God. I thought..." Stella mumbled confusedly, staring at the compressor near her on the deck, wheezing out its soft music. She looked up at Art and Lieutenant Commander Costello as their faces slowly came into focus. Behind them were more faces of the usual crowd of men to be found at any moment on their part of the deck. With Costello's assistance, she fumbled her way to a seated position and struggled to take in the scene around her. The rain had stopped for now, but the seas were still high and the night sky was filled with storm clouds.

"Sorry to break into whatever nice homey dream you were having, but we need you to do your scientist thing now," Art explained. "Murphy—"

"Murph? Is he still down there alone in the water? Wait— Jake! What's going on with Jake? How long have I been asleep?" she demanded, her voice rising in confusion.

"Take it easy, Stella. Have a sip of coffee, and wake up a little more. You've been right here on deck all day, but you dozed off not more than an hour or two ago," Costello said soothingly as he helped her raise the mug to her trembling lips. "Webster is stable. He's doing well enough for now. He's still asleep," Costello assured her. "Murphy completed the salvage work. That explosion of Webster's actually did a surprising amount of good toward breaking up parts and moving them out of the way. Murphy cut up a few more big pieces of debris and then used the PDQ Mobile as a tow truck to pull them away. He cleared the *Skinny Eel*'s docking area and finished all the welding of the new rescue seat. The hatch works.

"Murphy was there to see the PDQ mate with the *Skinny Eel*'s hatch. The first load of crew is on the surface right now, and the PDQ is heading back down for a second load. Murphy is right in there behind you in the Big Dipper." He tapped softly with his knuckles on the metal surface near her head. "With all the Team now onboard, Doc Balinski is thinking we should seriously consider the issue of using hydrogen biodec. He wants to get his hands on Webster in a real hospital bed with real diagnostics as soon as possible. What do you say?"

Stella's eyes were slowly opening wide through the steam rising from her shaky hands. "We did it? That is, I mean, the Team did it? The crew is already coming up?" she asked with growing excitement.

Hank Johnson was impatiently listening over Art's shoulder. "Oh, stop pussyfooting around with her, dammit! Ask her a straight question, and for once get a straight answer out of her!" He stared at Stella, his head tipped to the most sarcastic angle he could manage. "Are you prepared to use those damned bug capsules of yours, yes or no?"

Stella set her coffee mug on the deck and carefully rose to her feet, politely refusing Costello's assisting hand. She stepped to within a few inches of Hank and looked up at him with her trademark penetrating gaze. Her arm rose through

195

the narrow space between them with languid grace. With her fingertips she grasped his collar button, and with a tension that his startled minimal resistance could not defeat, she lowered his nose to within a snake's lick of her own.

"Yes."

Her bark made most of the men present flinch, including Hank, despite his best effort not to. The two men behind her, both literally and figuratively, were well prepared for her response. Art and Costello did not dare to exchange glances with each other, for fear they would crack smiles. *Hoo-yah, Stella!* flashed through both their brains.

Stella released her grip on Hank's collar and stepped back. "Thanks to Art, we do have the case of biodec capsules onboard. Of course I was concerned from the start about such contingencies. I phoned him before you all left PC and asked him to bring them along. They are in my cabin. I assume the real questions are: should we take a chance and use them in this circumstance, even though we are exceeding current experimental confidence; do we have enough of them; and do I have a schedule for administering them and monitoring their efficacy? Yes, yes, and yes," she spat out. "Straight enough fer ya?" she asked in sarcastic imitation of Hank's drawl.

Too flustered to know what else to do, Hank turned and walked away, mumbling something inaudible. Most of the other men hanging around thought of other places they needed to be as well.

Costello succumbed to temptation and flashed a tense smile at the deck before speaking up. "Stella, you were right the first time when you said *we* did it! I thought you'd say you were up for using the biodec capsules in this situation. That's what Murphy and Soaps and Sorensen have all said as well, but they wanted you to make the real call."

Stella slowly bent down and returned to her seat on the deck, retrieving her coffee mug in the process. She studied the coffee, her mind racing. "Soapy said so too? Meaning he's back with us?" she asked hopefully.

"He's back and looking pretty good," Costello assured her. "Well, most of him is. There was a bit of an awkward conversation with him regarding what hurt and why, since of course he has no memory of getting hydrogen happy. But never mind that now. We have another important issue to consider. We need to have you weigh in on whether to start the capsules immediately. There's still that last crewman, Harris, for Murphy to go back down and pull out. Murphy's telling us he's a little winded right now, but once he gets a chance to regroup and warm up, he'll be ready to go down again and pull Harris. Even if he were ready right now, we have to wait for a couple other things. One is the arrival of the PFC. It's being medevaced in from Miami, but we don't know when it will get here just yet. The other is that the PDQ Mobile needs to finish pulling all the crew from the dry sections before it's available to assist Murphy and Harris. And of course only when the dry sections are evacuated is it safe to flood the environmental controls room. But with as many men as they can pull per run, that job should take less than twelve hours at this point. So how about it? Should you go grab that case of capsules and send the first round in to the Team, and get those bugs heading to their jobsite?"

Stella mused some more over her coffee. "I'm worried about Murph doing all the work alone and taking all the risk when he's so worn out. I wish there were some way we could give that last job to another Team member…"

"It would be great if we could give Murphy a break and send Soaps for the last guy. Soaps has even volunteered to do it. We should be following Navy safety procedures and sending both of them, keeping Soaps in the bell for backup. But Doc Balinski thinks we can't risk Soaps doing anything as complicated and stressful as run an op like that in seventeen hundred feet of open water, no matter how sharp he seems now. And Sorensen's hands are full with Webster's care. Sorensen wants to do it and leave Soaps in charge of watching Webster, but Doc Balinski is against that also, both for Soaps's and for Webster's sake. So Murphy's our man. He swears he'll be up for it with the amount of rest he'll get waiting for these other elements to come together," Costello assured her.

"I guess this last rescue is either something that works within an hour or two of launch or not at all," Stella mused. "OK, I'll go get the biodec capsules, and we'll send in the first batch to the Team. Oh! Jake! Can he swallow capsules in his current state?" she asked worriedly. She glanced from Costello to Art, unsure which man had the latest medical update.

"Yes," Art interjected. "Cal can wake him and sit him up. He'll swallow down your horse pills with a little water, no problem. Cal has been getting him to eat and drink before now."

"Good." Stella had still not stirred from her spot on the deck, despite her claims of heading to her cabin. She started to wobble uneasily onto her feet, her head spinning and her stomach reacting to the growing volume of black coffee in it. She turned, struggled her way to the nearest deck railing, and fell against it, retching miserably.

Art extended to her a bottle he had been nipping out of himself. "Have some Blue Tongue Water," he urged her. "That might be better than coffee for you right now."

She took the bottle gratefully and pressed it to her lips for a few sips before handing it back to him. "Going for those biodecs, now. Really," she insisted in a weak voice. Costello helped her get her momentum up.

Once in her airless cabin, she realized the need to find what she wanted and leave quickly, or risk repainting her cabin in blue. She dug into her duffel bag and found the case Art had packed, with her full supply of precious biodec capsules neatly in their blister packs. When she pulled the case out, she noticed for the first time one more item Art had thoughtfully packed into her duffel for her, folded neatly the Navy Way, of course. She hastily pulled off the plain T-shirt she had been wearing and replaced it with this treasured one. *We are certainly not just putting on airs around here!* she thought, with a trace of a smile and a friendly pat of the shirt's cover art.

Stella made her way back to the deck and found a safe, dry place near the Big Dipper and comms station to stow the case of biodec capsules. She pulled out twelve capsules and carried them to Costello. "Incoming," she told him with more cheer than he was expecting from her. That, combined with the new appearance of her beloved Team T-shirt with the ridiculously hairy-chested diver on it made him smile in return. He borrowed Art's bottle of blue sport drink again and handed it to her as he took the capsules from her. He nodded and made the necessary preparations for pressure locking the capsules into the Big Dipper.

She switched on comms to the Team and placed herself at a porthole. All four men were awake and awaiting her and the capsules. "OK, buddies, drum roll please!" Their smiles grew even bigger when they noticed her T-shirt. "You've already made Navy history by making Operation SECOND STARFISH a mission success that is saving over a hundred lives. Now let's make it a scientific success with the first in-field use of hydrogen biochemical decompression! Gentlemen, start your bugs!" She held out her bottle as they saluted her with their paper cups of water, preparing to wash the large capsules down.

Murphy, who had been seated on his bunk edge, rose slowly to his feet in the tight space. Stella was startled to see how pale and tired he looked. He held his paper cup high aloft and swiveled to face each of his teammates and Stella in turn. "May the farts be with you!" he announced, with a gravitas they had never heard in him before, and that was surprisingly not much diminished by the squeaky hydrogen delivery. He tossed back his three capsules and water with a grand flourish. The other three men repeated the toast and the gesture. Hydrogen-infused laughter, brotherly back slaps, and high fives filled the chamber for quite a while. Stella repeated the toast to the men on the deck with her, with only Art finding it as amusing as all that. Oh well. Stella had long since become reconciled to the fact that a good fart joke was a hard sell to adults, even to a good sport like Bob Costello.

Stella turned away from the porthole and leaned her back against the Big Dipper, smiling. Costello joined her, wanting to stay near that smile for as long as possible. When she turned her smile to him, he was glad he was already leaning against something. "We did it? We really did it? And the rest is easy-peasy load guys into the PDQ Mobile, shoot them to the surface, slide them into the surface decompression chambers, repeat, until more than a hundred guys are not going to die young and badly? How amazingly cool is that?" she marveled.

"Well..." Costello mulled her questions. "The amazingly cool part is exactly right, but as for easy-peasy, you are leaving out a few things. Step one, get a bunch of brilliant scientists together to decide that on-site decompression is the only viable way to manage a major DISSUB scenario with many survivors. Step two, get Navy Brass to buy into the concept. Step three, get a bunch of talented engineers together to design entire systems of high-precision and custom-purpose equipment. Step four, get the Navy to cough up a bazillion dollars to fund the systems. Step five, train all the guys on the *Voo2* to load the equipment quickly enough and operate it skillfully enough to do their jobs. But yeah, from our viewpoint at this minute, considering everything the Team went through to gain access to the DISSUB, what's left to be done to save over a hundred submariners you may as well call easy-peasy."

Stella nodded. "My dad was one of those scientists in your step one. And from stories he told me, your step two was painful. Not that the rest of your steps were any easier than the first two, but I do know a little something about the start of that process." Her smile widened. "And here I am today."

Costello smiled along with her. "I'm grateful you are," he assured her.

"It is rather odd to realize all these submariners, each with their own lives, with fears and aspirations and reasons for not wanting to die this week, will be brought up in the next day and locked directly into their decompression chambers without us over here, right next door, ever seeing them," Stella observed.

Costello chucked at the thought. "True! We'll see the PDQ Mobile coming and going as our sign that the rescue is in progress, and that's it! Until we're back in Key West and see those chambers opening to let the crew out of them, we'll have to take the word of the *Voo2* crew we actually saved anybody!"

Stella laughed with him. "We'll see my buddy Harris some time tomorrow. He has one wild and scary ride ahead of him." Her expression turned solemn as she faced Costello directly. "I'm terrified of that."

"I know you are. Rightfully so," he responded. "But it's braver than hell of you to have thought up a way to pull him, and get him ready for it. Maybe we should both turn in and get a little rest to face that tomorrow," he suggested.

Stella bid him good night and after a brief visit with Art, she headed toward her cabin.

April 8, 2013
0530 Hrs
Aboard *Whatever*
Straits of Florida

"Stella, wake up, hon. We need you again." Art gently shook Stella's shoulder as she lay in a knot on her narrow bunk, a sheet pulled up tight under her chin.

Her eyes flew open. Before she could cry out in alarm, Art smiled reassuringly at her. "It's for something good," he said soothingly.

She sat up as quickly as she could and rubbed a fist over her eyes to clear them. "Something good? Do tell!" she urged him.

"We've moved up the rescue of Harris. The remaining crew members still on the *Skinny Eel*, which of course includes the Captain, are reluctant to leave Harris alone on the ship and picked up last, after they've all bugged out to safety. Harris's water and food ran out a while ago, while all of them are doing OK where they are. There are only one and a half loads of the PDQ Mobile worth of crew still down there. They've seen enough runs working smoothly that they're confident in their own safety at this point. So they want us to take Harris with them on their next run. They've already agreed to load only fifteen men inside the PDQ so the weight of Harris on the outside won't mess up the lift of the vehicle," Art explained.

"I thought we could not risk pulling Harris until all the other men were out because that would mean flooding and shorting out the environmental controls," Stella remarked.

"True," Art agreed. "But the last handful of crew who are still down there are confident their air will be good enough for so few of them, for the brief period of time they'd still be on the sub. And they want to make that gesture of support for their shipmate."

"That's both kind and brave," Stella responded. "What does this new sequence of who is pulled when do to the loading of the crew into the surface decompression chambers?"

"Not a problem," Art assured her. "We can adjust on the fly who goes into which surface chamber, and there's more than enough space in those chambers for Harris plus a medic to tend him. There's only one thing we'd like you to help us with now. We need you to come and talk to Harris to keep him calm until the final details are in place. He likes you. Can you do that?" Art added unnecessarily.

"Where are we on the preparation for this? Where's Murph? He didn't get the amount of rest he was promised. Is the perfluorocarbon here?" Stella asked in rapid succession as her brain switched into a higher gear.

"Murph looks a little the worse for wear to me, but he says he's rested enough and wants to go. He's in the Little Dipper and headed for the bottom. He'll be in position shortly. He has his map of where to go in the *Skinny Eel*, and barring any difficulties inside from mine damage, he's pretty confident he can navigate to the environmental systems control room quickly. The PFC isn't onboard yet, but the medevac from Miami brought it to Key West a couple of hours ago, and the Navy chopper they transferred it to is in transit to us now. They delayed a bit, hoping to do the transfer to our deck in daylight," Art explained.

Stella threw off her bed sheet and hastily struggled into her jeans. This was the first time in many hours that she had bothered to remove any clothing before lying down. She was totally forgetting the need for modesty about flashing undies at Art as she dressed. Being a gentleman—oh, who are we kidding? Of course he peeked. They were one of the pairs he had to dig for under the boring white cotton ones in her dresser drawer back in PC: little bikinis with big pink Hawaiian flowers. You're welcome.

"Let's go!" was the full text of her response to Art.

In the time it took for all the necessary elements to be in place for the rescue, Stella knew the following details from her pleasant chatting with Harris:

> • He was from Hermann, Missouri.
> • Hermann, by virtue of its location on the Missouri River, was subject to heavy and frequent flooding.
> • Stella was the first person he had spoken to in a long time who had ever been to Hermann, which she passed through when she and *Red Chief* were on their Lewis and Clark Trail ride. Stella had been to his favorite ice cream shop on the riverfront.
> • His wife of the past year and a half was named Cody, which rhymes with *soda*, but you write them differently.
> • He was not prepared to say that Cody was the prettiest girl in his high-school class, but he would swear she was the sweetest girl ever to walk this Earth.
> • At their wedding reception at the VFW Hall, every male relative of his and hers had insisted he drink a shot with them. Consequently, when they were leaving to head to their wedding night

accommodations at the Heavenly Daze, fortunately just a couple of blocks over on West Second Street, he and Cody had their first fight regarding which of them would drive. A man's gotta drive, don't he?

• He remembers nothing more until the next morning, when he was in bed, she punched him repeatedly in the shoulder and ordered him to "wake up, you sombitch!"

• He succeeded in sweetening her up. She don't call him "sombitch" no more.

• If what they were going to do today didn't work, there were notes in his pockets. One was for his mother, one was for Cody, and one was for their daughter, who was expected in July.

Stella heard the Navy helicopter flying away after having delivered the perfluorocarbon emulsion to the *Voo2*. She heard Hank, who was on comms with Murph, say Murph was in position inside the *Skinny Eel* and just outside the environmental systems control room. The PDQ Mobile was outside the *Skinny Eel*, its load of fifteen crewmen anxiously awaiting their shipmate. This crazy-risky rescue mission was really going to happen.

"OK, buddy, we're ready to go. My diver, Murphy, is just outside your hatch. Give him a 'shave and a haircut' with a wrench or something on the hatch, and he'll give you back your two bits. Hear him? Great!" she said as enthusiastically as she could with a knot in her belly. "Your suit is all zipped up, right? All you need to do now is open that valve and stay completely clear of the shot of incoming water. It would drill a hole right through you. And try to hang onto something for as long as you can, so you don't get swept around and bashed up in the flowing water. We'll do the rest. Ready?"

"Doc Stella? Is it OK if I get scared now?" Harris asked, his voice shaking, his hand frozen on the air intake valve.

"Yes, buddy. I am too."

"Doc Stella? Will you pray for me?" he asked again.

"Sure, buddy."

By the time Harris was so old he had told the hair-raising story of his rescue for the umpty-bazillionth time to still-delighted grandchildren (and their bored parents), he had long since forgotten all the horrors and agonies of that day whenever he was not blessedly passed out, comatose, or temporarily dead. But he could still hear Stella's velvety-sweet voice in those last moments before he let the ocean crash in on him. And "Amazing Grace" would always be his favorite hymn.

April 8, 2013
0730 Hrs
Aboard *Whatever*
Straits of Florida

The early morning sun found Stella collapsed over the rail of the vessel, retching in agony, and soaked with the cold rainwater that pounded her back mercilessly. She had been dry heaving so hard her jaws ached and popped. But that was nothing in comparison to the terror she felt over waiting to see if she had just helped to save or end a young man's life.

She felt a gentle but insistent tap on her shoulder. She turned to find Master Chief Tom White, the vessel's Medical Corpsman, next to her.

"Doc Balinski said I should come and talk to you, Ma'am. I have questions, and he doesn't have the time to field them right now," he told her. He offered her yet another bottle full of the blue liquid that was keeping her alive these days. She took a few sips, passed the bottle back to him, and instantly upchucked the drink into the stormy ocean. "Can we go somewhere out of the rain to talk?" he asked hopefully.

"Aaaaaaagh," she said decisively.

"Yes, Ma'am," the corpsman agreed sympathetically. He handed her the bottle again and urged her to drink more. He helped her to stand upright and led her toward a nearby overhang. "Do you think you're up to answering a few questions?" he asked doubtfully. He dug inside his rain jacket and found Stella a kerchief for drying her face and hands.

"I'll manage," she mumbled through lips that had already

208

been blue before the drink had arrived. She clutched the precious container with one hand while she steadied herself with the other hand on his sympathetic forearm. "What would you like to know?"

"I was hoping you could tell me what the heck this PFC stuff is that the chopper just flew out to—what do you call the SUBRESCUE ship—the *Voodoo*?" He pointed across the short stretch of water separating the *Whatever* from its sister ship on this mission.

"I suppose *Voodoo* does have an interesting ring to it, but I've been calling it the *Voo2*. Because it is, like this ship, a Vessel of Opportunity, and thus a 'voo,' too," she explained.

"Oooohhh. I never heard anyone try to make a word out of V-O-O before. *Voo2*. I get it!" White chucked. "A Medical Corpsman buddy of mine over on the *Voo2* is supposed to infuse the PFC into the submariner they're hauling up through the water and then follow him into the decompression chamber for medical support. So what's the deal here?"

He pointed down the deck of the *Voo2* to a spot near the empty cradle for the rescue vehicle. A rain shelter was being hastily erected and provisioned. Dr. Balinski, who had taken a launch across to the other ship a short time before, was directing traffic. His nervousness was detectable even from the distance separating the ships in his rapid movements and in the way he kept checking and rechecking each item as it arrived. White scanned the small group of men with Balinski until he spotted his buddy. He let out a cattleman's whistle to catch his buddy's eye for a moment of traded arm waves.

Stella took a few deep breaths to try to clear her head. "You know why we transferred the crew we picked up dry from the forward compartments of the sub straight into those decompression chambers, right? They'd been breathing some elevated pressure of air for the past several days in that leaky sub of theirs, so their tissues were loaded with more gas than they would have here on land. Hence the need to keep them compressed and schedule their decompression back to one atmosphere, so they don't get decompression sickness.

"The same applies to Harris. But we don't actually know what the air pressure was in his space, compared to the air pressure in the forward section. Then there's the problem with the way his air space on the sub became pressurized as it flooded for his in-water rescue. So he may have far more gas in his tissues than all the other crew members do. Just how much gas he has we will never know because it depends on if and when he stops breathing. He's all but guaranteed to do that somewhere along the rough ride to the surface. So we will need to send Harris in with his buddies, but their decompression schedule might not be long enough, or initially deep enough, for him. And it's likely that Doc Balinski will need to restart his heart and breathing when he gets to the surface and get him stabilized enough to send him into the chamber. We don't know how long all that may take. If we keep him for more than a few minutes at one atmosphere before we can re-pressurize him in the rescue vehicle and air lock him into the decompression chamber, he may take a hit of decompression sickness we can't bring him back from. With me so far?" she asked White.

He nodded briskly.

"We think that intravenous infusion your buddy is responsible for is Harris's best chance of surviving the next forty-eight hours. It's an emulsion of perfluorocarbon. That's the PFC you're hearing about. It's capable of holding a lot of gas in solution, more than any other liquid that you could dare expose your body to. You may have seen it in science fiction movies being used for liquid breathing. Sometimes they show a rat being dropped into a jar of this stuff, and he fills his lungs with the liquid and then swims around in it."

White shrugged. "Not the sci-fi films I've seen," he admitted. "And what I've been able to find online," he said, with a tap of something hard in a pocket, "makes me even more confused. Stuff like PFC being used to replace fluids inside eyes. PFC as adjunct therapy for laser removal of tattoos. What the heck?"

"There are a number of medical uses for PFC, but I must admit that the eyes and the tattoo removal are both news to me," Stella responded. "Because PFCs can carry a lot of oxygen in solution, they're used in hospitals for things like temporary blood replacement and filling the collapsed lungs of premature babies. The PFC your buddy will infuse is expected to take up the extra gas in Harris so it doesn't come bubbling out and cause an immediate and severe case of DCS. Then when we compress him back into the chamber and decompress him on the schedule of the other men, the PFC will slowly off-gas and evaporate away across his lungs, taking the extra gas harmlessly with it. Clear?"

White gave her a quick thumbs-up.

"Any more questions?" Stella asked him.

White shifted uneasily. "Ma'am, what happens if it takes them longer than ten minutes for Doc Balinski to defibrillate the guy and to get the IV line in? Collapsed veins can be

211

tricky to cannulate. I know that firsthand. And anyway, what good is a vascular infusion if his heart isn't beating?"

Stella considered her response carefully. "We have to hope his heart will restart within the time your buddy is setting the cannula. Of course you're right that if Harris's heart will not restart, the PFC is useless. But we don't want to think of those things now. As for what happens if the PFC goes into circulating blood after more than ten minutes, truth to tell you, I'm not one hundred percent sure. This approach has never been tried on people in a genuine diving emergency. The basic research was done ten or twenty years ago. Doc Balinski and I looked up the publications online a couple of days ago, to teach ourselves as much as is known. Some Navy researchers put pigs into a chamber at five atmospheres overnight and then brought them directly to the surface. The pigs that did not get any PFC within five to ten minutes after reaching the surface had more than a ninety percent chance of serious to fatal DCS. The ones that got PFC within that five- to ten-minute time window had only about fifty percent hits, and few of them fatal. The number of hits went up quickly if they waited more than ten minutes to get the PFC in."

"Pigs? Ten or twenty years ago? And no better than a fifty-fifty chance of success?" asked White incredulously. "That's what we have to go on here...Ma'am?"

Stella nodded and shrugged. "The Navy put the results and the PFC on the shelf, in case of just the kind of situation we have today. They could hardly test something like this on people outside of some genuine emergency, now could they? But to get back to what you really are asking: what will it look like if Harris starts to develop serious DCS, either while he is still on the deck or after your buddy is in the decompression chamber with him?"

She hesitated. "It could look bad. Really bad. Could be pulmonary DCS, which will fill his lungs with so many bubbles he'll cough up foamy blood, maybe die that way. Or it could be neurological DCS, caused by all those gas bubbles stopping the blood flow to his brain and making him go into seizures. Or both. And there will probably be nothing that can be done for him if those severe things happen. Your buddy and Doc Balinski will have to agree on the spot what to do about milder symptoms. That's why they need someone with medical experience in there with Harris."

Stella and White watched the activity at the shelter slow as the setup came to completion.

"We should be able to watch everything from right here, see how it goes," he assured her. "I want to run and grab my binoculars, so we can see better."

"Yeah. Great. Watch life-or-death scenes helplessly from the sidelines. My favorite activity this week," she responded ruefully.

"Thanks for all the information. I really appreciate knowing what's going down here, Ma'am," he said. As he started to leave, he turned back to Stella. "Oh, I meant to mention something a while ago. Begging your pardon, Doc Stella Ma'am," he said hesitantly, "but it doesn't look like you've mastered your sea legs yet."

"They don't issue us those in New Mexico," she replied.

"Oh, they don't issue those to anybody, Ma'am. You have to make your own. You like music, right?"

A smile flitted across Stella's face. "Yes."

"Well, just try thinking of some kind of music that's got a rhythm like the ship's motion, and then dance to that beat as if you were dancing with the ship, instead of fighting her all the time. Let all the 'motion of the ocean' stick in your knees. Steadies your head right out," he assured her. He hurried away to find his binoculars.

Stella closed her eyes and thought. As so often happened for her, she found a moment of solace in a beloved Elvis song. She softly chanted,

> "Are you seasick tonight?
> Did you blow chunks tonight?
> Are you sorry we're drifting at sea?

She let her knees take up the rhythm. It was nice to focus on something calm for a moment. The welcome interlude inspired her to keep going with this silly project.

> "Is your face pale and gray?
> Do you feel stuffed with hay?
> Should I make you a cup of hot tea?

A trace of a smile slid across her face. Her box step picked up more gentle sway in synchrony with the deck. She dug around in her head for more couplet rhymes.

> "Do the chairs on the deck slide to left and to right?
> Do you gaze at the ocean and view it with fright?

That fleeting smile made another appearance.

"Is your brain down the drain?
Will you see land again?
Tell me, dear, are you seasick tonight?"

When she opened her eyes, there were still war drums in her head, but they might have been a little softer, and the vague layer of haze in front of her eyes seemed thinner. She finished the bottle of Blue Tongue Water she had been death gripping all this time and stuffed the crushed empty bottle into a pocket. And she did not feel like breaking for the railing and tossing any of it. "Huh," she marveled. "A long way from well, but better. Music therapy. Amazing. I wish I'd known that years ago."

From their vantage point on the *Whatever*, Stella and White watched the whole terrifying drama of Harris's recovery as the PDQ Mobile swung up into its cradle on the *Voo2*, carrying a shockingly small and limp orange bundle. She winced as sailors grabbed the bundle and hastily extracted a man-shaped lump that was immediately soaked with rain. Poor Harris!

Once Harris was laid out on the deck under the shelter, even with White's binoculars there was not much to be made out beyond scrambling men on hands and knees. Stella could actually hear Dr. Balinski calling "clear" over and over, not daring to check her watch to see how long the resuscitation was taking. Finally she saw Balinski straightening up from the deck and nodding enthusiastically. White's buddy, squatting on the deck next to Harris, pivoted on his heels, looked around for White and Stella, and shot them double thumbs-up. He pointed to a rack holding a perfusion bag of clear fluid and pantomimed that it was emptying its contents.

Stella remained watching until Harris and the medical

215

corpsman disappeared into the PDQ Mobile to begin their short but vital trip into the decompression chamber. Harris would be reunited with his crewmates for the first time in five days. He was one welcome guy in there.

White thanked Stella again and headed off at a trot, leaving Stella rooted to her spot and too dazed to know what she should do next with herself.

"That went as well as it could have and better than we had any right to expect." Stella had no idea when Lieutenant Commander Costello had materialized beside her. "Art says you probably need more Blue Tongue Water by now," he said as he passed her yet another bottle of cool blue liquid. "What's the deal with that name, anyway?"

"Blue Tongue Water, that's what my Grandma Nellie back on the Rez used to call this stuff when I was a kid. She knew I liked it, so sometimes she would treat me to a bottle of it from the trading post near her hogan. Her English was not so good, so she had her own names for a lot of stuff, and she knew what this did to my mouth when I drank it, so that's what we called it," she explained. Stella took several long sips, holding each in her mouth briefly. Then she stuck her tongue out at the Lieutenant Commander.

"Oh! You mean that literally!" he said, surprised.

"Sure," she said, puzzled that he would be surprised at something so obvious to her.

"Actually, it's dawning on me now that you always speak literally. Even the funny nicknames you choose for everything are selected for their literal value. I know men who think that when you speak as slowly and carefully as you do, you're trying to hide your real meaning in elaborately disguised language. Like a lawyer with a dirty trick up his sleeve. But that's not it, is it? You speak the way you do to make sure people know exactly what you mean!" he concluded, still surprised and pleased at his own insight.

"Thanks, Bob. I'm glad you get that." And then Stella smiled. It was a full-blast signature Stella smile. Just for him! Costello felt his heart jump in his chest. That was a moment and an image of her he would long remember. But alas, it was only a moment.

"Murph! Where is he? And Jake! How is he?" Stella blurted out, suddenly realizing time was flying and she was losing track of important events transpiring around her.

"Murphy made it safely back into the Big Dipper at about the same time Harris went into his chamber. Murphy's understandably pretty pooped, and not in your biodec sense. Webster is stable. He still has eye tics and a bad headache, but he's coherent. We'll go see them," Costello assured her. "And then I propose you try to get some rest yourself."

April 8, 2013
0845 Hrs
Aboard *Whatever*
Straits of Florida

Lieutenant Commander Costello strode toward Hank
Johnson and the comms connecting them with the Team
inside the Big Dipper, a concerned look on his face. "We've
got a problem," he said flatly. "They've just passed on the
news to me that the PRM can't dock with the *Skin*—
DISSUB," he hastily corrected himself, "to pick up that last
batch of men. The DISSUB used to be sitting close to level
on the bottom, but it shifted its position since the last rescue
run, and it's now listing at a steep angle. The PRM is
designed to handle up to about a forty-five degree rotation in
any one plane and still make a hermetic seal with the
DISSUB hatch, but not more. Flooding the room to pull
Harris out must have made the DISSUB slide on that rocky
bottom to where it's now rolled to more than a fifty degree
inclination."

Hank slammed a hand onto the nearest smooth surface.
"Damn! I knew that was a crappy plan! We save one guy,
maybe, but we lose the last half a dozen, including the
Captain. And there's one poor sap down there who gave up
his seat on the last PRM run to let Harris get his free ride
strapped to the outside."

At the sound of Hank's angry voice, the usual assortment of
men assembled, some with authorized roles they could play
in the situation.

"What do you think of this idea: if we can find a heavy-duty
ratchet strap onboard somewhere, do you think one of you
men can strap the PRM over far enough to adjust its trim and

218

manually assist the mating with the DISSUB?" Costello asked the Team. The men surrounding Costello on the deck began to nod seriously. "If you think that plan could work, then we need to run this op immediately, because the men still on the DISSUB don't have a working life support system in there. Not sure how long they've got, but it's not night and day anymore."

Hank made another angry growl. "Like that part was my bright idea too!" Costello ignored him, his attention focused on the Team on the other side of the porthole in front of him.

Petty Officer Bill Murphy, who had been lying flat on his bunk, struggled upright, his face haggard and pale. "OK. On it," he said with as much energy as he could muster.

Chief Byron Soaps stood as quickly as the small space inside the Big Dipper permitted. He had acted calmly enough for long enough that Dr. Balinski had stopped ordering tranks for him. Soaps leaned down and placed a friendly hand on Murphy's chest to restrain him. "No, bro. Not you this time. You've done more than enough already, and we can all see you're half dead from exhaustion."

Chief Calvin Sorensen stood and headed for the Little Dipper. "Yessir, Lieutenant Commander. I'll suit up."

Soaps straightened and looked through the porthole at Lieutenant Commander Costello and the other assembled men outside. "Yes, I know. Nobody trusts me to keep my brains in my head if I'm working in the water. But look at me. Really *look* at me," Soaps demanded. "I'm *here*! All of me is here. Now look at Murphy." He pointed to his prostrate buddy. Murph's attempt at an apologetic smile and a feeble wave conveyed more than Soaps could have. "Trust

219

me! Trust me at least enough to let me be the backup diver for Sorensen. As stable as Webster is right now, surely you'll agree that Murphy can be left in charge of him. Webster doesn't need two nurses nearly as much as Sorensen needs a backup." Soaps stared fiercely at Lieutenant Commander Costello, waiting for his response.

Senior Chief Jacob Webster nodded his agreement as well as he could with the neck brace in place.

Costello glanced quickly over one shoulder, hoping to find his Diving Medical Officer and get a medical clearance for Soaps. Instead he found Stella quietly watching nearby. He beckoned for her to come toward him. "You know this man better than I do. Is he OK?" he asked her. "Can we send him down?"

Stella put her face near the porthole separating her from the men inside. Soaps was still fiercely gazing out from his stand in the chamber. "Tell him, Doc!" Soaps urged her, in a gentler tone than he had used with his senior officer.

"Yes, it's him. *All* of him," she assured Costello without taking her eyes from Soapy. "There isn't a better man on the planet for the job. Or for any other purpose," she added, sharing a fleeting half smile with Soapy.

Lieutenant Commander Costello quickly debated the question with the other dive supervisory men. "Agreed. We've been skating on dangerously thin ice for too long, sending Murphy down alone. Go. Back up Sorensen," he authorized Soaps. "You," he said, pointing to one of the nearby men, "call over to the other ship, and get someone to tell us what a strap can be secured to on both the PRM and the DISSUB that will meet our needs. You," he said, pointing to another man, "find that strap, and get it ready to send down."

April 8, 2013
1000 Hrs
1700 feet below the surface
Straits of Florida

Sorensen heard the *clack!* as the Pressurized Rescue Module finally mated with the rescue seat of the *Skinny Eel* for its last run. "Whew! That was harder than I thought it'd be, and I didn't never think it'd be easy!" he told the anxiously waiting people on the surface. "Yessiree. We are *that good*!" He performed a little touchdown dance of victory, gingerly minding his balance while standing on the tilted submarine's surface.

A garbled chorus of hoo-yahs assaulted his ears inside his helmet. But he still needed to wait until the PRM had loaded its men before he could dare release the strap holding the vehicle at its awkward angle. If he released too soon, the fittings at the rescue seat could bind and prevent the PRM from undocking.

Minutes ticked by. Finally the word was transmitted to him that all the men were onboard the PRM, and it was preparing to undock. Sorensen grabbed the quick release on his strap, ready to remove it as soon as he was given the order. Nothing happened. "We doin' this?" he asked his people on the surface.

"Hang on a second. The seat seems to be binding. They're shifting men around inside, trying to rebalance their load," Costello informed him. More minutes passed.

Finally, Cal heard the *clack!* he was so anxious to hear and saw the PRM shift up slightly as its propellers immediately started to spin. He hit the ratchet release, but it did not budge. The upward movement of the PRM, initiated too quickly and without warning to him, had caused the strap to tighten too much for him to release the ratchet mechanism. He tried again. Still no release. He transmitted the request as quickly as he could, from seventeen hundred feet below the ocean's surface, to the deck of the *Whatever*, across to the *Voo2*, and back down seventeen hundred feet to people just a few feet in front of him: "please shift back into neutral, so I can release the strap." This message relay was taking way too long. The strap was being strained far beyond what it was rated to hold. Cal was fearful that if the strap failed in some random location in front of him, it could whip back and injure him.

He dug for his knife and started quickly to cut the strap at a level he hoped would do him the least harm. Suddenly the strap parted somewhere over his head, sending the metal ratchet mechanism snapping down toward him. He heard the crash of metal on the side of his helmet. For an awful moment he thought his helmet might have been cracked; instead it was his helmet-mounted light that was destroyed. He lost his precarious balance on the inclined surface of the submarine and slid on his back, his umbilical cable linking him to everything he needed in the material world slithering behind him across the *Skinny Eel*, like a much smaller member of the same genus. He had no hope of gaining purchase on anything until he had slipped completely from the top of the disabled submarine and down its side, toward the rocky bottom.

As he slid, he watched the PRM rise, its running lights disappearing quickly from his sight. With his helmet light gone, he was now slowly falling in absolute darkness, with no way of guessing what he might land on. He heard the emergency come-home gas bottle on his back hitting metal sheets that skittered around him. One of his feet caught on something, causing him to tumble slowly forward. There was a shot of cold and a stab of pain in the front of his right thigh. His umbilical cable suddenly came up short, leaving him dangling upside down, his arms flailing helplessly in the darkness through something that felt like a giant spider web.

"Sorensen? What just happened? We're hearing strange noises," he heard Costello ask him. In the rush of events, the disorienting blindness, the upending, and the pain, it was difficult for Cal to sort things out. The black ocean suddenly seemed immeasurably vast and lonely. He was not sure what to answer.

"Sorensen? Where are you? What just happened? Can you get back to the bell?" Costello pressed him louder.

After a distressingly long pause, they heard: "fell off the DISSUB. Not sure…think there's something poking me in the leg," with the labored breaths between syllables more audible than the words. The topside listeners looked at each other, horrified. Then more silence.

"Soaps!" Costello called into the comms to the Little Dipper.

"Aye, Sir, bailing out now," Soaps responded immediately. Jumping out of the bell, always positioned ten or twenty feet above the bottom to prevent it from being pounded on the bottom in case of surface swells, and floating gently to the bottom was something Soaps usually enjoyed doing. But today, when he was anxious to go and find Cal, this playground game seemed irritatingly slow.

Several more attempts at hailing Sorensen failed to get a coherent response from him, only heavy breathing and disjointed muttering.

An excruciating number of minutes passed. Suddenly they heard Soaps report, "I see him! I have to go down a slope of metal sheets to get to him. This must be pieces that Webster and Murphy cut up from the *Mad Cat*. Boy, this is slippery. No wonder Sorensen skidded down here and landed hanging ass over teakettle. I could do the same thing myself if I don't watch out. Wow, what a mess! He's tangled himself up in a giant pile of electrical wires or some kind of cable. He's buried in it from the top of his head to his chest. How in the world did one mini sub have that much electronics on it? It's going to take forever to cut him out of this stuff! Hang on, bro, I'll get you out of here," he told Sorensen.

More weird sounds of metal groaning and squeaking were heard. "What's going on down there? Talk to us, Soaps!" Costello urged.

"I'm trying to find a piece of metal I can move out over the wiring so I can stand on that, instead of getting bogged down in this mess like Sorensen," Soaps explained, the effort involved clear in his breathless voice. "Almost there. How you doing there, bro?" he asked Sorensen, whose response was unintelligible.

Costello frowned in thought. "Oh! Of course! You're standing in jettisoned SEPIRB cut up by the ADS2000 pilot before we arrived. It's not one long coil anymore; it's chopped into lengths," he told Soaps.

"Now I get it! I was yanking on this stuff, and it was just making more knots and tangles. If I pull on a piece gently, or maybe even just shake it, it loosens right up and I can lift it off. See, bro?" he told Sorensen. "I'll have you out of this mess faster than you can say amen!"

"Amen" came Sorensen's response, the first the people on deck had understood from him for a while.

"OK, maybe not that fast, but faster than you thought a couple minutes ago," Soaps reminded him.

"Uh-oh. Now I see why he thought there was something poking him in the thigh. There's a long, sharp piece of metal sticking through his suit leg. Hang on a second, bro. This might hurt a little. There. It's out. Could be worse, I guess," Soapy informed them.

Two or three more bursts of reports came from Soaps as he worked to free Sorensen and return him to his feet. Sorensen had little to say for himself throughout the process. Then Soaps had to climb his umbilical back onto the upper surface of the submarine and help pull Sorensen up by his own umbilical, all by only the meager light of Soaps's headlamp. The piece of metal debris in Sorensen's thigh turned out to have penetrated less than an inch, without doing any serious damage to his leg. The greater problem was that the puncture let cold water enter his heated suit. Sorensen's increasing hypothermia did not make matters any easier for Soaps to direct Sorensen's movements as the two men made their way slowly back to the Little Dipper. The final climb up their umbilicals to reenter their elevator to safety was exhausting for both of them.

The crowd of people awaiting every word of news from below was now frozen in silence. Suddenly Sorensen's voice was heard clearly from inside the Little Dipper. "Well? Are ya gonna pull this trash can up, or are ya gonna make us walk home?"

226

Cheers went up from all over the *Whatever* and the *Voo2* as the good news spread.

Stella had been standing within hearing distance but out of the way throughout the whole operation. She was struck, as she had been before, by the calm and almost banal way in which everyone managed this crisis. She closed her eyes and tried to imagine the utter blackness in which Cal was entangled and the small spark of a headlamp by which Soapy had to work to free him. She was so proud of these men and so honored to see them at their best.

Cal would have liked to tell people that during what should have been a short walk for him back to the Little Dipper, but then things took a bad turn and it got a little confusing for a while, he thought of his wife, his daughters, his mother, his Lord and Savior—something life-affirming and noble that bore him up through his trials. He was an honest man, so he never did say those things. But he was also too proud a United States Navy Diver to admit how fuzzy in the head he actually became and how little he remembered from his ordeal.

Soapy knew. Soapy had looked through Cal's faceplate into his glassy eyes. But his bro Soapy would never rat a buddy out. There was one fact of which Cal was certain: if Cal had been down there alone, as Murph had been for so many hours, Cal would not have been able to free himself. Soapy saved his life, no doubt in Cal's mind about that.

For Soapy's part, he was proud and relieved to have finally had a significant role in this operation. He would never have been able to forgive himself if anything terrible had happened to Cal or Murph while he sat high and dry, drooling into his lap.

April 8, 2013
1200 Hrs
Aboard *Whatever*
Straits of Florida

"Methane production has spiked," Stella informed the men clustered near her gas chromatograph, awaiting her news.

"All righty, then!" Hank Johnson announced with dramatic energy, his outstretched hand reaching for the valve to start the decompression on the Big Dipper. Stella, Art and Lieutenant Commander Costello were shuffling with the excitement of the moment. "You know the first words spoken from the moon, right?" Hank quizzed them.

"The *Eagle* has landed!" Stella responded.

"One small step for a man…" Costello offered.

Hank nodded to them both. "Now, how about the very last words spoken from the moon?"

The three listeners shook their heads.

"Let's get this mother out of here!" he informed them with a proud grin.

Stella and Art exchanged dubious glances with Lieutenant Commander Costello. "Consider the source," Costello murmured.

"Or did you need me to come up with some old Navajo quote for you?" Hank needled Stella, offended by their skepticism.

229

"Actually, I'd say you were quoting quite a few old Navajos," Stella rejoined. On that note, the decompression of the Big Dipper was off at the blazing pace of six feet of seawater pressure drop per hour for as long as hydrogen was in their breathing mix. Not an impressive speed by most standards, to be sure, but twice what it would have been without the hydrogen biochemical decompression capsules tucked in the four bellies inside the chamber.

With all the *Skinny Eel's* crew now safely onboard the *Voo2*, the PDQ Mobile locked in its cradle, and the Little Dipper secured on the deck of the *Whatever*, Captain Gilchrist gave orders for both ships to head back to Key West, where everyone could continue their decompression at dockside. Art insisted on taking Stella's afternoon shift at chamber tending and sent her off to her bunk, assuring her that she could pay him back some other time.

April 8, 2013
1500 Hrs
Aboard *Whatever*
Straits of Florida

"Stella. Stella. We need you again. You have to wake up. I'm so sorry, but we need you," Art said as he insistently shook her shoulder.

"*Yá'at'ééh*, Art," she mumbled. Stella smiled up at him until her eyes were open enough to see Art's expression. Then she sat up quickly enough to make her woozy. "What's happened?" she asked in alarm.

"It's Murph. He's in trouble. Belly pains. Doc Balinski needs you to come and help him evaluate," Art explained.

Stella shook off her sleepiness as quickly as she could. "Abdominal pains? Where exactly? Fever? Any nausea, diarrhea, any other symptoms?" she asked, trying not to sound as panicked as she felt.

"Pain is about here," Art fingered a circle over his right abdomen. "Fever, yes. Diarrhea, no, and according to him no bowel movements of any kind for longer than he can remember. Nausea, yes, but he's eaten so little in the last day or so that he's not puking anything but water as fast as he tries to drink it."

"Right upper quadrant?" Stella asked, puzzled. "He had his appendix removed last year, didn't he?"

"Yes, and the most tender part he says is pretty much under the appendectomy scar," Art responded.

231

Stella stared in thought. "What does Doc Balinski make of it?"

Art shrugged. "He was hoping you'd know if it could be the biodec capsules, and if so, what to do."

Stella scurried to the deck as fast as her trailing shoelaces permitted. The all too familiar cluster of alarmed men was already assembled at portholes of the Big Dipper when she arrived. She pressed her face against the nearest available porthole and switched on the comms. When she spotted Murphy inside on his bunk, she gasped. He was gray in the face and sweaty. His body convulsed with pain.

"Murph, buddy, what's going on with you?" she asked with as much cheerful sympathy as she could muster through her fears.

Murphy looked around at the sound of her voice in the chamber, but it took him a moment to locate the porthole with her face in it and focus on her. His brave attempt at a smile was heartbreaking to see.

"Been better" was all he could manage.

"When did you start having these abdominal pains? Was it right after you took the biodec capsules? Some time since then?" she asked him.

"No, I'm sure it's not that. Had some pains way before I took the biodecs," he assured her.

"Way before? How long before?" she insisted. "And you didn't say anything about it to us?"

"Dunno exactly, but I know it was a long time before. Like…a day or two, three maybe. Honest! It's not the biodecs!" he protested. "Something else…" He suddenly curled even more tightly, and his face twisted in a paroxysm of pain.

Dr. Balinski, anxiously watching and listening at another porthole, cut in. "Murphy, we're going to take care of you. Try to relax now. We're going to give you something for that pain, and it's going to knock you out. I couldn't do it sooner, till we had Doc Stella have a moment to talk with you. But Chief Sorensen is going to hit you up with the good stuff. Hopefully when you wake up, you'll be feeling better, OK?"

Murphy was in too much pain even to nod.

Balinski and Stella switched off their comms and stepped a short distance away from the Big Dipper. Costello quickly joined them. Stella did not like the depth of worry she could clearly read on the doctor's face. "What would present like that?" she asked him. "In anybody else, I'd be guessing appendicitis, but he doesn't have an appendix."

Balinski slowly shook his head. "Any number of intestinal ailments or blockages. With such a vague point to his abdomen, it could also be gall bladder or liver. If we could just get our hands on him, get him into an MRI, maybe even into surgery, we could figure this out and get something going for him. Damn it! He's close enough to see but not to touch!" Balinski shook his head again in frustration and concern.

"Sorensen drilled a hole into Webster's skull, right there in the Big Dipper. Sorensen isn't a surgeon, and that's not a surgical suite, but he did it anyway, and it seems to have worked. Could you direct Sorensen to perform abdominal surgery and see what's going on in Murphy's belly?" Costello asked hesitantly.

"Oh, no!" Balinski responded immediately. "Opening an entire abdomen is a very different thing from drilling one discrete hole in the skull, not that there wasn't plenty to be afraid of there," he informed the Lieutenant Commander. "It's too much to expect of Chief Sorensen, smart and competent Medical Corpsman though he is, to perform that level of surgery. And I cannot possibly see from here what's going on in Murphy's belly, even if Chief Sorensen did open him up. Worst of all, if there is some major rupture or infection of an abdominal organ, and we opened his belly up in that confined space, it would create a biohazard for the other three men in there with him."

The doctor frowned for some time at the deck. "I suppose we have to expect there is a septic or necrotic event taking place and have Chief Sorensen put him on a broad-spectrum IV antibiotic. I can't imagine such an approach would do him any harm, regardless of his real problem."

Stella looked alarmed. "Wouldn't an antibiotic wipe out his biodec bugs and mess up his decompression profile? Assuming of course it isn't the biodec bugs that are causing the problem to begin with?"

"No, not necessarily. Antibiotics are designed to kill bugs that are pathogenic, but they usually don't mess with the native and nonpathogenic ones, such as yours," Balinski assured her. "But I'll do some looking up before I choose one."

Stella sighed. "Poor Cal has to stand right there where he can touch him, but without diagnostics all he can do is knock him out and blindly shoot stuff in." She returned to the porthole on the Big Dipper. Cal had just injected Murphy with morphine. Murphy's face, relaxed and free of pain, looked like his boyish self again, drenched in sweat like a kid who had been running around on the playground too long. "Hang in there, Murph buddy. You're our hero, and we'll all be praying for you," she muttered to the glass.

What if it was a contamination of the biodec capsules that had already been given to the rest of the Team, or would be given to them in the days ahead? Stella slumped to the deck and stared into space, lost in her own terrifying thoughts.

April 8, 2013
1700 Hrs
Aboard *Whatever*, Naval Air Station Key West
Key West, FL

Stella was on deck to see the *Whatever* arriving in Key West, lighted by one of its legendary glorious sunsets. Murphy was still burning with fever. Sorensen was giving him sponge baths to try to reduce his temperature but with little success. At least the pain meds were working.

Dr. Balinski had sorted through his drug cabinets and consulted multiple references before choosing an antibiotic to send into the Big Dipper for Sorensen to start as an intravenous drip. As yet there were no indications the antibiotics were doing anything useful. But as Dr. Balinski had predicted, there was no indication of harm from them. None of the other three Team members had any abdominal issues of their own, beside those attributable to concern for their buddy. Even though Webster's status was still listed as stable, his ongoing spasms of eye muscles and headaches bespoke a man who needed a hospital sooner rather than later. His neck brace was becoming a real annoyance to him, but there was no way of guessing if it could be removed safely.

The decompression of the crew of the *Skinny Eel* progressed without incident. Even Harris was doing pretty well for a guy who had been legally dead for a while.

Stella had insisted on taking the last couple of hours of her assigned shift at chamber tending so Art could get some rest of his own. But by 8:00 p.m., Art was back on deck and assumed his usual shift. Stella returned to her preferred seat on the deck next to the Big Dipper. Art did his best to ply her with a bit of food and the never-ending stream of Blue Tongue Water, and he eventually offered her a blanket. But Art knew better than to try persuading her to retire to her bunk. And Costello knew not to try to say anything Art was not willing to say to her.

Nor would anyone else leave. Dr. Balinski, Lieutenant Commander Costello, and Hank hovered along with Art and Stella and a variable crowd of others outside the Big Dipper. All of them were long past having anything casual to say to each other, let alone anything profound. They were even out of energy for much idle movement. But none was prepared to just walk away to a game of cards in the galley or a warm bunk, with Murph hanging on to life by the barest glimmer of spirit inside that suddenly ugly chamber. They were inches away from reaching out to him, but they could not.

And if the people holding vigil outside the chamber were beside themselves with concern, just imagine the emotional state of the three men inside with Murph. None of these men had been deployed in a theater in which buddies met violent deaths beside them. They had all witnessed some frightening accidents, and all had had the sad duty of burying loved ones. But they had never watched with empty hands as a life drained away. A life they knew well and loved. They realized they were fortunate never to have had that experience before. And how they wished and prayed today would not be the day they would. *Come on, Murph, buddy. Hang in just a little longer. Mission is complete. We're at the dock. Just hang in till we can get you out, please* was the message all three men kept thinking.

April 9, 2013
0202 Hrs
Aboard *Whatever*, Naval Air Station Key West
Key West, FL

Dr. Balinski was the first of them to vent his frustration at his inability to do anything in the face of this crisis of Murphy's. "I'm gonna go get a cup of coffee in the galley. Somebody come and get me if anything changes," he told the group clustered around the Big Dipper.

No one responded. Shortly after Balinski left the deck, Lieutenant Commander Costello shrugged tiredly and headed toward the galley as well. "I'll be with him," he mumbled over his shoulder.

Inside the Big Dipper, Jake Webster and Byron Soaps lay on their bunks, staring at nothing, lost in their own thoughts. There was not enough room in the tiny space for all of them to be seated on the edge of Bill Murphy's bunk along with Cal Sorensen. Cal was alternately sitting with closed eyes and murmuring lips and leaning to listen to Murph's ragged breathing. Suddenly he leaned forward and listened intently. His fingers slid to Murph's neck. He gave his buddy's sweaty forehead a brush to push back the sticky hair on it and to give himself a small space on which to plant a kiss.

"Dudes?" he called softly to Soapy and Jake. They materialized beside him in the dim chamber. Two more kisses were gently planted. The friends lingered together for silent farewells. Cal slowly rose on shaky knees and stepped to the comms switch.

"Doc Stella?" he called. "Art? You guys out there?"

Art jumped to his comms switch. "We're all here. What's happening in there?" he asked pointlessly, already knowing the answer.

"He's dead."

Stella's head drooped forward, loose strands of her long black hair veiling her face. The two men standing near her stared at the deck, slowly shaking their heads.

"Doc?" came the voice again over the communications system. Stella did not look up from where she sat on the deck. "Doc Stella? What do you want us to do now...? Doc...? Are you there?"

The two men looked at Stella. She had begun to rock gently to her own rhythm, her arms wrapped around herself, her face still obscured by her tangled hair.

"Stella?" drawled Hank Johnson, a tall, lanky Texan in his fifties. "You have to say something. The Team is waiting. We're all waiting. I want to know how you're planning to talk your way out of this one, Little Miss Know-It-All."

"Shut up, Hank, you jerk!" hissed Art Moore.

Yeah, Hank. Shut up. We're all sick of hearing you.

April 9, 2013
0500 Hrs
Aboard *Whatever*, Naval Air Station Key West
Key West, FL

Stella sat up, aching and weary, in her small bunk. Time to give up on the possibility of any sleep, she figured. Slowly she rose, pulled on her belt and shoes, and headed down the corridor to the deck. Crew members stared at her strangely but greeted her politely as usual. When she came on deck, she was momentarily startled by the view that now included palm trees, buildings, and other ships in the pale light of early morning.

Hank Johnson and Art Moore were standing by the Big Dipper, talking in quiet tones with other men. At her approach they turned toward her. Both men looked startled.

"What the hell kinda craziness is this? Some weird Navajo thing er what?" Hank blurted out.

Art hurried toward her and ushered her to a spot along the deck railing where Stella and he could confer in private.

"Stella, honey, what have you done to your hair?" Art asked her. Her glorious mane of thick black hair, worn usually in a long braid at work, had been chopped short and badly. It was now sticking out in irregular tufts all over her head. "Is this some part of a Navajo tradition of mourning for the dead?" he asked, hoping the explanation was that sane.

Stella shook her head slowly. "No, not Navajo. In fact Navajos have rather minimal funerary activities. This is just me. When my mother died, I did not want to load extra work onto my dad by making him help me wash, comb, and braid

240

my long hair. It had been such a ritual for my mother and me to get me up in the morning and have her comb out and rebraid my hair that it felt wrong to go on the same way without her. Plus I needed somehow to look as different as I felt with her gone. So I cut it off. Now with Murph...The scissors were in my hand, and my hair was on the floor—last night? This morning? Not sure when, but doesn't matter—without me even giving it that much thought. I didn't have a mirror or anything. Does it really look that bad?" she asked, running stiff fingers through the scruffy mess.

Art debated his response for a moment. He settled on "it'll grow back." They walked together toward the Big Dipper. Behind her back Art pantomimed to Hank that the situation was OK, and he would explain later.

Hank, characteristically, was less diplomatic. "Looks like you need to sharpen the blades on your lawnmower, girl!"

"Can we stop discussing my hair and get to business, please?" she demanded pointedly. "Where are we with poor Murph?" Stella began peering through portholes in the Big Dipper as she spoke.

"Murph is taken care of as best we can right now," Art assured her. "He's been laid out in the Little Dipper and packed with ice. Lieutenant Commander Costello has ordered us a steady delivery of ice from the base mess hall. We pressure lock in more ice bags every couple of hours, and so far so good. Since the rest of the Team needs to get into the Little Dipper to replenish the ice, we won't be able to completely isolate Murph from the Big Dipper. That means we won't be able to accelerate his decompression the way we'd like to. Or to spare the feelings of the guys in there with him. The best we can hope for is to keep him in shape

241

for a useful autopsy." Art ground to a halt, unable to think of euphemisms for terms like *decomposition* and *overinflation*. He knew she would know all the grizzly details anyway.

Stella nodded gravely, staring at the deck. She suddenly looked up at Art. "What the hell? What the hell? What the hell?" she demanded in frustration.

"Do not jump to conclusions. Do not jump to conclusions. Do not jump to conclusions," he responded as patiently as he could.

She nodded gravely again, and made a visible effort to compose herself. "How is Jake?" she asked. She could see him dimly in the chamber's night lights. He appeared to be asleep, as were Cal and Soapy at that hour. Or at least they were in their bunks with their eyes closed, as she had been.

"Stable. Coherent. Still has that headache, but Cal doesn't see as many eye tics in him. Doc Balinski says he is guardedly optimistic," Art assured her.

"Methane release rate?" she asked, stepping toward the latest printout from the gas analysis system.

"Tooting along just fine," Art responded. "Remember that with every passing hour of good methane, it becomes less likely that Murph's problem was the biodec capsules or that the other Team members will have problems with their own biodecs. We should let them all sleep as long as they want to. What are the odds we can get you back into your bunk for a while? Your watch is hours from now," he reminded her.

She glanced at her watch and gave him a wry look. "You're one to talk about watch hours! Seems like you're always on deck," she countered. "But yes, now that you mention it, I might try to do with a bit more time in the bunk. Not sure I'd call any of it sleep. Looks like everything is as much under control as we can make it for now, anyway," she said resignedly. She turned and headed back toward her cabin. And managed to sleep for several hours when she got there.

April 11, 2013
1000 Hrs
Aboard *Whatever*, Naval Air Station Key West
Key West, FL

The crew of the *Skinny Eel* had all completed their decompressions and their one-atmosphere observation periods. Harris needed more medical observation in the nearest hospital; his eyes had not fared well in the massive pressure changes. His ears were of course a mess, but with time and antibiotics they were expected to heal themselves. Everyone else from the crew was cleared for release. They left the *Voo2* as fast as one hundred-plus highly motivated men could move down a gangway.

Not to worry. They were not a bunch of thoughtless clods who ran off without trying to meet and personally thank the people who had saved them from deaths that would not bear serious reflection. The crew did ask for permission to go onboard the *Whatever* and meet the NEDU people. It was denied in the name of security. They were granted permission to hand to their captain, who in turn handed to Captain Gilchrist, a stack of eight sheets of paper. Each sheet was completely covered with the single word— "THANKS!"—written in over one hundred different hands.

Seven of the recipients of those sheets considered theirs treasures they kept with them for many years, until they faded into illegibility and needed to be thrown away. The eighth sheet was folded into a Team T-shirt and became a pile of brittle yellow fragments the better part of a century later.

There was one member of the *Skinny Eel*'s crew who had not learned his lesson about disobeying orders. On second thought, perhaps he had. Stella found a folded note slipped under the door to her cabin. It said she would always be in his family's thoughts and prayers, and if she was ever in Hermann, Missouri, she should come by for a visit. Stella took him up on that invitation. It was easy to find him. By the time she and *Red Chief* were making their second Lewis and Clark Trail ride, enough years had passed that Stella Grace Harris had her own listing in the Hermann phone book.

The departure of the crew of the *Skinny Eel* signaled the reversal of the process that had brought in all the submarine rescue equipment to the *Voo2*, docked next to the *Whatever*, albeit at a considerably more leisurely pace in this outgoing direction. As the deck of the more-than-usually-aptly-termed Vessel of Opportunity emptied, the noise and pace on their end of the dock subsided into something approaching loneliness in comparison to the past week.

April 12, 2013
1100 Hrs
Aboard *Whatever*, Naval Air Station Key West
Key West, FL

The first few days of decompression of the Hydrogen Team were rough on everyone from the NEDU group. Not difficult in terms of the decompression per se; that was sufficiently familiar to everyone that it went without incident. And if there were ever going to be problems with the decompression profile, they would be expected at much shallower depths. But each member of the group had his or her own reasons for thinking he or she was uniquely qualified to take the blame for the loss of Bill Murphy. Reasons ranged from "I should have demanded a greater role in leadership" to "I should have been stronger," "I should have been more careful," "I should have been more observant before things got out of control," or any combination of those vague and unquantifiable reasons. Having to service poor Murph's body in the Little Dipper with steady deliveries of ice only dug the guilt and anger in more deeply. Tempers were painfully short, and hours were painfully long.

It was Art who thought of a way to change everyone's mood and move from angry frustration toward resigned remembrance of their dear buddy as a happy influence in their lives.

On the previous morning, Stella had spent several minutes digging around in her duffel bag, unsuccessfully searching for her beloved "If you're not diving hydrogen" Team T-shirt. A hunt around her tiny cabin also failed to locate it. She pulled on another shirt and immediately went looking for Art to ask if he knew where the missing shirt might be.

246

Art would only say, "Don't worry. It's safe. Trust me." What the heck?

When Stella returned to her cabin to prepare for an early lunch, there it was on top of her duffel bag. Neatly folded the Navy Way, of course. When she eagerly unfolded it to pull it on, she noticed the back of the shirt. It bore a freshly silk-screened message in bold letters: "May the Farts be With You."

She ran on deck to the Big Dipper. There stood Art in his newly embellished T-shirt, smiling calmly at her. Even Hank was wearing his redecorated shirt but was trying to look nonchalant about it. Lieutenant Commander Costello was on hand as well, but in his mandated working Navy uniform. He did look a bit envious of their team finery, a problem Art would solve within the next few days.

Stella hurried to the nearest porthole of the Big Dipper. Yes, Soapy and Cal had their shirts on, and Jake had his shirt draped across his neck brace and chest. Murph's words, which he had offered as a silly toast, had metamorphosed into a touching benediction. There was one more shirt folded the Navy Way on a now-empty bunk. The marks of those folds could still be seen on that shirt when little Billy Murphy's grandchildren finally threw it away as a faded old rag filled with paper fragments and bearing the cryptic legend "arts be Wit."

April 13, 2013
1000 Hrs
Aboard *Whatever*, Naval Air Station Key West
Key West, FL

Art found Stella pacing the deck like a caged panther. "Stella, we need to get you to unwind a little now. Jake is stable. You can see that for yourself. And Murph is just Murph until we can get him out. All of Key West is before you to relax in and enjoy for the next week or so. You need to take your off-shift time and do some mindless sightseeing. Stroll Duval Street. Have a strawberry daiquiri. Something!"

Stella paused in her pacing and shot him a look of frustration. "I know. Jake is stable. Murph is stable…ish. But that's the problem! Everything is moving at a glacial pace—literally—at this point. I need something to change faster. But change in a good way, please! Plenty of stuff might still go wrong, and when it does, it will probably be far too fast. But I can't just relax and go play tourist right now!"

"Stella, you can't just stay like this either. You aren't doing yourself any good, and if there are any further problems, you won't have a clear head for dealing with them," Art reminded her. She inclined her head in acknowledgment of his point. "Well, there's one thing I have in mind to get you into another gear," Art said as he looked around the deck. "Ah. This should work."

Art directed Stella to what had been a rain shelter and was now conveniently acting as a sun shade. At this warm morning hour, it was free of sailors. He grabbed a folding chair from a pile in a corner, placed it behind her, and nudged her into taking a seat. From one of his many pockets, he pulled out a small towel, which he draped across her back and shoulders. A pair of scissors, a comb, and a small spray bottle quickly followed. Stella was reluctantly enlisted as bottle holder; her suspicious sniff failed to detect anything more ominous than water in it.

"I used to cut my boys' hair when they were growing, and I got pretty good at it, if I may say so myself. They were pleased and even took to asking me for my 'attitudy' cut. Your hair is even thicker than theirs was, so it ought to take an attitudy cut pretty well. At least I can't make it look any worse than that hatchet job you gave yourself. Oh. Hope that expression wasn't offensive," he added, knowing full well that it would not have been to her.

Stella relaxed a little into the chair under the calming influence of Art's hands, rough and knobby though they were, running through her hair. Since the day she had cut it, she had been unable to bring herself to really look at it much in a mirror or even to comb it when she gave up tossing in bed and dressed for the day. She knew from the odd look in people's eyes when they spoke to her that they were staring at something pretty bad up there. "At least you didn't call it a *tomahawk* job. That I would have gotten *all savage* about," she said with more wry humor than she had used in days.

The two old friends remained in companionable silence for a while, both enjoying the gentle snip-snip-snip of Art's scissors, punctuated by an occasional susurration from the spray bottle.

"Must be nice..." Stella said slowly, her eyes lazily following a few gulls. "Must have been nice for you, I mean...meeting the love of your life while you were still really young, getting married, having kids, raising all of them well, slowly growing old together, sharing lots of

249

happy memories..."

Art did not respond. Puzzled by his lengthy silence, Stella turned her face up toward him.

"No moving," he said, tilting her chin back to horizontal. Another long silence ensued. "Well..." he began. And ended.

"A single woman in her thirties wants to know about these things. I need to know if I'm really missing out on something important here or not. Don't we know each other well enough by now for you to have something more to say to me than 'well'?" she asked.

Art sighed heavily. "You're right. I should be able to tell you what you want to know. It's just not a subject I like talking about," he added. "Yeah. Betty and I were high-school sweethearts. Back in Detroit in those days, graduate from high school, get a job in a car factory, get married, start having kids, with all those things in any sequence you wanted, was all my classmates expected of life. I wanted more for my life than just standing in an assembly line. Sure, Betty and I were crazy excited about getting married and making a home and family together. But I wanted also to see the world, do interesting and adventurous things, make a little more of a mark than it seemed possible I could make if I just stayed in Detroit. So a few months after we got married, I enlisted in the Navy and shipped out pretty quickly after that."

Art clipped on in silence for a little while, expertly wielding a comb with one hand as he trimmed with the other. Stella understood she should let him take his time in relating whatever it was that was not what he liked talking about.

"Eight and a half months after I went to sea, there was an announcement on the PA system of my ship: 'Attention on deck! Seaman Arthur Moore is now the father of a healthy baby boy!' And everybody applauded and cheered. It was another month before I got to see my firstborn son. But when I got home, Betty was all crabby about the weirdest stuff. I didn't know which kitchen towel was for hands and which for dishes, I didn't know what days to take the trash out, I didn't know anything about the routine she and the baby had, so I was always in the way. And a crying baby at two a.m. and four a.m. and six a.m. is hard for most men to take. So pretty soon I went out for another tour of sea duty. And eight and a half months later, same announcement on my ship. By the time Betty was having the fourth baby, the announcement on the ship was just, 'Yo! Moore! Another boy!'" Art chucked softly at the memory.

"After a decade of this shipboard stuff, I was done with it. I got out of the Navy. That's when I converted to civil service and started working with your dad at the Navy lab in Bethesda. I thought I was so smart, realizing I could get a pretty nice house big enough for a wife and four boys and a spread of land, all on a lab tech's salary. Only catch was I had to live in West Virginia and commute to Maryland for work, about an hour and a half each way every day. I got the idea from a couple of the other guys who were doing the same thing, and they and their families were very satisfied with that arrangement.

"Betty and I were getting along pretty well for a lot of those years, or so I thought. She seemed happy enough to me, taking care of the house and the boys. I spent those hours of commuting time each day plus longer and longer hours at the lab, working on the overnight chamber dives of your dad's.

251

Then came the order to dismantle the lab and move some functions across town to the new Walter Reed building and some functions to Panama City. By then the boys were all out of the house and getting on with their lives, so the choice for us was easy. Betty was so happy to be moving to Florida! She thought it would be like retiring early. She hoped we would finally start spending what she called 'quality time together.'"

Art sighed again heavily and lowered his scissors. He stared at the deck for a long time before continuing his narrative. "But of course I got caught up in work stuff at NEDU and was not around as much as all that. We had next-door neighbors we liked a lot—Anna and Nick Bates. When I was at home, we did a lot with them, like backyard picnics and card games. Then Anna up and died of cancer. Betty felt so sorry for Nick. She spent a lot of time over at their place, taking him casseroles, cleaning house for him, stuff like that. Then about six months later, the day came when she told me she was leaving me for Nick. She finally admitted how much she resented all the years she'd had to raise the boys by herself, run the household by herself, live her life effectively alone, but still had to clean up after me like some stranger who showed up for dinner once in a while. So we got a divorce, and she moved into the house next door with Nick."

Stella let out a gasp despite her best efforts not to interrupt.

"Yeah. That was rough. Seeing your wife over the fence with a new husband is not something a man can easily take. Hearing her laugh at his jokes, watching her dance a little to his radio…" Art's voice trailed off.

"But I saw Betty at the Christmas party! You mean you aren't married to her anymore?" Stella asked in

252

astonishment.

"Yes. We are married. Long story short: Nick had a heart attack and dropped dead after he and Betty had been married only about three months. Betty was devastated and lost. So she remarried me and moved back across the fence to our house. Most of our friends and relatives don't even know we were divorced for part of a year. And you're not going to tell them, are you?" Art asked her pointedly.

"No, of course not!" Stella assured him.

"So. To get back to your original question about marrying young, having kids right away, growing old together with lots of happy memories. It's not necessarily everything it's cracked up to be. That does seem to work for some people, sure, but not everyone. There are no pat formulas to a happy life, young lady. If you're doing what you love and you're not harming anyone else in the process, you're doing the best you can. Thus endeth my sermon," he concluded, intending to soften the somber mood a little. "And thus endeth my barbering!" he added with a flourish of scissors and comb. "Whaddya think?"

Stella ran her fingers gingerly over a stiff ridge of hair running from forehead to just past mid-crown and feather-cut short hair on the sides. She slid from her chair and moved to a porthole that gave her a dull reflection of her image. Tipping her head from side to side, she appraised the cut with increasing satisfaction. "Won't I be accused of changing tribal affiliations?" she asked Art, who was waiting impatiently for her response.

Art shrugged. "Is Mohawk the worst thing you've ever been called?"

Stella smiled. For the first time in days, she really smiled.

"You look stunning!" he assured her.

"Attitudy! Now I get what your boys meant by that. Yes. Definitely attitudy," she concluded.

"Whenever you go into town, maybe you can get yourself some hair gel and make it a nicer and more lasting shape up top than I can do with just plain water," Art suggested.

Stella continued to tip her head and inspect her reflection.

"My little Indian paintbrush," Art murmured.

Stella spun to look at him, startled. "What did you say?"

"Something just occurred to me that your dad wrote in a Christmas letter to me, when you were a new baby. He called you his 'little Indian paintbrush,' apparently because of the way your baby hair stuck up all over your head, like a brush dipped in wet paint. Kinda like now."

"My Grandma Nellie used to call me that when I was little. You may not know it, but that's also the name of a Western wildflower. Here…" Stella pulled out her i-whatsit, as Art would call it, from her hip pocket. A few punches of buttons later, she showed him an image. "This is the flower by that name. It has red petals, and it's definitely wet-brushy shaped. I didn't know why she called me that except that she and I both liked red things and wildflowers." She smiled at the memory.

Stella glanced at her watch and fixed Art with a firm gaze.

"Looks like I have more than an hour, and you have a lot more than that before we need to take our shifts at chamber tending. Thanks! You were right. I needed to get out of my head for a while. Maybe we could take a stroll together, and you can show me how to get to Duval Street?"

"I thought you'd never ask, my dear!" he responded, dusting off his own smile for the occasion.

"By the metric of suns over yardarms, not to mention impending chamber-tending duties, this is maybe a little early for a strawberry daiquiri. Got any other Key West delicacies to suggest?" she asked.

"Do I!" he enthused. "We can start with a Key lime freeze—that's nonalcoholic—and work our way from there to some conch fritters for lunch. I can show you where to go this evening, when your shift is done, for a great strawberry daiquiri."

"Let's go!"

April 14–24, 2013
Aboard *Whatever*, Naval Air Station Key West
Key West, FL

After their rocky start, the NEDU people outside the Big Dipper settled into a rhythm during their days in Key West that they found surprisingly comfortable. Art Moore and Hank Johnson had both gravitated to dark-hour chamber-tending shifts over the years because they liked the quiet and privacy. But this chamber tending in the late night or early morning hours in the soft, salty breezes of Key West was amazing. To be the last one watching the world fall asleep and the stars shifting around in the velvety black sky over the ocean or the first one watching the sun rise and the sea birds awakening to a fresh morning: wonderful!

Chamber tending inside the echoing and slightly musty operations facility at NEDU would never be the same for either of them. And, of course, the waking hours they had off from chamber tending could be put to excellent use in a town made for seafarers. They were certainly still sad over the loss of Murph and concerned for the health of Jake, but with nothing they could do about either of those things, they put these thoughts to the backs of their minds most of the time.

Lieutenant Commander Bob Costello needed to get back to his assigned work for the Navy Experimental Diving Unit. This work kept him on his laptop and cell phone for large blocks of the day. He slept a mostly normal night now, but he also put in respectably long shared chamber watches at the start of Moore's night shift and in the early morning with Johnson. He got a detailed update on the progress of the biodec component of the decompression in the afternoon from Stella. Working an eighteen-hour day had never been this convenient or enjoyable.

Now that he was free to contact his children again, he called them every day after they were home from school. The kids were great. He had been able to hastily arrange for them to stay with his sister-in-law, Lois, and her husband, who had a spacious home near their own home, with a swimming pool and some friendly dogs. Lois loved her niece and nephew and pampered them almost as much as their mother had. She was a far better cook and more comfortable homemaker than Costello was and a better helper with their schoolwork. It was good to hear his kids' happy voices on the phone and know they were enjoying a few weeks in their aunt's tender care.

He had lingering breakfasts with Stella each morning. He liked that new Mohawk haircut of hers; it suited her. It was fine to send her off for her morning excursions into Key West while he turned to his NEDU work. She and he had agreed the two of them should never be absent from the ship simultaneously, as a safety issue for the dive. She always promised to return with a detailed description of where she had explored and recommendations on where he should go when he was ready for his own leg stretcher. She brought him little treats from her walks: a lime cookie, a piece of dark chocolate studded with pink sea salt, a sandy seashell, a colorful leaf, a watercolor art card. They were charmingly girlish treasures. She also began bringing him books, some of which he thought he might actually read someday.

He usually kept working through lunch, but he always checked in with her and the Team sometime in the afternoon. His concern for Webster's health diminished as Dr. Balinski's reports improved. As for Murphy, there was nothing to be done at this point except what they were doing: keeping the ice coming. Then more afternoon NEDU work, maybe a quick walk around town, and finally the calls to his kids.

The best part of his day was in the early evening. He would join Stella on deck to admire the sunset and to watch the stars appear. Then he would run into the ship's mess and collect a couple of trays of food to make a picnic dinner for the two of them in the moonlight. Conversations would drift away from work to anything that came into their heads. He enjoyed her tales of her childhood in that exotic place she called the Land of Enchantment. And she was the only woman he ever knew who was interested in his old motorcycle—adventures, mechanics, spills and all as he explored the verdant hills of his native Maryland as a teenager. He had put the bike up for sale the day his bride told him he would be a father. But it sure had been fun to tool around on his bike as a young man with fewer responsibilities, and it was fun to reminisce with her about it now, one biker to another. Oh yes, a man could get used to a life like this one. And they were giving him hazardous duty pay right now?

What he had been missing most since he'd lost Katie was not so much the physical intimacy, not that there was a thing in the world wrong with that, but the warm company of a good woman. Only a good woman could listen to a man's musings so attentively or laugh at his jokes so heartily. Soon they would all be back in PC, and life would settle down again. When that happened, could there be more? He knew Stella was concerned for Webster, but she was concerned for all her Team. She was reading them bedtime stories, for heaven's sake! She was kind to Moore. She was considerate of him. She was just flat-out a warmhearted woman to everyone. Could a new chapter in his life be only a few weeks or months away? Didn't a man, even one self-aware enough to know he was a simple man with simple needs, have a right to dream? He did not know what those dreams should realistically include, but under the Key West moon, many beautiful things seemed possible.

Stella had really needed that jump-start from Art to get her head cleared out from her grief over the loss of their dear Murph. Her lingering anxiety that his death was in some way her fault had been keeping her from functioning properly. Good old Art! And she really appreciated, now more than ever, what a good man Bob was to have with them. His initial insistence that he did not have sufficient expertise in ultra-deep diving issues she quickly recognized as modesty. He knew plenty. Not about hydrogen per se, true enough, but he had a wealth of operational experience that was invaluable. She could never have managed everything that was expected of her on Operation SECOND STARFISH without Art and Bob supporting her.

What a silly name Art and she had come up with for such a momentous week of activities! It suddenly hit her that the Neverland implied in that title was not the site of the DISSUB, as she had become reconciled to calling it, but Key West. This funny little place at the end of the wettest road in America had all the right elements to be Neverland. It had boys who were trying desperately not to grow up but to party forever. It had pirates. It famously celebrated its gay pride, which in turn filled local costume shops with Tinker Bell outfits. It might even have had crocodiles. She checked her i-whatsit. Crocodiles could be found nesting on Big Pine Key—close enough. Hank was Hook. The ticking clock everyone was afraid of was the decompression schedule.

Oh no! As a child listening to Grandma Curtis reading *Peter Pan* to her, she had identified with the character Tiger Lily, an American Indian princess. But in her Neverland today, she realized with a shudder and then a laugh she was cast in the role of Wendy, providing motherly ministrations to Lost Boys. Luckily there was one important difference in her real-life version from the original: her Peter Pan was suddenly itching to grow up. Yes, Key West was an oddly perfect place to see out the end of Operation SECOND STARFISH. Bob was right about many things, including the fact that she definitely preferred dealing with literal concepts and speech, not figurative ones. But as overworked metaphors go, this Neverland one was hilarious.

Once Stella got on a roll wandering around in Key West on her hours off, she discovered it had good used book stores. Having been an avid reader all her life, she knew the value of books for making time pass in a way that felt profitable. She knew the Team was becoming blow-their-brains-out bored (with one man already having the requisite hole in the head) and hoped that sending a stream of cheap paperbacks into the Big Dipper might help relieve some of that boredom.

Her earliest offering to the Team was admittedly a hard sell. *The Journals of Lewis and Clark* had looked too dauntingly thick and dry to three young men. It had been a childhood favorite of hers, and she was sure she could convince them of its value if only they would give it a chance. She did have one advantage over a high-school English or history teacher: she controlled the comms switch to a captive audience with no other entertainment.

"Listen, buddies," she urged them, "there are all sorts of amazing things that happen in this book. Boats that get caught in storms and swamp with non-swimmers aboard, including Sacajawea's new baby. Bear attacks. Falls down slopes that might have killed people but miraculously did not. Loss of critical equipment like compasses that turned up again. Lewis getting accidentally shot by another team member, and then the shooter running away and leaving Lewis bleeding and assuming he'd been ambushed by Indians. No work of fiction could ever be as exciting as this for an adventure story. Just let me read a few passages to you, and then you judge if you want to read the rest or not." What could they say?

Our vessels consisted of six small canoes, and two large perogues. This little fleet, altho' not quite so rispectable as those of Columbus or Capt. Cook, were still viewed by us with as much pleasure as those deservedly famed adventurers ever beheld theirs; and I dare say with quite as much anxiety for their safety and preservation. we were now about to penetrate a country at least two thousand miles in width, on which the foot of civilized man had never trodden; the good or evil it had in store for us was for experiment yet to determine, and these little vessells contained every article by which we were to expect to subsist or defend ourselves. however, as the state of mind in which we are, generally gives the colouring to events, when the immagination is suffered to wander into futurity, the picture which now presented itself to me was a most pleasing one. enterta[in]ing as I do, the most confident hope of succeeding in a voyage which had formed a da[r]ing project of mine for the last ten years, I could but esteem this moment of my departure as among the most happy of my life. The party are in excellent health and sperits, zealousy attached to the enterprise, and anxious to proceed; not a whisper of murmur or discontent to be heard among them, but all act in unison, and with the most perfict harmony...[excerpt from p. 92, *The Journals of Lewis and Clark*, edited by Bernard

Susan R. Kayar

DeVoto, copyright © 1953 by Bernard DeVoto, copyright © renewed 1981 by Avis DeVoto, Houghton Mifflin Harcourt Publishing Company.]

They were hooked. Sure, it was a great all-American adventure that oddly resonated with some of their own experiences. But it was Stella's mellifluous voice that lulled them into a peace they had not felt in far too many days at this point. She could probably have read them the Key West police ledger to equal advantage.

Her reading from *The Journals of Lewis and Clark* at their bedtime became a daily ritual they all looked forward to. Art, captive audience though he was at the controls of the Big Dipper at that hour, seemed genuinely engaged in the book. After the first evening's reading, Bob pulled up a stool to listen as well. It pleased Stella to see Bob's face relax and his eyes become dreamy as she read. She knew he missed his kids like crazy. She noted that each day, after he spoke with them on the phone, he came looking for her for solace and distraction she was happy to provide.

Never far from Stella's mind, no matter how hard she tried to focus on other subjects, were her thoughts of Jake. In the past week she'd had to consider the possibility of his death before her eyes. Within the first forty-eight hours, that had become an unlikely outcome. But had his promising young life, on the verge of great new undertakings, been spoiled by a moment of carelessness? With each passing day of improvement, that seemed decreasingly likely as well.

On the day when they shared their motorcycle ride, had she understood correctly that he was speaking with seriousness about a future role for her in his new life, or was that either wishful thinking on her part or a passing fancy he was ill advised to have mentioned? She did not think of him as one to speak lightly on serious matters. Those ears of his had turned too red to suggest a casual whim. Meriwether Lewis had phrased it, if not spelled it, so well: when her imagination was suffered to wander into futurity, the picture that now presented itself to her was an increasingly pleasing one. The Key West moon was working its magic on her as well.

The Team, prisoners that they were inside the Big Dipper, did not have happy recollections of their time in Key West. They were the ones who had to treat their fallen brother like a tuna on its way to a distant fish market. Back at NEDU, during their long experimental stays in the chamber, it had been possible to rig up a video screen outside a porthole so they could occasionally watch movies to relieve their boredom. That was not logistically possible in this case. Decks of cards lost their minimal charms on the first day. Board games, they would declare, did not use the proper spelling of *board*. Stella's supply of books came as close as anything they had to relieve the agonizing tick-tock-tick-tock passage of time during their decompression. The Key West moon could work no magic on them, and little wonder: they were stuck where the moon don't shine. Literally.

The Team had to remind themselves that no matter how long and boring this decompression felt, without Stella's ridiculous fart-fest biodec capsules, the decompression would have been almost twice as long. They were also aware that during decompression, there is no exciting event that is welcome. Every night when Cal Sorensen said his prayers, they always included one message: "please, God, keep this decompression boring."

The only small newsworthy event for them was when the

Big Dipper reached the pressure equivalent to three hundred feet of seawater. This pressure allowed them to safely flush out their chamber gases to remove all the remaining hydrogen and replace it with the same pressure of helium and oxygen. From there to the surface, they would have to decompress at a conservative rate of 2.9 feet of seawater per hour. And of course, if there were going to be any problems with decompression sickness, this would be the time to be most vigilant.

When the hatch on the Big Dipper finally opened on April 22, there was a brief welcoming party for the Team. Jake Webster was carried out on a stretcher and was taken quickly from the deck to the sick bay for a thorough examination by Dr. Balinski. There he would stay in preparation for his medevac back to the hospital in Panama City, once his twenty-four-hour no-fly observation time was past. Cal Sorensen and Byron Soaps walked out and were immediately swept along with Hank Johnson and Art Moore into the service of dismantling the equipment they had brought from NEDU and preparing to go home.

Art and Hank waited for everyone to move well away from the Big Dipper before they slipped in unobtrusively to retrieve the frozen remains of Bill Murphy. For the sake of not being too offensive, details will not be provided on what a man looks like when he has been breathing at over fifty atmospheres of gas pressure and who travels back to one atmosphere without a functioning cardiopulmonary system. Let it just be said the geometry of Murph exiting the chamber was a lot more awkward than the geometry of his walking into the chamber. And rest assured the coroner would be fully advised on the subjects of ample room ventilation and nonelectric tools in performing the autopsy.

Having slipped back so quickly into business-as-usual mode, it came as a shock to all the NEDU contingent when they were ready to disembark from the Good Ship *Whatever* for the final time, to receive their heroes' farewell and formal piping ashore by the vessel's crew. The Navy Way, of course.

April 25, 2013
0800 Hrs
Office of Diving Medical Officer, Navy Experimental Diving Unit
Panama City, FL

Stella sat in the small and excessively brightly lighted office, staring vacantly. Her brush-cut hair, as yet unstyled that morning, held the imprints of a serious battle with her pillow, which her bloodshot and bruise-ringed eyes demonstrated she had lost. Lieutenant Commander Ron Balinski, Diving Medical Officer, marched briskly into the room and greeted her.

"Stella, I know you're on pins and needles here, so I'll get to the bottom line first: it was not the biodec capsules," he said firmly.

Stella did not respond.

"Stella? You there?" Balinski tried snapping his fingers at her.

"How will we ever know that for sure?" she responded softly, still staring vacantly.

"OK." Balinski sighed. "I'll read you the autopsy report, and then you'll see we know it with a capital K, no doubts or ambiguity about it."

He took a file of papers from his desk and, scanning them quickly, found the section he was looking for. "Extensive adhesions in the vicinity of scars consistent with prior surgery for acute appendicitis, creating herniated loop of ileum with ischemic necrosis and gangrene." Balinski stared up at Stella, waiting to see if the information was sinking in. It was not. Balinski read further. "Three enteric-coated capsules found intact in ileum, anterior to ileal blockage and rupture point."

"Wait. What? The capsules? Found intact? Where?" Stella said, lifting her face for the first time to look at the young doctor.

"Aha. You are there. Good! Now we can get somewhere," Balinski said warmly. "A year or so ago, Murphy had acute appendicitis, as you remembered. It took him so long to tell anyone he was having abdominal pains that it actually ruptured. They got him into the hospital and took care of it. Should have been a done deal, no further issues, so he was of course returned to duties. But in some small percentage of people, especially when there is the mess made from a rupture of an appendix, the body responds by throwing out large quantities of connective tissue adhesions that adhere to everything, as an over-reaction of the body. That doesn't have to be a problem either, unless the adhesions do something like throw a lasso around a loop of intestine and squeeze it shut. That's what happened to Murphy."

"Couldn't he feel that?" Stella asked incredulously.

"Initially, no. Eventually, yes, but he wouldn't have known what to make of it," Balinski explained. "He was having digestive issues that made him eat less and less for the past couple of months, which we know from his regular weight charts. But he didn't actually mind losing a few pounds, and the symptoms were too vague, and he was probably too stoic, to report any of that to me or another doctor. That stoicism is what nearly killed him with the appendicitis he ignored for too long last year.

"As that lasso of adhesions tightened, it would have first squeezed shut the venous outflow of blood from the loop of intestines, making the loop swell. Then the swelling would have made the lasso even tighter until even the arterial blood flow was cut off. At that point, with no oxygen getting to the intestinal wall, tissues would have started to die. That was the point at which he started telling us he had horrible belly pain, while he was in the chamber and we had no way of getting to him. The dead tissues in the intestinal wall would not have been able to hold pressure. The wall would have split open, and intestinal contents and dead cell debris would have spilled out into the belly. The IV antibiotics we administered were too little, too late. At that stage things went downhill very fast," Balinski said with a sad shake of his head.

"So the actual cause of death was…?" Stella asked.

Balinski searched for the exact line in his documents. "COD: overwhelming intra-abdominal peritonitis from ileal rupture."

"Why did this situation reach the critical point at the one time you couldn't treat him? You know absolutely it wasn't the biodec capsules because they never got to the large intestine and thus never dissolved. But could it in some way have been the stress of the dive that made this happen when it did?" Stella asked, her serious eyes focused so intently on the young man that he had to glance away.

"No," Balinski responded firmly, after the briefest moment of thought. "Emotional or physical stress should not have been a precipitating factor here."

"Then why last week?" Stella said, confused.

Balinski shrugged. "Bad luck."

Stella sat silently for a long time, reflecting. "Our Murph is gone. Gone badly. Gone when he didn't want to go and lots of people still needed him. I can't feel OK about that, no matter what. But I have to say that knowing it wasn't my fault, or generally speaking biodec's fault, or even the mission's fault, is some small comfort. And he did an incredible job of saving lives on the way out, which is more than most people accomplish in a longer lifetime. Thanks, Ron," she concluded.

Lieutenant Commander Balinski rose with Stella to formalize her departure. He extended a hand toward her but was surprised at the ferocity of the hug she gave him instead. And oddly disappointed at its brevity.

April 25, 2013
0900 Hrs
Gulf Coast Regional Medical Center
Panama City, FL

Stella stood in the hospital elevator, nervously tugging at the new dress she had hastily changed into that morning, after her conference with Dr. Balinski. Her spare hours in Key West, possibly slightly influenced by some strawberries, had led her to purchase it. The sundress, turquoise with cream polka dots, was so cute and so unlike her usual comfortable and sensible work clothes. It fit her perfectly. But now, realizing she would probably be seen by every man she worked with, she felt self-conscious and awkward. She straightened herself, composed her face, gave an unnecessary pat to her freshly moussed hair, and prepared to exit the elevator. Her best pair of flip-flops squeaked on the waxed floor.

Heading down the corridor toward her was indeed the gaggle of Navy men she expected to see. She made an effort not to notice which ones chimed in with wolf whistles but simply smiled a bit formally and wished each of them a good morning as she passed. Bringing up the rear of this group was Art Moore. Unlike the others, he was not smiling at her. He was staring carefully into her eyes and shaking his head. She walked on past him with a pleasant but puzzled nod and into the open doorway the group of men had just vacated.

Two steps later she stopped dead. There in the room, standing next to the bed where Jake Webster lay comfortably propped on pillows, his head neatly bandaged and neck collar notably missing, was the daintiest painted doll of a woman Stella had ever seen. "Dr. Curtis," Jake greeted her with a formality that felt like a slap, "may I please present to you my wife, Barbara. Barbara, this is Dr. Stella Curtis, about whom you've heard so much. The woman who saved my life."

Stella lifted a hand in modest protest at that introduction. "I think the lifesaver distinction goes to Chief Sorensen. I'm more like the ambulance driver in this case." She made a short cough that in another mood might have been a laugh. "World's slowest ambulance driver at that. Took more than two weeks to travel the thickness of one hatch."

Barbara gave her an oddly birdlike smile, fluttered toward her, and extended a delicately manicured hand that felt like a moist dishrag in Stella's callused palm. "Oh," Barbara gasped, "although I have heard so much about you, I didn't realize you were..." She gave a nervous giggle and let her voice dribble away. She stared fixedly at Stella's new brush-cut coif.

Stella stared back. "Navajo?" she ventured.

"Oh, no. I knew that. I mean..." she said, vaguely waving a hand toward her own blond helmet head and then extending a dainty finger toward Stella's hair. The finger continued to wobble everywhere over Stella's body. Her smile was increasingly cracking at the edges.

Stella still was clueless as to where this conversation was going.

"Maybe I just mean *sturdy*." Barb offered a little Popeye the Sailor Man pose in illustration. "Now I can see how you play so well with the boys. Well, anyway, live and let live, I know, right?" she chirped. "Have you heard Jake's wonderful news yet? We're getting back together! That

271

really is wonderful, I know, right?" she said brightly.

Stella did not respond.

"Barb, why don't you run out and take a break, get yourself a cup of coffee, and maybe when you're done, you could bring us some too?" Jake proposed.

Barbara nodded. "Certainly, sweetie. That is, if Dr. Curtis is still here that long. We wouldn't want to keep her from…whatever it is she's dressed up for. I'm sure the girls are just dying to get their hands on her!" She minced out of the room; Jake and Stella both waited until they could no longer hear the click of her stilettos on the linoleum hallway.

Jake was reluctant to meet Stella's solemn gaze. "I guess Barb has heard that you had a long braid, and she's surprised to see the shorter cut," he lied. "In fact it's the first time I've really seen it with both eyes in focus. Looks nice on you, Doc. Pretty dress too," he said with nervous enthusiasm.

Stella did not respond.

Jake swallowed. Struggling to control his voice into the tone required for the circumstances, he said, "This is not how I wanted you to hear about this."

Stella did not respond.

"What I told you about my plans—things…changed with this." He pointed to his bandaged head. "The Navy won't let me remain on the Hydrogen Team, or as any kind of diver, with this hole in my skull. There's an early release from my enlistment in the works. My dad has persuaded me that if I am going to go the MBA route after all, I should really be enrolled back in Harvard, not University of Florida. Name recognition, famous program, you know, all that. But it's a package deal." Jake squirmed in his bed, still unable to meet that gaze.

"It's long overdue for me to mend fences with my family. Barb wants us to give our marriage another try, with me out of the Navy and back in Boston. My parents and her parents really want that too. And Jacob Junior. My boy would really like a few years with both parents around him. He wants a real father in the home, not one he sees a few days a year or even a couple months in the summer. Barb has promised me that if we try to make a go of it together for at least six months...maybe a year...two years tops, and if it still doesn't work out, she'll let me have a divorce with shared custody of my boy. If I had gone through with the University of Florida plan, she would have demanded full custody on grounds of abandonment, and I would never have had an opportunity to play a real part in my boy's life. My boy, Stella!" he pleaded.

Stella did not respond.

He floundered on in what little speech he had prepared. "I had the Team get me this as I guess a kind of special thank-you gift for you." Jake fished in a small drawer next to his bed and dug out a rumpled paper bag. "I know there's no way to give you something that truly says 'thanks for saving my life,' but this represents what I think of you, the only way I could think to express it."

Wordlessly, Stella took the offered bag and looked inside for a long time. "I'm a washed-up, smelly old starfish?" she asked dryly as she pulled out the contents.

"Stella! Please don't. I'm trying to be…I'm trying to say…something important when I can't say what I really wanted to be saying to you today. You're a star, Stella. You're *my* star." Jake struggled for every word.

Stella did not respond.

"I know I haven't the right to ask…" His voice trailed off when he saw the sudden shooting of flames in her eyes, and not in response to her one-word command. He would remember the look in those eyes for years to come, more years of regret and longing than a young man knows he has. It eventually occurred to him that an Aztec high priestess with her dagger in both hands over her head could not have been more blood-chilling to a man than Stella was at that moment.

Art Moore was waiting for her in the corridor, a look of concern and sorrow on his face. She did not need to repeat her command to him; he already knew better than to say a word as she passed.

Before she could make it out of the hospital lobby, her cell phone was ringing. It was Commander Richter, and he wanted to speak to her in his office. No, immediately.

April 25, 2013
0900 Hrs
Office of the Commanding Officer, Navy Experimental Diving Unit
Panama City, FL

Commander Lewis Richter sat at his desk, his head hanging as he cradled the phone to his ear. "Yes, Sir. Yes, Sir. Yes, Sir" was ninety percent of his end of the conversation. When he hung up, he called out, "Marcy! Get Lieutenant Commander Costello in here, ASAP!"

Moments later his XO appeared at his office door. "Something up, Commander?" Bob Costello asked pleasantly. One good look at his boss's face erased his calm smile. "What's wrong, Sir?"

"Get in here, and close that door behind you. We got some real bad shit incoming," the CO responded curtly. Richter waited impatiently while Costello hurried into the seat across his desk. "The fallout is just now hitting from all those adverse event reports we had to file on the Hydrogen Team. Three out of the four divers, including one death, and now one man having to be processed out of the service early from his injury. The Flags in Washington in our funding line are spitting-tacks mad that things went so far awry. They want a head to roll, and they've focused on Curtis's. I have to fire her and out-process her *tooot sweet tooo-day*, and I need you to be onboard with this, and I need you be consistent with me on all the details."

"But Sir, none of those AERs were Dr. Curtis's fault! And if she didn't have her Team and their knowledge of hydrogen diving ready, we'd have lost a whole boatful of submariners," Costello remonstrated. "I was the Senior Dive

Officer in charge. Why come down on her?"

"Yeah, sure, you and I know all those things. And Curtis knows them. And the men whose lives she helped save know them. But the DISSUB rescue is classified out of the funding line's chain of command. All they know is that the Hydrogen Team was out on a training mission, and they did stuff in training that was not in the program to be tried for another year or two, according to Curtis's own proposal schedule. So from their point of view, the adverse events *were* her fault. They have to be somebody's fault. You know that as well as I do. I just got off the phone with Admiral Burns. Of all the Flags they could send, he's the one who has always been hardest against Curtis and the biodec effort. He'll be here tomorrow morning on the first flight in from DC, and you can bet he'll be here with blood in his eyes."

Lieutenant Commander Costello shook his head slowly in dismay and disbelief. "This just isn't right," he protested. "Have you seen or talked to Dr. Curtis this morning? She gave me a call less than half an hour ago. She's just seen the autopsy report on Petty Officer Murphy, giving the program the all-clear. She's overjoyed that the hospital reports are great on Senior Chief Webster. None of the Team bent on the way out, so she considers her part of the mission a complete success! And instead of congratulating her, you're calling her in here to fire her and throw her out? And if you don't, an Admiral who doesn't know the facts will chew her face off tomorrow? Are we just supposed to let this play out so badly?" he asked in alarm.

"We gotta complete her out-processing papers and send her as far away from here as we can get her today. And you and I need to be consistent on our story of how we were so motivated to take immediate action regarding the AERs that we could not even wait for the Admiral to show up because we wanted to fire her ourselves," Richter insisted.

"Jesus," responded Costello softly. He felt as if he had been kicked in the gut. "Are you sure, Commander, there isn't some other way...something maybe you or I could say to explain that she was being pressured to advance the milestones quickly enough to prepare that DARPA proposal, and her end of it worked, but, well...shit happened that could not have been predicted, and—"

"You're using logic, Bob, and that's not what's called for here," Richter responded wearily, raking his fingers through his perpetually raked hair. "We can use some of that logic to at least keep Admiral Burns from hunting her down and trying to send her to prison for criminal negligence. But that's the best we can expect here."

Lieutenant Commander Costello continued to shake his head slowly. "This isn't fair. It isn't fair. It can't end this way," he repeated slowly. "We could not have left her behind. We needed her."

Richter bent forward. "No, of course you wouldn't have wanted to run a hydrogen op at that depth without her. But that's what's letting us fly this under the black ops radar, as her experiment. If I can out-process Curtis today, then her permanent record is locked in place that she was fired for three adverse events, which is the truth, regardless of whether or not it's fair," he added hastily in anticipation of Costello's remonstrance, "and that's what will make this at least survivable. She's a tough woman, Bob. You know she is. She'll lick her wounds for a while, and then get up and go look for another job. She can go to a university or a diving industry job interview, and when they look into why she was fired from here, they'll see three unclassified AERs listed and will file for permission to read them. One death from an unrelated health condition, one cutting torch accident, and one deep-water narcosis, which she properly managed," he ticked these off on thick fingers, "and they'll conclude on their own that she was not guilty of any negligence. The AERs won't stand in her way of getting hired if they otherwise want her," Richter concluded.

"And we'll look like a bunch of jerks for firing a good employee for unfortunate accidents that weren't her fault!" Costello interjected.

"I don't give a damn what somebody else might choose to second-guess me on; this is my command and my decision!" Richter spat out. Then, more gently he added, "No, Bob, I honestly don't see it that way. We will look like what we are: an organization with very strict rules regarding numbers and severities of AERs. And this is how we have to be to avoid charges of being too lax with the safety of the people under our command. Everyone, *everyone* takes adverse events deadly seriously and understands it is always a judgment call how to demonstrate to the world that we took steps to prevent recurrences of these tragic accidents," Commander Richter concluded.

Costello was still unconvinced. "Curtis did something great and heroic, and she did it because she knew it was the only right thing to do. She thinks the success of the hydrogen biodec part means she'll be assigned new Team members and have greater support than ever to advance the project. Even if the Navy wants to use the three AERs to shut down an expensive and mixed-popularity program, we have multiple other programs she could be reassigned to. Why can't we do that?"

Richter sighed deeper and squirmed in his seat. With exaggerated slowness, he said, "I'm trying to keep this situation from exploding into a repeat of the mess with Dr. Colman. She was before your time, I guess. Nice woman, really. She was guilty of the sin of being better funded, by virtue of being a better researcher, than her erstwhile colleagues. One of them overheard her making a casual— and I might add correctly cautionary—remark about how if she didn't manage her chamber experiment properly, she could blow the building up. That remark was taken out of context and twisted into her making a terrorist threat. She was not only fired but facing jail time before some cooler heads interceded. They could undo the jail part, but as part of the deal, she had to stay fired. She took her case to court, and a civil judge saw right through the dirty politics, and she won her case. But so what? Her lawyer took the lion's share of her settlement, and the Navy insisted on a gag order, so she couldn't tell anyone the grounds on which she won her case. The proceedings on all this were so long and messy that her reputation as a researcher was thoroughly ruined. She couldn't get another job anywhere. Two years later she blew her brains out.

"If we let Burns get here while Curtis's records are still open, those goons of his will go around and collect every story they can find about her and twist them all into vicious criminal acts she will never get untangled from. Like, she's a schizophrenic because she thinks she's Elvis, and she sings 'I Want to be Your Teddy Bear' because she's a pedophile. Stuff like that. If she's fired for schizophrenia and pedophilia, nobody will ask what's the evidence. They'll just believe those lies and run screaming from her. I would rather have Curtis think I'm the meanest old bastard on the planet while she's sitting comfortably in her new office as a professor at the University of Whatsadoodle than have you bringing her cookies every week in the psych ward or taking flowers to her grave," Richter said, finally looking directly at his friend, whose face he had been avoiding.

Richter took a slug of now-cold coffee to clear his throat before continuing. "And I'm not just worried about Curtis. I'm worried about you. Colman was not the only one ruined in all of the mess around her. The officer who helped her the most suffered for his role too. His support of her was the beginning of the end for Captain Whitehall. Remember him? One of the best men I've ever known. The claim, from the same jealous and then butt-covering idiots, was that he supported Colman because she was sleeping with him. Pah! I knew John and Marie Whitehall for decades, and he would no more have cheated on her than you or I would step out on our wives. He was allowed to retire with his pension intact, but just barely. I cannot let you throw your career away on this!" he said with heat.

Lieutenant Commander Costello had sat attentively through this speech, his eyes on the desktop between the two men. Now, as he looked up at his commanding officer, his pain and sorrow were noticeable even to a man as gruff and usually unempathetic as Lewis Richter.

Commander Richter studied his old friend for a long time in silence. "This is a lot more to you than just fairness toward some girl with a shapely backside, isn't it?" he asked.

"Sure," Costello answered simply.

"Hoo boy," Richter breathed. The two sat in silence for some time. Finally Richter spoke again. "Look, Lancelot, like I said, I need to worry about your career—and for that matter mine too. When Admiral Burns rolls in here tomorrow morning, we both need to be squeaky clean on this. We must be able to tell him the hand-to-Bible truth that I fired her today for excessive adverse events on her watch, no mitigating explanations given to her, no apologies, no mercy, no nothing. You cannot undermine my authority on this or embarrass the Navy. Neither you nor any other Navy officer can explain to her what we are doing here or why it is better this way than letting a Flag rip her head off and put it on a spike by the gate while his goons assault the rest of her. We are under oath to maintain loyalty to the Navy over loyalty to any individual under our command. And as far as personal loyalties go, I'd toss a hundred Little Green Running Shorts to the Big Bad Wolf before I'd let any harm come to you! Are you listening to me?" Richter demanded, getting irritated over the preoccupied look on Costello's face.

"Aye, Sir; no Navy officer can contact Curtis to explain or assist or apologize. What Admiral Burns hears must be the literal truth. Loyalty to the Navy above all. You're concerned for me. That it, Sir?" he enquired politely and oddly calmly.

"Glad I got the message across," Richter grumbled with some dubiousness. "Now, you'd better be heading outta here because as fast as I can call your damsel in distrust, she'll be stomping her cowboy boots through that door, and I doubt you'll want to be around to watch Annie Oakley get that ass whupping."

Costello stopped his rise from his seat to look squarely at his commanding officer. "You've got that wrong, Sir, begging your pardon, but she's not Annie Oakley. She's Sacajawea."

The full significance of the reference was lost on Richter, but the sincerity with which it was spoken was clear. Costello resumed his rise and headed toward the door. "I don't envy you your job today, boss," he commented over his shoulder.

"That's why they pay me even bigger bucks than you, Lieutenant Commander," Richter responded.

Costello turned back to face Commander Richter. "Boss? Speaking of big bucks, can I by any chance borrow some money?" he asked casually.

Without comment Richter heaved a heavy cheek from his chair, fished into his hip pocket, and tossed a thoroughly nasty old man's wallet on the desktop. "Leave me enough to buy some lunch, but you can keep the rest," he said.

Lieutenant Commander Costello took the wallet and pulled out a stack of bills thick enough to make his eyebrows rise. Curiosity got the better of his sense of courtesy; he fanned the bills quickly, his eyebrows rising higher as he counted.

"Thanks, boss!" he said enthusiastically, slipping the bills into his own pocket as he slid the wallet back across the desk.

"Don't mention it. And that's an order," Richter added unnecessarily.

February 14, 2013
0400 Hrs
Office Wing, Navy Experimental Diving Unit
Panama City, FL

He slipped the envelope, neatly typed with her name, under the door to her office in the 0-dark (forget the :30) hours. He could not sleep anyway, thinking about her and this. His expectations? Hazy. A valentine poem to her? Really? He pictured her a few hours from now marching down the hall to her office, dusty boots drumming softly on the concrete floors, and on opening the door, finding the envelope. She would bend down slowly (oh yeah!) to retrieve it. Surprised, she would open it, standing right there in the cool, dim, and quiet of those early morning hours before starting work. He could imagine her solemn, dark eyes opening wide as she read and reread the lines he had written and erased so many times before painstakingly typing them. But then what?

Most of the men she knew here were locked in a chamber today. Surely she would reflect on her positive interactions with him, coupled with the unavailability of others, and realize the valentine came from him. So then she would…That was where his imagination left him swinging from the yardarm. He had not done anything like this since he was a high-school boy, so his playlist of romantic thrusts and parries was woefully inept for adult interactions.

He was surely not mistaken that their conversations were always more pleasant than merely polite, but was he off course in thinking she liked him well enough to consider him as a potential, um…romantic interest? After all, he did have some years and some of life's experiences that she did not, and she might not want to have them thrust upon her. A couple of half-grown kids would be hard for a younger single woman to accept, he knew. That was always the point at which the lump in his gut would turn hard and cold, and he would wonder why he had this overwhelming compulsion to admit his feelings for her and test those waters. He could not bear the thought of confronting her directly and seeing any look of hesitation or confusion or rejection in those magic eyes.

But he had to know if he had any chance with her at all. He had to put the ball into her court to see if she would be willing to come to him if he asked. As a worst-case scenario, he could pass it all off as a meaningless joke if she seemed disinclined to consider it a legitimate romantic gesture. After all, with rhymes to *valentine* of *Frankenstein* and *Palestine* and *turpentine* and *calamine*, how hard could that be? Besides, every man in the place was making cruder jokes to her than this and getting away with it.

The actual outcome of leaving that letter under her office door was far worse than his wildest nightmares. Boots drummed down the hall, door opened, harsh fluorescent lights switched on. Jean-clad backside tilted fetchingly up as she retrieved the letter, surely enough, but his envelope had unanticipated company. She fanned through the pile of envelopes with a chuckle at their various scrawls and doodles, squinted only briefly at the typed envelope before stuffing the stack of envelopes into her day pack, did some thisenthats in her office, switched off the lights, relocked the door, and drummed those boots back down the hall. His heart's outpouring was read aloud later that day to a chamber full of laughing men. It was years before she knew who wrote it and with what intentions.

April 25, 2013
1200 Hrs
Stella Curtis's Apartment
Panama City, FL

Art Moore tapped on the sun-bleached door with increasing volume for some time before it finally opened.

Stella was still in her turquoise polka dotted sundress, barefoot and pacing agitatedly even as she held the door open for him. "Looks like crappy news travels fast around here," she said. He brushed past her and entered the apartment without waiting for an invitation.

"Listen, Stella, I know this is a lot to have flying down the road at you, but you don't have to do it all alone, and you don't have to run off and do anything half-cocked. You have friends who are going to help you," Art said earnestly.

"What the hell, Art? What the hell?" she demanded. "Adverse events? Hell yeah, they were adverse, but blame them on *me*? How does that help?" she spat indignantly. "And just what am I supposed to do here? With the apartment? With my stuff? With *me*?"

Art walked briskly to the kitchen and returned with a tall glass of water. "Stella, sit. Here, drink this. We'll answer all those questions. Just let's get you calmed down enough that you can hear me."

The two settled themselves together on the small flowered sofa in the tiny room, Stella tense as a cat ready to spring.

"OK, question number one," Art started, waving a finger. "This apartment. This is PC. Landlords are accustomed to

285

Navy people getting deployments on short notice and cutting and running on their leases. No big deal. You give me the phone number of your landlord and your key, and I'll call him to take care of the rest. Might not be able to get your security deposit back, but no worse than that. If they can rent this place out right away, we might even get that back."

Art interrupted himself for a quick walk to the kitchen for his own glass of water. "Number two," he said, waving another finger, "your stuff. One of the things the Navy does really well is to help people deploy quickly by bringing in professional movers to help pack personal effects and store them until there's a new address to ship them to. They are very good and surprisingly reliable. Again, you just leave me your key, and I'll make the calls and take care of it. Done it dozens of times. And that includes *Red Chief*, by the way. There's also closeout maid service that could be arranged, not that you need to worry much there," he said, surveying her Spartan and tidy room.

"But if I've been fired, am I eligible for all those Navy services?" Stella interjected.

"These moves happen so often, there is no way anyone wants to monitor for situations like that," he assured her. "And besides, the Navy would rather have your stuff cleared out of here, even at their expense, than sitting where you might come around to reclaim it and make trouble. If it is ever questioned, you get the services up front and pay the bill yourself later, whenever you can. What can they do to you—fire you?" he asked with no humor intended.

Stella took another sip of her water. She folded her legs and tucked them under her skirt, visibly relaxing a little. "OK, you're doing pretty well so far. Now make sense of them firing me for stuff that was not my fault, and tell me where I'm going this evening," she taunted.

"Sure. I can do both of those if you'll give me a couple minutes. Number three," Art continued. "Why? The short answer is that with bad stuff of this magnitude happening, they need a scapegoat. You've been elected. But by getting you outta Dodge this evening, they keep your scapegoatage limited to those three accidents, which are factual, not personal, and did actually involve you. If they waited until DC Brass showed up, the accusations could include a lot more than these three charges. They'd run to anything bad that ever happened, back to Eve handing Adam the apple, and they could get very, very personal."

Art sipped his own water meditatively while Stella sat silently, still puzzled and unsold. "You mean I should be grateful they aren't doing anything worse to me than firing me for stuff that's not my fault?" she demanded.

Art continued unperturbed. "You aren't actually a stranger to things like this. Consider your own father's career. Why is he mostly doing admin at a Rez hospital and rarely seeing patients or doing surgery anymore? Is it because he likes admin? Is it because he can't handle surgical tools anymore?" Art asked pointedly.

Stella did not respond for some time as her gaze turned introspective. "My dad spent a lifetime taking on patients other doctors wouldn't because they were afraid that if a high-risk patient didn't make it through their procedure, they would have to take the hit through their own adverse event reporting system. No board of inquiry ever found Dad guilty of malpractice. But he has had so many high-risk patients die on or just after the surgical table, he can't get malpractice insurance anymore, even though nobody has ever actually sued him or charged him with malpractice," she finished.

Stella lifted her fierce gaze to Art. "My dad is proud to have been the kind of doctor who would do the right thing to the best of his ability, for people who really needed someone to try to give them one more chance, and the occasional bad outcomes were never his fault. He always said he wanted to live his life according to the old Navajo saying 'wisdom, compassion, and courage are the three universally recognized moral qualities of man.'"

"Confucius," Art corrected her.

Stella looked momentarily confused. "Really? Well, OK. But in all my dad's cases, he was the attending, he was the one standing over the dead body with a scalpel in his hand. I was seventeen hundred feet away, either literally or effectively, when all the shit hit the fan!" she said with indignation.

Art returned her gaze as best he could. "You know AERs must list a person in charge. Should we name Captain Gilchrist? Lieutenant Commander Costello? Jake? Murph?"

"No, of course none of those people would be any better or fairer as scapegoats. But you can hardly expect me to be thrown under this bus cheerfully to protect everyone else, just because there's a blank on a stack of report forms that needs a name in it," Stella retorted. "I helped save lives a couple of weeks ago! Doesn't that count for anything this week?" she demanded.

"What lives would those be? As far as the incoming Brass is concerned, you were running a training mission of your own devising. You must not lose track of the fact that the *Skinny Eel* and all of Operation SECOND STARFISH are entirely classified, even within the Navy, and cannot be used to mitigate your situation," Art reminded her.

"Oh yeah, that's classified," Stella said, her head ding-donging to match her sarcastic tone. "So how do I go on from here? Who will ever hire me once I'm fired from here, if I cannot defend my actions as part of a life-saving rescue mission?"

"Why does the Rez hospital still employ your dad?" Art countered.

Stella was quiet again for a long moment. "Because they know he's a great doctor, and anyone with half a brain could read his AERs and see he was doing the right thing, and there are the board of inquiry decisions to formalize that," Stella said slowly.

"There is no equivalent of a board of inquiry here, because no board is permitted to inquire into the full situation. So you don't have that for protection. But remember, Stella, you are not being charged with malpractice. You are only being fired for having your name listed as the lead scientist in charge when bad stuff happened on three rapidly sequential occasions," Art reminded her. "And you were large and in charge, woman! Don't you downplay your importance on that resc—er—training mission!"

Stella squinted at him. "I am still really confused on one critical point. If this *reskertraining* mission is such a highly classified black op, how is anyone outside the Navy accessing my AERs to see I did not commit malpractice?"

"Hmph indeed," Art responded. "That's the weird betwixt and between of this situation that is giving everybody fits. Your funding line, your biochemical decompression and hydrogen diving programs are all non-classified. Hence the AERs must be non-classified. But the situation that had your Team members getting into their adverse events was a black op. So the chosen method for dealing with this has been to write up the reports as non-classified documents, but with anything that is considered sensitive to the black op and not strictly relevant to explaining the nature of the Team's injuries redacted. So an AER will indicate, for example, that one of your men had an accident as a function of a cutting torch gas explosion but not the location where this happened, or why he was cutting up anything. Same sort of description for the other two: only the what and not the where or why. Described in only the terms of the non-classified facts, there is nothing damaging to you in those reports. Get it now?"

Stella began to breathe more easily as the importance of Art's message sank in.

"Now, did your dad ever tell you a story from back in his DC days about a doctor friend of his at the Naval Hospital who tried and failed to save the life of a kid who turned out to be a Senator's son?" Art asked.

Stella shook her head. "Dad was always very discrete about telling us anything bad about colleagues."

Art nodded. "Should have known. Well, I'm going to tell you now. There was a boy, son of a Senator but a real mess of a worthless kid, who spent every moment high on every pill and bottle known to mankind. One night he caused a terrible traffic accident. Killed a young couple and their baby in a car he hit head-on. They took him to the Naval Hospital, not because it was close but because the Senator thought he could keep a lid on the story better there than in the nearest public hospital. Kid was smashed to bits, and one of your dad's buddies tried to put him back together again but wasn't able to. The Senator wanted to punish somebody for the loss of his boy and take away some of the shame and embarrassment from his family for how the kid went and who died with him. When the AER on that case was not enough to destroy the doctor, because anyone with half a brain could read that it wasn't his fault, the Senator's lawyer implied that the tox report on the kid was actually the tox report on the doctor. The board of inquiry was left with the impression that the doctor was the one higher than the Washington Monument, and that was what destroyed the doctor!" Art ended with a sad flourish.

Stella stared at him with growing alarm.

"Yup," Art said eloquently. "The DC Brass who want to take you out have no limits to the harm they are willing to inflict and no limits to the lies they will tell to do it. Yes, you do have friends who are doing you a huge favor by firing you and quickly getting you out alive, with only the truthful AERs assigned to you. Do you get that now?"

Stella nodded slowly. "Yes, I get it. I don't like it one bit, of course, but I get it." She sipped a little more water and studied the worn carpet before her.

"Have you called your dad yet?" Art asked her.

"Yes. He said to tell you 'hi' and asked me to give you his phone number, so you two can catch up a little, and so he can thank you for helping me all this time," she told him. She fished on her coffee table and handed him a crumpled scrap of paper.

"Well? What was his reaction?" Art pressed.

"With my end of the conversation limited to 'I've been fired,' 'that's classified,' and 'I don't know,' the call did not last all that long," she responded. "He asked me if I had done anything bad, and when I said 'no, I did all good stuff,' he seemed to understand more than I was able to actually tell him. And he was not mad at me at all. I was afraid he would be."

"Oh, honey!" he protested sadly. "No, of course he wouldn't be mad at you! I'm so sorry you ever thought he would be. And yes, I'm sure he understood perfectly."

"He reminded me of something he's told me many times before: that I need to get past what he calls my Annie Oakley syndrome. That's my failure to understand that if I can easily out-ride, out-rope, out-shoot, out-cuss, and out-spit every galoot on the prairie, why don't the boys like me?" Stella said, with a slow hunch of her strong and shapely shoulders.

Art chuckled. "That's maybe the best description of your dilemma I've ever heard! I have actually heard you referred to in passing as Annie Oakley more than once, but I never thought of it in just those terms. Yeah, I'd say he nailed it. I always did like your dad's way with words."

"Oh, and he also said not to panic, but to trust you, and do whatever you recommend," she finished. After another long drink of water, she turned to him again. "Art? Tell me the truth on one more thing here?"

"Always," he responded gravely, without realizing how

quickly he would be breaking that solemn vow. And without realizing how quickly she would understand.

"Was I set up to take this fall from the very start?" she asked him bluntly.

Art did his own analysis of the carpet wear patterns. "First of all, in the case of Lieutenant Commander Costello, the answer is a resounding no. He would never do that to you." Stella immediately threw up both hands in protest at the thought. "As for anyone else...yes and no," was what he finally settled on. "I think the room full of officers who originally briefed you on the sinking and asked about using biodec and got your take on hydrogen gas mixes could smell a career-ender mission. They knew from the get-go it was unlikely for anyone to pull off something as complicated as a rescue SAT dive to seventeen hundred feet without mishaps and AERs. They surely did not expect you to volunteer to participate. But once you did, the advantages of that approach really sank in. You saved them from the dilemma of drawing straws to see who among them would join the mission and thus be in a coin toss with Lieutenant Commander Costello on who would have to take the hit to their career. But..."

He shifted his position to face her squarely and raised a finger. "I swear to you, I honestly believe none of those men was so evil or so selfish they would deliberately let a mission go sour by sending you on it if they did not have total confidence that you could manage your end of it at least as well as any of them could, if not better. They wanted the mission to succeed, for heaven's sake! Which it did. Proving that their faith in you was well placed, and I can't say that too many times to you here. But are they sorry their careers are safe and yours—with the Navy—is ended? You know that would be asking too much of almost anyone," he concluded.

Stella slowly nodded her understanding. And then she let out a deep breath. "That was such an amazing event, and it was a privilege for me to be there. The Team risked *everything*. What the Team did, and what took place on the *Voo2*, were marvels of human endeavor and technology such as few people on Earth ever witness. But I was not just a spectator; I was an active participant! I cannot be sorry for my role in any of it. It would be a betrayal of Murph for me to whine now about losing a job. And no, it would not make me feel any better to have Bob lose his job instead of me. Or Captain Gilchrist either." She took another long moment to sort through her racing thoughts. "I did something important. Life *should* be spent trying to do something important, maybe even something impossible. Otherwise what's the point? We *must* make the sound and fury signify *something*. In the end only cowards will have no scars."

Art smiled at her. "She's back!" he announced.

They sipped their water and reanalyzed the analysis of the review of the carpet. But the tension in the air was fading.

Stella stirred in her seat. "OK, Houdini, now how does my disappearing act go?" she enquired.

Art grunted softly. "I told you that you have friends looking out for you, and there's not just a plan for you. There's a good plan. Here's some background information," he said, handing her a manila folder full of pages.

Stella took the folder and slowly began to shuffle the pieces of paper and to scan a few. Then she really start to read, a look of growing interest and wonder slowly appearing in her eyes. She read in silence for a long while. Suddenly she snapped the papers down and stared at Art with an open mouth.

"Holy crap!" she blurted out with ladylike grace. "Is this the King of Farts that little thug Kratz mentioned back when I was being briefed before the mission?"

Art nodded, a faint smile on his lips.

"So let me see if I've gotten this straight. This Professor Ron Crane at the marine school campus of the University of Miami uses the metabolism of various deep-water marine bacteria, some of them sulfur-compound metabolizing, hence the farty smells from his lab, to power batteries that are actually microbial fuel cells. The fuel cells in turn power whatever deep underwater sensors and data storage devices you might want. One advantage to using the bacterial batteries is that they are already adapted to the pressure, which conventional batteries are not. Another advantage is that they are effectively infinitely operable as long as the bacteria have their normal living and growing conditions, whereas conventional chemical batteries die and need frequent replacing. The only maintenance to the system you would need would be to periodically transfer the data collected by the sensors."

Art nodded.

"Kratz made such a big deal about secrecy! I don't get it. This file is loaded with publications from the open scientific literature. I don't see anything in here that would trip his cloak-and-dagger reflex." Stella shook her head in confusion.

"Your hydrogen-metabolizing biodec bugs are well published in the open scientific literature too," Art pointed out. "But a few weeks ago, you used those non-secret bugs as a critical element in a black op. It isn't the basic research that makes these things classified; it's the uses the Navy may choose to put them to."

"Hmmmmm," she responded with more enlightenment than verbal wit. Stella was quiet for a long time, lost in thought. Slowly she fixed Art with another of her trademark penetrating gazes. "Do you think it's possible the *Skinny Eel* was transferring data from a string of Ron Crane's fart-powered sensors when it got nailed by the *Mad Cat*?"

Art smiled. "Well, you know of course that the true answer to that is 'that's classified.' I certainly don't know myself. But my wild imagination runs that way too. There's also that other little submersible you heard was the first to arrive on the sinking site so conveniently quickly. It might have been out checking fart-charged trap lines of its own."

Stella frowned slightly. "If this guy Crane and I are both working on unclassified microbial products for the Navy, how is it possible I've never met him?"

"Good question. By now you should have met. Must be either by chance or because his applications are all things that show up in microbiology or engineering or information tech meetings, and yours are presented at physiology and diving meetings. He's a really nice guy. I think you'll like him," Art concluded. "Now for that disappearing act you've been waiting for. A call was made. By someone who has your back and who has standing with Crane. You have a job interview with Dr. Crane in his lab tomorrow morning at ten."

"What do I know about chemical engineering or information technology or sensor development?" Stella asked with alarm. "I've been using bugs for a novel application, yes, but I need bacteriologists to help me with handling them."

"So does he. Crane's a clever guy with lots of applications for his research yet to be considered. Who knows what he might do if he had a physiologist like you to bounce new ideas off of? Like, I dunno, engineer nitrogen-fixing bugs for novel uses in diving?" Art proposed.

Stella's wide eyes widened further. "Whoooa!" was her throaty response.

"He has a variety of funding lines, so if he hires you, it can be independent of any Navy funding and thus out of the Navy line of fire. Or at least for as long as it takes the Navy to lose interest in trying to shoot you down, which is never infinitely long," Art assured her.

Stella looked shocked. Then she smiled. It was the full-on Stella signature smile Art had been waiting for. "You did it! You pulled the world's coolest rabbit out of the hat. Thank you, thank you, thank you!" Stella began hopping up and down on the sofa hard enough to risk sloshing water out of their glasses.

Unfortunately her delight did not last as long as he had hoped before she once again descended into gloomier thoughts. Stella stared blindly out the window and sighed heavily. "So whatcha got in that bag of tricks of yours for a broken heart?" she asked softly, without looking at Art.

Art shook his head. "Nothing," he suggested usefully.

"Doesn't take Sigmund Freud—or is that sangfroid?—to see I have a thing for boys who have Bostonian accents like my dad's," she said sadly.

"Well, yeah, you might wanna give that some thought in the future. But then again, if you're subconsciously looking for a man as good as your dad, you're on the right course. But make sure the next one really acts more like your old man and doesn't just sound like him," Art concluded.

Stella studied the dust streaks on the window a little longer. "I know, I know. It's shallow and stupid at a time like this to think of such a thing. But something that is really bugging me right now is the thought that Hank was right all along about Jake. That jerk was right, and I didn't see it."

"Bah!" Art waved the thought away with an impatient hand. "Hank Johnson donno jack about jack, never did, never will!" he spat out with irritation. "Hank had no insight whatsoever into Senior Chief Webster's mind, heart, soul, or any other part of his anatomy. What he said was based solely on his stupid jealousy that a young and good-looking woman was more attracted to a young and good-looking man than she was to him."

Stella shot him a look of disgust and horror. "No."

"No which?" Art asked. "No that Hank hoped you'd be attracted to him, or no that it suggests he's attracted to you?"

"No, no," she clarified.

Art shrugged. "He's a man."

"I disagree," she responded flatly.

"Never mind him. I wanted to make an important point to you about Webster," Art insisted. "Webster is not a dirty dog; I honestly don't think so. You had as straight a shot into his true and unguarded soul as one human ever gets of another. You heard him raving out of his head when he thought he was going to die, and you never once heard him call out, 'Oh Barb!' now did you? We all heard a lotta 'oh Stella!'"

"You all heard that?" she asked hesitantly. "Oh. I was hoping that got lost in the commotion."

"You know what I think is Jake's biggest problem? He makes lousy snap decisions. Almost got him killed. He's an intelligent guy, and he figures things out well in the long run. I think he actually has a good heart, for whatever that's worth to you. But the man does not think on his feet worth squat. You don't need a guy that slow," Art summarized.

Stella did not respond. But her expression was considerably softened.

Art took Stella's empty glass from her and, slowly heaving himself off the sofa, headed for the kitchen counter. "OK, Annie. Time to saddle up. We have big plans for this afternoon, before you head to the airport and ride into the sunset. We're going to a picnic. We better start moving."

"Really? On a weekday?" she asked.

Art shrugged. "Shore leave."

"Will there be barbecued shrimp there?" she asked hopefully.

"Best damn shrimp on the Red Neck Riviera, I hear," he assured her.

"And Key lime pie? Old school style, with meringue?" she said, brightening further.

"Yup. And bring your little boom box and your cape. There's going to be a concert. Stellvis and the H-Bombs in final performance," he informed her.

"Oh God. I don't think I'm in the mood for that today," she said wearily.

"Lots of people will be there, and they're all counting on you. Billy Murphy wants to fill in for his dad on air drums. Ida Murphy has requested 'Danny Boy,' in honor of Murph." Art raised a hand to stop Stella's frantic objection. "Yes, you can. And yes, you will. You cannot honorably refuse either of them this request. You are Stella Nellie Goddam Curtis comma P-H-D, and you will go out there with that ridiculous cape flying, and you will sing the *hell* outta that song!" he said with fervor. Then, more gently he added, "Wisdom, compassion and courage are the three universally recognized moral qualities of woman too."

It took several minutes of reflection and deep breathing before Stella slowly nodded.

"Oh, by the way," Art added, "Ida is not the train wreck you're expecting to meet. She took her rehab seriously. She's cleaned herself up, lost a ton of weight, and she looks pretty darned good. You can see why Murph fell for her.

And she's ready to bring Billy back to living with her."

"Hoo-yah, Ida," Stella responded softly, her head and shoulders rising a little higher.

"Tick tock, Doc," he urged her, tapping his watch. "A little less conversation, a little more optimized engagement of back parts, please."

Stella half chuckled, half choked. "Oh dear. Do I really sound that bad?"

"Yeah," he acknowledged. "But it's why I...I've enjoyed getting to know you these past years. Now really, move."

Stella sighed. "I'll need to get changed out of this first," she said, rising and patting the sundress.

"Keep the polka dots," Art said flatly.

"At a barbeque?" she asked.

"Keep the polka dots."

"But if we're going straight from there to the airport, what do I take with me for tomorrow?" she asked with confusion.

"Keep the polka dots."

"Tomorrow I'm going to a job interview! I can't wear this! It's much too...too..." she said, tugging self-consciously at all the locations not normally highlighted when wearing jeans and T-shirts.

"Arright, wait a sec..." Art marched quickly into her

301

bedroom and fished in her small closet. He returned with her navy-blue blazer, the one she had worn for her NEDU job interview and at the occasional scientific conference. "Put this in your smallest duffel, along with a change or two of underwear and your toothbrush, and that's it. You'll want to be on and off that regional with no check-in luggage and in and out of your interview without dragging some silly-looking suitcase. You can't know right now how to fill a suitcase anyway, so don't. Once you know what things you actually need until we can ship you your own stuff, you can buy them. That's what money is for."

"Speaking of which...I'm a little stuck between paychecks and bankomat runs," she confessed with embarrassment. "I guess I can put the plane ticket and a hotel room on a credit card, but..."

"Oh yeah. Here." Art dug in his hip pocket and tugged loose a thick wad of bills, which he thrust at her rather more forcefully than he would have wished. "We took up a little collection" was his only explanation.

Stella's eyes opened wide. "Are you sure? This looks like a lot." She knew it would be rude to count it, but she had to marvel at its heft and the denominations of the bills in view. "I'll pay you back when I..." His raised palm made her stop. "Thanks. Please thank...everybody," she concluded sheepishly.

She hiked a hip in preparation for stuffing the cash into a pocket before she remembered she did not currently have a hip pocket. Smoothing a nonexistent wrinkle from the dress to try to cover her gaffe was not the success she thought it was. She disappeared into the back of the apartment for a few minutes and returned with a sparkly cape over one arm.

Over the other arm was a small duffel and her only purse. Its earlier incarnation as a flour sack was cheerily warbled by the bluebird stenciled on the heavy fabric.

"The Miami airport has some nice handbag stores," Art hinted. "And shoe stores," he added, trying not to look at her flip-flopped feet.

As they headed to the door, Stella stopped and stared at Art. "Um...will Barb and JJ be at the picnic? I know Jake will be in the hospital for a while longer, but—"

"Oh hell to the no!" Art said with heat. "We would never do that to you. What's-Her-Barbed-Tongue's invitation got lost in the mail or something. And by the way, Barb has every reason to know you're straight. And that haircut is stunning *and feminine* on you."

"Ohhhh...that's what that was all about? Huh. Thanks for filling me in. That's OK. Why should I care what that idiot thinks anyway? I know, riiight!" Stella simpered in fairly accurate caricature. "While we're on that subject...could we maybe swing by the hospital on the way to the picnic? I think I need to say a few words. I really shouldn't leave things as roughly as I did," Stella mused.

Art shook his head emphatically. "My most important commission today is to make sure you don't do anything stupid, like try to show up back where anyone with stripes will see you. And Jake did have a lot of that coming, anyway. If you want to thank him for his work on the Team, he knows that. If you want to say good-bye parentheses forever, he knows that part too. So just what do you think you need to say that he doesn't already know?"

Stella studied her toes. "That I understand and respect his need to put his son above all else. And...keep two wheels down," she said barely audibly. Art looked puzzled. "It's biker talk. It's like saying 'fair winds and following seas' to Navy people," she clarified.

Art grudgingly nodded slowly. "I'll give you his phone number. At the airport."

"Why are you being so good to me?" Stella asked him softly.

The honest and exactly correct answer flashed through his brain. Instead he said, "I know these are not your favorite words right now, but this is the Navy Way."

Years later, as he lay dying, he smiled in remembrance of her response: "I love you too, Art."

Stella accepted his gentle press in the back toward the door. She had tried so hard to hold herself together, but this final touch of kindness was the last straw. Dropping the armloads of things she had been carrying, she turned, threw her arms around Art's broad but world-weary shoulders, and cried.

Art held this most precious of cargoes in his arms for some of the best—and worst—moments of his life. *It's true*, he thought later, when he had the capacity to think, *when the gods want to punish us, they give us what we ask for*.

April 26, 2013
0940 Hrs
Rosensteil School of Marine and Atmospheric Sciences
Virginia Key, FL

Stella pulled some bills from her cream calfskin purse to pay the cab driver and walked through the gate of the place she had usually heard called by its acronym 'Razmus'. The morning sun was already hot. Her navy-blue blazer pulled over her sundress felt sticky and odd on her bare shoulders. She checked her watch and, squinting at a scribbled map on a piece of cheap motel stationery, calculated her trajectory among the collection of massive buildings. Through the palmettos on her left, she saw a dock lined with an odd flotilla of dinghies and small canvas-topped boats along with one impressively large boat. The dock was swarming with sunburned and bug-bitten young people in faded and salty barely-theres and floppy wide-brimmed hats. She felt an odd mixture of queasiness and optimism.

The dark of the entrance hall was a relief after the glare of sun on gravel outside. She checked her map again and chose the nearest corridor. Her soft cream wedgies clacking ("why can't anyone make dress shoes a real person can walk in?" she had asked the salesman) on the tile floor sounded frighteningly loud, so she slowed her pace. The bulletin boards lining the hall and clustered at each closed door came into focus.

Since she was a little ahead of schedule anyway, she stopped to peruse a few of them. They were a thumbtacky collection of research papers, slightly off-color and/or nerdy cartoons and jokes, and snapshots of clowning kids, both young and not so, on beaches and boat decks. At the far end of the hall was a door that, unlike all others, had no name tag beside it.

305

As she stood there confused as to whether to knock, the door opened.

Stella and the small man in the doorframe, who looked like he could not be a day less than seventy, exchanged startled looks for a moment. "Yes? Come in, come in," he urged her with a happy grin. "May I help you?"

"Excuse me, Sir," Stella stammered, the butterflies in her stomach going crazy. "Dr. Ron Crane? I'm Stella Curtis. I have an appointment with you this morning?" she ventured hesitantly.

"Oh, darn!" the man responded. "I was so hoping you were coming to see me. Nope, Ron Crane's office is one hall over from this one." He waved his fingers to indicate directions. "But please, come in and have a chat with me for a moment, if you have one. Stella, you said? I'm Joe Levante, and pleased to meet you."

She could not politely refuse the invitation. "Professor Levante," she responded formally, taking the hand he offered.

"Please, please, call me Joe," he urged her. He noted her eyes scanning the cluttered room behind him, which was crammed with books and specimen jars. "Come in, come in, there's lots to see," he urged.

Taking a slow step forward into the cramped space, Stella closed her eyes and sniffed appreciatively. "Mmmm. Dead fish...seawater...ethanol with a hint of formalin...and a faint finish of musty paper. Ahh, Woods Hole!" she sighed. She opened her eyes to see Joe's approving grin. "I spent a summer there in grad school and really loved the place."

"You've gotta love that!" replied Joe, not referring to Woods Hole. "I'm what my granddaughter calls an *icky theologist*, and boy, do I hope she never knows how right she is." He chuckled at his favorite joke. "I'm rapidly becoming the regional authority on the lionfish invasion of the Caribbean. You know about that? *Pterois volitans*? Exotic, fancy-looking stripey thing from the Indo-Pacific, lots of pointy fins and nasty toxins? About six or seven of them got away from Florida aquarists in 1985, and their descendants are now munching their way through a dangerous number of endemic fish species all over the Caribbean. Well, I'm working on some novel ways for getting rid of them. Since they are all descended from such a small founder population and thus have almost identical DNA, I'm hoping to find some weak spot in their genes that I can exploit. Gee, I sure hope I don't have a weak spot in my jeans!" he said with a laugh at his other favorite joke as he patted his receding backside.

Stella nodded vaguely, not sure how to respond to this rapid monologue.

Joe grabbed a large glass jar from the corner of his cluttered desk and held it toward her. He swished the jar gently to make its contents more enticing. The improbably spiky fish spun slowly in its pickling liquids. Stella tried not to see the accusatory look in its bulging, clouded eyes as it pirouetted to face her.

"Cool" was the best she could manage. "Thanks, but I have to be going now." She turned toward the door.

"So. You are really going to leave me so soon to go talk to another man? Ah, well." Joe sighed theatrically. "You can't miss Ron's office. It will be the one with that trashy hillbilly music incessantly blaring from it." The back of Stella's head barely nodded her acknowledgment. Joe could not resist the urge to get Stella to turn once more toward him. "You can't really blame me for trying, can you? After all, you are a veritable goddess in polka dots," he said, with the kind of charm that, alas and alack, only a man too old to truly profit from it can muster.

Stella turned her face toward him. And then she smiled. The smile was too full of pain and confusion and fatigue to be what a true connoisseur would call a signature Stella smile, but it was more than enough to knock the old boy backward a half step. "If this visit works out, maybe we'll have that long chat over coffee some other time," she suggested politely.

Stella walked back down the dark corridor and made the recommended turns. As she headed toward the door at the end, she began to hear soft music. And then she recognized the velvety voice and familiar tune. It was one of her all-time favorites—the one about sweet lips at a phone. She loved the way Elvis's voice rose so passionately as he begged his sweetheart to tell him those special words he wanted to hear. Even better was that magnificently rumbling low note from the jukebox. Stella's head and heart were so brimming that the touchingly sad song filled with longing was too much. She staggered toward the nearest wall for support but wound up slumping to the floor to form a puddle of long, rubbery limbs and polka dots. And, of course, that was the moment when the door before her opened.

The fresh-squeezed Florida sunshine pouring through the doorway so brightly back-lighted the man holding the doorknob that Stella could make out nothing of his features.

He stopped when he saw her.

"Ah, Dr. Curtis! I'm Ron Crane," he said, unperturbed. He tipped his head to study her briefly. "Well, you're on time, that appears to be a right shoe, and a very nice one, on your right foot, and…" He held up an index finger and slowly slid it back and forth before her perplexed gaze. "Your eyes appear to be tracking properly, so all in all I'd say you're in better shape this morning than might be expected, from what I've heard. And I've heard a lot," he added emphatically. "I'll go put on the coffeepot for us. Whenever you feel up to it, do come on in, and we'll talk. I've been looking forward to meeting you for a while." He turned to reenter his office but stopped and looked back at Stella. "Oh, and do you prefer Stellvis or just Queenie?" he asked with cheerful innocence.

Stella smiled.

About the Author

Susan R. Kayar holds a doctorate in biology from the University of Miami. Her research career in comparative respiratory physiology spanned more than twenty years. She was the head of a research project in hydrogen diving and hydrogen biochemical decompression in animal models at the Naval Medical Research Institute, Bethesda, Maryland.

She currently resides in Santa Fe, New Mexico, with her husband, Erich; they met when they were both performing research at NMRI.

Dr. Kayar was inducted into the Women Divers Hall of Fame in 2001 for her contributions to the study of diving physiology and decompression sickness.

Made in the USA
San Bernardino, CA
18 December 2017